TENDAYI O. CHIRAWU

# The Glitter Horn

*This book is dedicated to all the women who are trapped in relationships with abusive partners, to the ones who got out and still struggle while institutions protect their abusers, to the ones who stay because they have no choice, and to the ones who leave and start new lives — you are not alone, and you can and should get help. You can be free.*

# Acknowledgement

*Thanks to my Baba, Dr. Tapera Onias Chirawu, who was the anchor of our family and ran his race with dignity and integrity. Thanks to my mum, Maureen Saviye Chirawu, whose unwavering cheer leading got me much further than I ever could have on my own.*

*Thanks to my daughters, Léna and Shamiso — the stars who light my path in the darkness.*

*Thanks to my sisters, Ngambo and Arisa Chirawu— my first and remaining best friends whose merciless teasing and interminable laughter give me strength and joy when I am in the valleys of life.*

*Thanks to Michael Klapper, my love.*

*Thanks to the American Church in Paris Writers Group members Patricia Killeen, Yvonne Hazelton & Rose Burke, who walked with me as I brought in chapter after chapter for scrutiny and refinement.*

*Thanks to my brilliant editor, Sara Richmond, whose professionalism, heart, and honest feedback took this work from something I rustled up in the kitchen to a gourmet meal.*

*Thanks to Malik Figaro the wonderfully gifted artist for giving this book a proper face.*

*Thanks to God and the universe for gifting me with storytelling and an indefatigable drive.*

*Thanks to God, the great I am who was and is to come.*

# 1

## One

The doorbell rang as Malaika was emptying the dishwasher. Her husband had dropped Aila off at school and she was well into her morning routine. She put her coffee mug on the white counter next to the coffee machine and headed to the door. Hanging on the adjacent wall was a wooden keyrack. It had hooks on different levels that hung car keys on the top level and house keys on the second. Except, the second rack was empty. Malaika blinked, hoping this would make the set reappear on their usual hook. They did not. Damn it. Her husband had taken both sets with him. She tapped the intercom screen.

"Je viens!" she said, with so much irritation she worried the delivery guy might have picked up on it.

She went to the kitchen and opened the double window. She got the stool she normally used to reach the overhead cabinets and dragged it over. She climbed on it. It had been wobbly for almost as long as she'd lived in the house, but today was the day its legs decided to go weak and give out under her weight. She tumbled out the window like a graceless, drunk gazelle.

"Crap!" she yelled to no one in particular.

The kitchen was at the back of their house so she hobbled around to the front, down the narrow walkway, and opened the small gate, still wheezing and panting. The man from La Poste handed her an electronic device and told her to sign with her finger. He handed her the package and wished her a 'bon journée'. It was a good-sized box and she fumbled trying to find the best way to carry it back to the kitchen window. Somehow she managed, and then launched it through the window, not caring about what happened to its contents. She proceeded with her ridiculous reentry through the window. A single, random piece of jagged plaster on the windowsill hooked on her leggings and ripped a small hole in them. She rolled her eyes to the heavens. Whatever. She closed the window and pushed her husband's package into the salon.

Malaika had gotten married thirteen years ago. She came to France as an exchange student for a semester. She met her husband while drunkenly stumbling home in the Paris streets in the 7th *arrondisement*. He was partying in an eight-hundred-year-old Haussman, with the window open. Malaika and her girlfriend must have been speaking at a blow-horn volume for Axel and his friend to hear them. Since the French are enamoured with America, American culture, and English in general, they did the only logical thing. They invited Malaika and her friend Maggie up to join the party (because what their storm-drunk behinds really needed was more wine). They went, of course, and Axel and Malaika hit it off. When it came time for Malaika to go back home to finish her degree, Axel did everything humanly possible to make sure she stayed in touch and came back when she was done. They were married a year later in a quaint little village at a rustic reception on an old French vineyard estate. Malaika didn't enjoy her wedding. None of it felt like hers. She was overwritten in all decision making by Axel, his mum and his sisters. The only great thing about it was her family being there.

In the beginning, things were great, but that changed literally the day after they wed. Malaika was newly graduated with her double master's degree and her prospects for employment seemed limitless. Eight years later after successfully failing to find stable, gainful employment, she now worked in digital marketing. It was a soul-sucking job that paid scandalously low, less than minimum wage, and whose only perk was that she got to work remotely and in her own time. She also taught English on the side, like most anglophone expats.

They had a 12 year old daughter, Aila. Aila was a good kid; she was also a serious gymnast. Malaika didn't mean to brag (okay, maybe just a little bit); she was impressive and being groomed for the national team. Most of Malaika's days comprised cleaning and taking Aila to her training and competitions on the weekends. She was young, but extremely talented. Her coaches were all about her regimen, and as a result, so was Malaika. Axel was initially very much against Aila doing gymnastics, but now that all these impressive people in the Federation Gymnastique were talking about Aila's prospects, he was onboard. Malaika wasn't complaining, just stating the facts. It must be said that he did work and support their family really well. A few months before their wedding, Malaika told her mentor about her plans to marry. Having lived in France for over 30 years, she had one question:

"Is he French?"

"Yes," Malaika answered proudly, wondering why that

mattered.

"Oh, that's going to be hard," she said. Malaika suppressed her mild offense, but also wondered why she would say that.

Now, more than a decade later, she thought she understood. After they got married, she had to begin the lengthy and painful process of getting French residency. It would enable her to work and stay in the country. For the first two years, she couldn't leave France. Her papers were still being processed; if she left, she wouldn't be able to come back into the country. This no documentation phase is called '*sans papiers*'. Axel seemed to change the minute he realized that, as his wife, Malaika wasn't going anywhere; being undocumented, she literally couldn't leave. He spent the first two years with his friends all- the- time. Malaika was depressed and neglected and he didn't care. She tried talking to him, and when that hadn't worked, she got everyone who would listen to try and get through to him, with no reward except looking like a whiney weakling. Eventually, she gave up. He didn't care about her tears or unhappiness.

One day, when she threatened to leave, he told her he didn't care and she could go. He went as far as to say she watched too many movies, and he would not run after her. So, she stopped caring too. Axel slowly began to resent her for not working, since she couldn't without resident status. When she finally did obtain legal documents, she went back to her parents' house and considered divorce. The truth was, she liked her life in Paris; she always had. In the end, she decided to stay out of optimism.

A little while later things between them started looking up and they had Aila. This was also the last time they had documented intimacy. Things worsened when, despite everything, she still couldn't get a CDI (the French permanent contract, a.k.a., the Promised Land). She was basically her husband's dependent, which he said he didn't mind, but then had constant fits of rage telling her, "You are not enough adoolt to do anything." Axel didn't speak English very well, but insisted that it be their home language.

So here she was in her would-be-nice home, getting on with her day. She had an enormous proofreading task for a client, which she was meant to start two days ago but because she knew she could do it in a day she was procrastinating. She blogged about her life in Paris and that actually made her a bit of money. Turns out, everyone wants to know what it's like to live in the City of Light. Her husband always talked about her blogging like it was child's play, and she contemplated giving it up for a long time. Her parents, however, told her to block everything out and keep on doing it. She really did love writing. Writing was the only place where she felt like she had some agency, and she did it pretty well. Her blog wasn't a powerhouse, but it was her space and helped her to not lose herself. After her coffee, she went into her home office and got through her to-do list, feeling particularly proud of herself after completing most of it before having to dash off to get Aila from school and shuttle her to the gym hall. She microwaved her lunch and put it in a thermal bag for the drive.

Aila ate in the car while Malaika tried to extract information about her school day and friends. The older she got, the less interested in talking to Malaika she became; at least, that's how Malaika felt. She guessed it was normal, but it didn't make it hurt any less. It hurt in the way parking attendants and car wash guys were replaced with machines. All through her bizarre marriage, Aila was her person and her being more interested in her own things now felt like abandonment. She knew it was not Aila's job to be her companion, but she thought she still had a few more years. Malaika thought Aila would only be over her when she got into the preteen years. Attempting to engage her in conversation was like pulling hen's teeth, so Malaika eventually directed the conversation to her competition this weekend. Her aunts, Malaika's sisters-in-law, whom she affectionately dubbed Goodness and Gracious (because goodness gracious they were the worst), would be coming. Aila was thrilled, unlike Malaika. A whole weekend when she'd have to endure thinly veiled insults and snark was not her idea of a good time. They were not completely evil incarnate; they could be nice. But they were also cliquish, gossipy, and terrible at hiding the fact. Goodness had looked at Malaika's long manicured nails somewhat enviously once and remarked "It's true, you do do nothing". Or that time Malaika had made apple pie for a family gathering and Gracious had commented loudly "It's not the best apple pie." Or even that time Malaika visited her monther-in-law's home and awoke to hear Gracrious and her husband complaining about Malaika being disorganized and how having her on the trip was disagreeable. Malaika always bit her tongue and smiled politely. Afterall all in laws were ass-hats right? Malaika remembered something her father always used to say: When people reach a stage in life which they never thought they would, they must tell everybody. Gracious and Goodness did. Malaika had the good sense to pretend not to know what they were doing and smile through it all. We all have our crosses to bear she thought."Right, maman?" Aila's voice snapped Malaika back to the present.

"Huh?"

"I said, you got enough places for tata Christiane, Fanny, and Anaïs, right?" This last person was Aila's cousin, Goodness' daughter.

Malaika nodded absently and mumbled a yes. As a family member of tournament participants, she always reserved a set of places for friends and family.

The rest of the drive was quiet as Aila played Fortnite on her tablet and ate the packed lunch. Malaika enjoyed music all the way to the gym. She never dropped her off. She was that over-protective mom and no one would shame her for it. She always stayed and watched her practice. Okay, watch is a stretch. She worked on her computer and looked up from time to time to see her practice. She'd never just left her, because she lived in fear that she might get hurt or one of these grown men's hands might go straying on a body part it had no business going to. She discovered it was an excellent way to get work done, since she was not wasting time and fuel driving.

She sat in the stands with her computer open, texting her sister. Malaika's sister, Chen, was eight years her senior and lived in Cape Town. Two years ago, she turned 40. Since she was a Libra 'fly by the seat of her pants' type of person she dragged Malaika, their cousin, and four of her closest friends to New York. Chen got married before Malaika, in her late twenties. She, too, had a daughter. Chen decided she wanted to hit a real club and party till she dropped again, just once. So, as always, Malaika was forcefully conscripted. Like that time she took her to a friend's wedding in a village with no running water, electricity, or indoor toilets. That was fun Malaika thought and did a mental eye roll. There was that time they almost missed their flight to the Christmas family reunion because Chen was having her makeup professionally done. When they got to the airport, the gate had to be reopened for them; their names had long been called on the PA system, and they sped through border control onto a plane full of people who gave them the stank-eye. This was like those times.

They left their daughters with their mum and partied like rock stars in the Big Apple. Chen splurged on a private suite in the fanciest hotel and a booth in a fancy club. She always was the spontaneous adventurous one. Malaika thought this with kindness and envy; Chen was always red carpet ready. The night of the big party the birthday crew wore custom African print gowns Chen's theme was Pan-African, which was befitting: her posse comprised people from different African countries.

As they left the hotel, they realized they were sharing a floor with celebrities of some sort, but seeing as they had their own mission, they didn't pay any attention. If Malaika had to guess, it was a sports team, given the hulking physiques of most of the men. Their fancy kente cloth outfits brightened the hotel lobby. Malaika, Chen and Delano got on the elevator and were greeted with starring eyes. The ride down would have been awkward so Malaika put some pep in her step. Two transformers disguised as men stepped in before the doors closed.

"I bet The Vuyo will be late," Chen said dryly.

They burst into laughter because they knew he most definitely would be. The Vuyo (so-called because he prefaced everyone's name with "the"), was the group's MVP. He was tall and absolutely gorgeous, but he also had a wonderful personality and possessed the ability to diffuse any situation with smarts, charm or his crazy triceps. Quads? Biceps? Whatever, Malaika didn't know the technical term. His body was perfection.

"Of course he will," she confirmed. "But it'll be worth it. He'll be looking like God's gift and he'll most definitely have something extra, like a vuvuzela or a flag. It's like his to-do list is: the absolute most."

Delano scoffed. "I don't know why you girls always say that. He's not that good-looking." Chen and Malaika shared a knowing smile, then looked at him with pitying eyes.

"The Vuyo is a fool, but he is gorgeous beyond what is physically comprehensible." Chen spoke.

"Sadly, he never lets us forget this fact," Malaika added. "He's the perfect male specimen," she said, just to tease Delano, who rolled his green eyes heavenward. Delano was extremely handsome too. His mixed-race skin was more on the mocha side and his wavy dark hair made his green eyes pop. He was average height and well-built. He and Chen had studied engineering together and ended up being best friends. There was a time when Malaika couldn't even speak normally around him because he was just that dreamy.

"Futsek," he grumbled in his language, telling them to get lost. They burst out laughing.

Malaika was checking her phone when it rang,... Aila's coach. When he called, Malaika always answered , because it was under his guidance that Aila had bloomed into a star gymnast.

"Bonjour Jean-Baptiste," she greeted.

"Merci. Ça va et toi?" She continued.

He wanted to know if Aila would be back in France for early training. He explained what it was for and how it would benefit Aila, but she couldn't hear him properly with everyone talking in the elevator.

"Attends, quitte pas." She muted her microphone and spoke to Chen and Delano. "Guys, can you keep it down,? I can't hear him."

"You're not in France shouldn't he *not* be calling you?"

Malaika rolled her eyes at Delano and, realizing that they were in a rowdy mood, punched a number on the elevator so it could let her off on the next floor. As she did, she stared sightlessly at the two huge men in the elevator.

"Dites moi," she said into the phone as she stepped out and watched the doors close.

When she stepped out into the foyer several minutes later, it was as she suspected. The Vuyo was there in a two-piece kente outfit with a cape, and a little drum tucked under his arm. He looked like an African Superman. She burst out laughing as soon as she saw him. He called to her,

"The Lo."

"The Vu," she replied. "And then?" she questioned, pointing to the drum.

"Ngoma yakwedu," he said,. 'Our drum' in Shona.

"Haibo uVuyo always so extra," Martha, Delano's fiancé, cut in.

The Vuyo turned on her. "Ungenapi Martha?"

Everyone shook their heads. 'Ungenapi' was like saying where do you come in or why are you inserting yourself in matters that don't concern you?

They smiled amorously and gave each other a hearty hug.

Martha and Delano'd been dating for an age and had three children together. They'd finally decided to tie the knot, so next year all roads led to South Africa for their big day.

He held her hand and let her twirl out from him so he could appreciate her traditional Zulu outfit.

Malaika looked for Chen and found her talking to, if she was not mistaken, the large men from the elevator. She was looking very chummy with one in particular who, now that Malaika was paying attention, was positively beautiful. She doubted her taste for a second, because she appeared to be finding every male person she laid eyes on, handsome. She did an internal eye roll. Chen was like their dad, the social butterfly who made friends everywhere she went. She called Malaika over. Malaika didn't want to go over and hoped no one could tell. She was neither like Chen or their dad. Malaika liked to freeze her form in the hopes that not moving would render her invisible. Then, she wouldn't have to do small talk and politely nod to things being said which she either had no idea about or didn't care about. When Malika got to where Chen was standing, Chen told her they were waiting for the two random men's friends because they'd be joining them. She introduced them as Vesuvio and Paxon. Malaika said a polite, but perfunctory, hello and nothing more. She spoke to Chen in their mother tongue, asking why. Chen waved her question off and tried to divert Malaika's attention.

"You" she said sounding the way she did when she talked to her daughter "Isn't this place great? I can't wait to see what birthday treats the club will have for me!" she said in a sing-song cadence.

That was all Malaika got out of her, so she didn't push. Instead she walked back to The Vuyo and Delano to complain and hoped they'd side with her. Sadly, they were not bothered. They meandered about until Vesuvio and Paxon's friends appeared. It reminded Malaika of that time she was flying to Cape Town from Johannesburg and these giants in green were lopping around occupying an offensive amount of space. It took someone else shrieking for autographs for her to realize that they were the South African national rugby team and world champions, The Springboks. These large men assembled in the foyer were not in green uniform; on the contrary, they looked super fashionable. Malaika counted six in total. They looked like a squad of something. They'd managed to charm their way in because Chen's crew had no self-control. In their defense, these dudes were varying degrees of hot. Why did she care? She was there to celebrate her sister and she'd never see these people again. God only knew when she'd be in New York again.

If only she knew then what she knew now. She didn't need to go to New York to explode her entire life; New York would be coming to her.

# 2

## Two

It was competition day.  Malaika sat in the stands with her sisters-in-law and niece, Anaïs. Aila was practicing off to the side of the floor. They'd been there for some time already. So far, Aila's score was really high. She only had the floor routine left, and if she could get a high score there, she would win the day's competition and move on to the next selection round. Malaika had a cardboard sign with Aila's name on it.  It had 'Go Aila' written in different colored markers on it dusted in glitter. She'd been cheering extra loud because her sisters-in-law, who liked to act super classy, got embarrassed by it. She was on her phone sending the results to her mother and sister when she heard a deep rumbling voice say,

"You weren't lying about your child being a phenomenal gymnast."

Malaika froze. It couldn't be. It simply wasn't possible. She was never supposed to hear that voice again, and yet she did, clear as if he was standing right beside her. It was still sexy as fuck, strong and warm. She turned to the side and had to look up to see him- standing right beside her. Towering beside her actually. Paxon freaking Dannis. Paxon Dannis who she had a fling with in New York at Chen's 40^th birthday celebrations. Paxon who she thought she would never see again, Paxon. What the fuck! Her mouth dropped open in horror. He must not have realized her emotional state, because he smiled, and she was blinded by perfect rows of white teeth. Malaika was rendered temporarily mute. Paxon raised an eyebrow and his dark green eyes shone with something she didn't understand. Seriously, why was this her life? She screamed in her head.

"How, how are you here?" She stumbled over the words. He furrowed his brows.

"I got on a plane, Polynomic Princess" he said using the nickname he had dubbed her when she told him how many names she had that night, two years ago. As if that explained how he was in France at her daughter's gymnastics tournament, he plonked down beside Malaika. The stands shifted to accommodate his weight. He nudged into her gently, which sent electricity zipping across all her nerve endings and said,

"You look amazing. How are you?" His deep voice snaked around her in a vice-like grip.

Her eyes doubled in size. Did he really just say she looked amazing? She wore a grey cotton ice-skater dress with leather loafers.

"Shocked," she managed honestly. He chuckled in that way that she remembered made her feel queasy.

"C'est qui?" Gracioius asked Malaika. Malaika had forgotten the in-laws existed the minute Paxon Dannis materialized. She tended to have selective hearing around them, and ignored the question.

"How did you..." Malaika started, still talking to Paxon.

"Find you?" he supplied. "Come for a coffee with me and I'll tell you about it."

"What?" She looked at him.

"You heard me," he said with a smug smile.

Malaika stared disbelieving at him. She managed to close her mouth, because it was drying up from being open for so long. She didn't know what to say to him.

He raised his eyebrows, questioning.

"I can't," she said, pointing to the floor beneath them where all the gymnasts were flipping, pacing, and shaking out their limbs. "Aila has her floor routine next." She saw something at work behind his dark green eyes that set butterflies loose in her stomach.

He nodded once. "I didn't mean right this second... after." "We can talk here," she said, not wanting Gracious and Goodness to get even an inkling of an idea of how she knew him.

"You sure? People might hear and next thing you'll be plastered all over the sports news," he was smirking now.

This was a joke. How could he be joking about this? She snorted and blurted out,

"Oh please, this is France. You're not a celebrity here. No one watches American football here, Paxon," She wished she had run that through a filter; it sounded so mean-spirited.

"Looks like I'm not the only one sleuthing. How'd you find out?"

"Vesuvio let it slip to my sister."

"He talks too much."

"I heard that, asshole." Malaika spun around and, sure enough, Vesuvio was sitting right behind them.

"S'up," he said to her, saluting with his head.

"Hey?" She answered hesitantly.

"You do," Paxon said over his shoulder.

"Man, whatever," Vesuvio waved Paxon off.

"Coffee, after," Paxon said matter of fact, but there was something more in the words something she didn't understand. Urgency? Humor? Mischief? He stood abruptly, and something inside her panicked.

"You're leaving?" She didn't mean for it to come out so surprised, so desperate for him not to go.

A smile tugged at the corners of his lips, and then he winked.

"I'll be back. I just need to tell the others we'll be here a while."

"The others?" She asked, not even trying to hide the shock.

He pointed over his shoulder. Further up in the stands stood Geneva and a woman Malaika had never seen before. The offensive tackle raised his head once to acknowledge her and the woman waved. She gave them all a hesitant wave in response.

She watched Paxon and hoped she wasn't drooling. His ass was firm and filling out his jeans like a dream. It was marvelous how proportionate his body was and deeply bewildering how quickly someone of his size could move. He was ridiculously tall, 6ft. 7 the internet had assured her. He was built with strong hard muscle, and a face that was both intense and inviting. He was in sports high-top sneakers, faded jeans, and a black t-shirt. The layers of muscle on his arms looked like they were fixing to tear through the dark fabric. The shirt would look ordinary on anyone else, but not on Paxon. Malaika stared at the black ink work on his arms. His hair was hidden beneath a mud green beanie that matched his eyes. He looked cool and laid back. Malaika tried hard not to look at his face as a preemptive measure. She didn't trust herself not to jump him. She noticed that his stubble was razed close. Paxon was masculinity wrapped in the most delicious packaging. There, she said it in her mind. He was maddeningly God-like hot. She quickly turned her attention back to the floor.

Gracious took the fact that Malaika's attention had returned to interrogate her.

"Who he is?" she asked in butchered English.

"A friend," Malaika said quietly.

Mercifully, the announcer's voice chose that moment to boom over the loudspeaker into the hall. Aila was up next. Malaika readied her board and glitter horn. It was not really a horn, but one of those vuvuzelas, which had a huge squeeze ball at the bottom. She had filled the ball up with glitter so whenever she squeezed it, the entire thing spat out fountains of glitter. Malaika was nervous, despite reminding herself that Aila was a natural. Sometimes though, nerves made her fumble.

Aila approached the borders of the floor and searched out her mother. When their eyes met, Malaika smiled brightly and pointed to the sign with her name on it in glitter. She gave her a thumbs-up and mouthed 'you are the best'. Aila gave her mother an anxious smile, nodded once, and turned back to the floor in front of her. She took her position and struck a pose. Her routine music started, Lindsey Stirling's "Anti-Gravity."

The routine was flawless to Malaika's eye, and she prayed the judges thought so too. Malaika could see Aila's shoulders rise and fall vigorously as she caught her breath. The entire hall looked to the scoreboard in tense anticipation. Then, it happened. Her score appeared next to her name Aila Herman, 10.0. The gym erupted in applause and Malaika released a breath she was unaware she had been holding and shrieked with joy. A deafening buzz filled the room.

Aila was jumping up and down on the floor and Malaika hopped in the stands, showering everyone with exploding glitter. She didn't even notice that Paxon had returned to stand next to her. He put an arm on her shoulder, and in her excitement, she turned to him and gave him an enormous hug. She even hugged Vesuvio, whom she suspected did not quite like her but who was shouting,

"Wooo, baby! That's what I'm talking about! That's that melanin baby!"

Malaika eyed him, but was drawn back to Paxon. Paxon, who smelled unbelievably good, delicious, spicy, and sexy, all rolled into one. How was that?

His strong arms gathered her into him and her face was plastered to his chest, so comfortably burrowed, like she belonged there.

"Congratulations," he said.

She withdrew quickly. This was not good. She should not be feeling or acting this way. Clearing her throat, she said, "Thank you. I'm just so proud of her."

She kept her eyes fixed on his shoes. She couldn't let him to see her this way. In fact, her greatest fear was that he would see her the way she saw herself, the way she told him honestly that she moved around in the world two years ago. She was suddenly hyper-aware of her shame of performing failed adulthood and because she was afraid that he knew- that in this moment he could see it playing out.

As if sensing her thoughts, he said, "You are obviously doing something right in the way you raise her."

Her eyes darted up to his and she saw him smiling at her in a way that may have been be kindness or the expression you give a little puppy. She didn't know. If it wasn't pity, could it have been compassion? Her whole life, she never had the tools to decipher social interactions or the motivations behind people's behavior. They always left her questioning reality. People thought Malaika was either too direct, rude, or too accepting. Malaika never knew how to respond appropriately and the effort required to constantly remember what her mother told her were socially appropriate responses always left her drained. It was part of the reason she usually kept to herself or just kept quiet. Her cheeks heated at Paxon's words.

"Thanks, that means a lot." It was an odd thing to hear from her husband telling her that she was unable to ingrain the simplest things in the child.

"Paxon?" a timid voice interrupted. Paxon turned to see a young boy of about fifteen looking at him, moon-eyed.

"Hey," Paxon answered, giving the boy a solitary wave.

"Oui c'est Paxon Dannis et Vesuvio James je t'ai dit!" the boy called to his friends, telling them that he was right; these were, in fact, Paxon Dannis and Vesuvio James. He motioned them over. The group of young boys came in a flurry of excitement and uncertainty. They were all talking at the same time.

Malaika was impressed by how these giant men answered the kids with patience, kindness, and wide, genuine smiles. Because Paxon's arms were abnormally long, he took multiple selfies as innumerable phones were handed to him. Grown-ups joined the frenzy. Malaika stood, not knowing what to do with herself, and then decided to get out of the way. As she did, she was met with what were either angry or expectant glares from Goodness and Gracious. Anaïs looked puzzled. Malaika shrugged to them, as if she didn't know what all the fuss is about.

Paxon called Geneva over and the small crowd rushed to him. "What was that about France and American football?" Paxon asked, making no attempt to hide the satisfaction in his voice.

Malaika rolled her eyes, - unimpressed. In Paris, where superstars frequent, she had met her fair share, and few, really only Eric Cantona, were nice. Now, she just didn't bother, and thought it was a little ridiculous how logically thinking humans lost their minds over these people, just because they had a lot of money and a million people knew their faces.

"Am I going to get to meet your superstar?" he asked with a cheerful smile, revealing his dimples.

"Aila? Sure. They'll present the medals and then she's going to collect her things, talk with her coaches, and then she'll be over." She rattled off the proceedings, still nervous.

He didn't take his eyes off her. Malaika felt the unwelcome but familiar feeling of anxiety going haywire. Her mind spun, wondering what he could be thinking. Why did she care? Oh, that's right, because of New York.

Aila waved to Malaika, who exploded yet more glitter above her head and waved back, blowing massive air kisses at her. Aila bounced away, and Malaika saw Paxon dusting the glitter off himself in her peripheral vision. Her sisters-in-law complained bitterly about her makeshift glitter horn and she grinned inwardly. If she was a villain, which she often felt that's what she was best suited to, her one-liner would be Kill them with kindness, accompanied by her own wicked theme music.

As Malaika watched Aila mount the little podium and get presented with the gold medal for best overall gymnast, her thoughts drifted to those nights in New York.

# 3

# Three

New York, New York the town so nice they named it twice, she had once heard someone say. She had been drunk, but not so drunk that she'd lost control of her faculties, a skill she thought she should probably thank Paris for. Parisians drank a whole lot, but it was always done with sophistication, and without the intent of getting shit-faced. People knew their limits and cut themselves off or had the good sense to pace themselves with intermittent water and food breaks. Malaika was pleased to announce that she was now part of the population that drank *avec la classe.*

It was a wild night at the club with her sister and posse; the African Power Rangers. She had a nice buzz and had already cut herself off. The honorary African Power Rangers, the giant add-ons from the hotel, were having a great time with them. She was only now noticing his wardrobe: white skinny jeans ripped in strategic places and what looked like a Hawaiian shirt. He wore black high-tops, a decidedly weird look to her eyes. When you'd lived in France for as long as she had, the number of poorly dressed men in or from other places did not escape your notice. She looked at Vesuvio, whom she decided was someone who took major pride in his appearance. He was in a black deep V-neck shirt and black, fitted jeans tucked into black boots. He was wearing reflective sunglasses but had a shimmery waistcoat over the shirt.

Malaika danced to her heart's content, which is saying something, because she really could not dance. She was stiff and uncoordinated. Chen likened Malaika's moves to spasms and was quick to kindly ask her to stop whenever Malaika got carried away, or laugh; she laughed at Malaika a lot. Malaika was terrible at small-talk. She tried, but things got awkward and people fled, so generally she didn't engage people she didn't know in conversation. That night though, she made an effort. She didn't want to spoil Chen's night. She didn't want Chen to have to worry about keeping her company, so she offered to be the unofficial DJ, which basically meant giving the actual DJ requests. Malaika practiced a few dance moves with Vuyo and Delano. Then, since she already cut herself off, she headed to the bar to get a glass of water. She stood there for an eternity; the barman seemed to be ignoring her. She wasn't sure if it was because she was short.

She was about to give up, when a pair of strong arms appeared on either side of her and came to rest on the bar, with her sandwiched between. A deep voice called to the barman, instructing him to get whatever Malaika was having and a whiskey for him. Malaika looked up and saw a chiseled, strong face looking down at her. A guy she didn't know. The barman brought her water at the speed of light. She said a quick, but polite, thank you, but when she turned to leave the man got gropey. She initially thought he was being chivalrous by getting her the drink, but then he started getting demanding. When she refused to kiss him, he hurled lewd comments and insulted her. C'mon baby don't be like that, quickly turned to, frigid bitch. As she attempted to walk away he grabbed her arm and pinned her to a wall. She was horrified, but also scared witless.

"You think you can just walk away, you cheap bitch. You owe me," he motioned to her drink.

She was about to knee him in the groin, but he suddenly fell away from her. He staggered back, bumping into people, cussing like the gross a-hole he was. Someone had pried him off Malaika and shoved him into obscurity.

"Whoah, what the fuck? What you do that for? Is she like your girl?" Before Paxon could answer, Mr. A-hat apologized. "Sorry, I didn't know she was taken. Didn't mean to ov-" He didn't get to finish that sentence.

"You should be apologizing to her, not me. Whether she's taken or not is irrelevant. She clearly was not consenting to anything involving you and intimidating her into doing what you want is what you should be apologizing for asshole!"

"Fuck you man! Who do you think you are? She's not even your girl."

"She doesn't have to be anyone's girl to be protected from pieces of shit like you." This got a rise of out Mr. Force-a-lot and he walked up to Paxon leaving no space between them and murmured in what he thought was menacing "You wanna take this outside?" Mr. Force-a-lot sized Paxon up and for what Malaika thought was the first time tonight for him, used his better judgement.

"Whatever." He mumbled "She's not worth it." Paxon wanted to go at him but Malaika put a hand on his chest and just like that, the tightly wound energy waiting to explode from him dissipated.

Paxon's hair was tied into a short ponytail, and Malaika looked into piercing, dark-ringed green eyes.

"Thank you?" she said.

He smiled. "Are you ok?" His face was a mixture of concern and anger. He was the reason the entitled, drunken harasser no longer had her cornered.

It was just her luck that she would find the creepy, gropey, club guy who thought just because he did you a favor, it entitled him to your time and body.

"What?" Malaika wanted to know why Paxon was looking at her the way he was.

"You don't seem too happy we joined your party?" He looked over to where the SADC Power Rangers still ruled the dance floor.

"It's not that," she said.

He raised his eyebrows expectantly. "Bullshit."

"You're right. I am sorry you noticed."

"You're sorry I noticed?"

"Yes."

"Not just sorry?"

"I'm not sorry about feeling uncomfortable around strangers."

"A stranger is a friend you don't know."

Malaika snorted and bit down a smile.

Paxon didn't miss it, and gave a triumphant chuckle. "So, you're French?" he asked.

Malaika shook her head. "I am from Africa. Those idiots just like to make fun of me because I live in Paris." She pointed to her crew. She hoped they could move on from this line of questioning.

"Where in Africa?"

"It's complicated," she took in a breath "But the short of it is, a couple of countries in the Southern African region."

He nodded. "Care to get complicated?" he prompted, with a smile that warmed her nether region.

She gave him a mildly irritated, sideways glance. Why did simple chatting with this man make her feel like she'd never been spoken to by a male in her life before? It was unsettling. "My mother is from South Africa and my father is from Botswana. I grew up in Zimbabwe."

"Nice combination," he said with a smile.

She shrugged.

"I like your moves," he told her, still smiling. For some reason, the laugh lines around his mouth made him look even more delectable.

She snorted because that was definitely a lie. No one liked her dance moves, she didn't even like her dance moves. Alarm bells blared in her head. He was flirting with her. Was he flirting with her or just being nice?

"I'm married." She blurted out, which made him laugh.

He leaned in and down to her ear. "How long have you been married?"

She wondered why he was asking. "Do you really want to know?"

"I do."

All of this was alien to her. "Twelve years." she said, looking at her hands, which were clasping and unclasping as she spoke. "Are you?"

"Married?" He shook his head.

"Girlfriend?" Another headshake. "How come?"

The right side of his mouth tipped up into a wicked smile. "My career."

"Married to the job," she said, trying to make light of the situation and hoping it was the right thing to say. The shows she watched had women saying this kind of meaningless stuff that filled in silences, but also gave them an air of confidence and savoir-faire.

He made a face, like he found her curious. "Your husband is a lucky guy."

She rolled her eyes. "Oh please, how would you know?" she said without thinking, and instantly regretted it.

To her surprise, he just laughed. "So, you're saying your husband is unlucky to have you."

Malaika gave an explosive sigh and wanted to say something but thought better of it. She didn't know if it was the latent alcohol, being in a city where no one knew her, or the fact that no man had given her attention in over a decade and a half, including her husband so, she asked about his friends.

"Are my friends single?" He didn't look like he was going to answer.

She shook her head and was about to apologize and return to the SADC Power Rangers when he answered.

"You interested in one of them?"

She shook her head, vigorously this time. "Well..." Malaika said, putting her empty water glass on the bar.

"Well?" he repeated.

She made a move to leave, when he asked,

"What do you do in Paris?"

"Errr," caught off guard, she stuttered. "I, I'm a freelance communicator." She tried to keep it as vague as possible. This wasn't entirely true because she was a content collector, but it was complicated to explain and this was close enough.

"Interesting," he said. His voice and face when he did so

was the stuff of dreams in an Idris Elba meets David Beckham kind of way. "Why do you guys call yourselves SADC Power Rangers?"

"You ask a lot of questions, detective." She said

"Digger is one of my qualities. Tell me," He said unfazed.

Malaika didn't know why, but she loved the ease with which he communicated given the intensely difficult communication she'd become accustomed to with her husband and the years of mistreatment she'd been subjected to. "We all come from countries in the SADC region and wanted a group name."

"Which Power Ranger are you?" .

"Blue," she beamed, pointing to her blue kente jumpsuit, which had a train. "I need to go to the bathroom." Though it was true, she suspected the announcement had been poorly segued.

"You'll come back; you're not ghosting me?" he said, reaching for her hand and holding it lightly. The feel of it almost rendered Malaika unconscious.

She smiled hoping to strike a balance between enigmatic and welcoming. "I'm not ghosty." She crossed her heart to emphasize.

He furrowed his eyebrows, then arched one.

"I'll be back".

Doubts assuaged, he released her.

She was walking to the bathroom when a thought crossed her mind. Would he be watching her walk away? She turned around ever so casually and found that Paxon's gaze was boring holes into her from the bar. If they were in her favorite video game, this would be his fatality move and the game master's voice would ring out "K.O." as she dropped to the floor in slow motion and her life-bar disappeared at the top of the screen.

The rest of his giant friends and the stunning girl with long, light-brown, wavy hair went over to join him. He winked. She didn't know what it meant but waved once and scurried away.

When she came back out, she spotted Vesuvio, a giant with blond dreadlocks atop of his head and a body like a Greek god which made sense since they all played for the same team. Geneva was built like Paxon but a little shorter and a lot wider, with bronzed skin and loose curls curtaining his head. Angus was built like a fridge and had a short blonde cut that was gelled back. Fern, the only woman with the giant men, was a bombshell, full stop. She was the partner of one of these athletic men. Malaika lost track of names thereafter.

Paxon stood beside her doing some mild dancing, but Malaika didn't pay him too much attention. She knew better than to try and engage him too much. She'd never had someone really want to dance with her except for the SADC Power Rangers. The song Malaika had practiced most to was Kupe by A-Star. When it came on, her group formed a gauntlet for her, chanting her name, "Lo, Lo, Lo, Lo." She sauntered down it like Beyoncé and prayed she didn't trip on her heels. All she had to do was follow the instructions in the song and then do the actual Kupe dance.

As she started to lead, yes, the horrible dancer leading the dance, Delano ran toward her and dropped to his knees, sliding to a stop just behind her. He grabbed her train, rose from the floor carrying it and the Power Rangers ululated and clapped. They all fell in behind Delano. The Vuyo pulled out a Namibian flag from his back pocket and tied it around his shoulders like a cape. He moved to dance in front of her, then danced in circles around her. Their cousin Shanya put her cup on her head and balanced it there as she danced. Paxon was still close. Malaika had no idea what he must have been thinking but killed those thoughts, determined not to mess up her energy.

Delano and The Vuyo always seemed to have some magical chemistry and did amazing complimentary dances together. They sidestepped to the beat, then dropped to the floor and rose repeatedly in tune with the music, and finally sort of vibrated on the spot like they were being electrocuted. It should have looked nonsensical, but they made it look incredibly cool. They clapped each other's hands and left the circle.

Malaika returned to the circle thinking she'd do her 'power move,' but Paxon slid in unexpectedly. He did some semi-breakdance moves in intervals, slowly making his way around her. She was nervous because she really did need to focus on counting off the beat. Somehow, she made it through her power move while Paxon did his dance and the effect was surprisingly well-coordinated. At least, that's how it looked to Malaika. Chen threw her a Botswana flag. Malaika caught it and waved it around a little until Paxon took it from her and used it as a faux lasso to rope her in. The Vuyo and the rest of the rangers chanted, "New Ranger, New Ranger," to Paxon, who rubbed his hands down his beard and hair before rubbing his hands together and doing a weird pose like he was chasing away a small animal. The rest of his massive friends did the same pose. Malaika didn't get it, whatever it was. She was laughing hard when it was all done and followed Paxon to the circle's rim.

"So, you practice dancing together?" Paxon leaned in again.

"Kind of, but we just follow the instructions. A lot of the songs are 'instructioned'. Is that a word?" She looked to him for confirmation. He gave none. She ploughed on, "Dance songs because I can't dance. But you can dance!" She exclaimed.

"Strange?" he asked amused.

She made a face that said, well.

"I'm a devastating force on the floor," he said, brushing a finger to her hand.

It was a tiny gesture, a whisper-light touch, but she felt it so acutely that her temperature went up a few degrees. His gaze never left hers; she was imprisoned by it. She needed to get away from this person. Now.

She announced she was going to the bathroom, again. While in the bathroom, she cursed because the damn jumpsuit looked amazing but was hell to get in and out of, a necessity to use the loo. Once she finally managed to zip herself up again, she heard another awesome song and danced out of the bathroom.

Chen came over to her and inquired whether she was having a good time. Malaika told her to get lost because she was not supposed to be fussing over her.

"Go have fun. You and Vesuvio seem to be hitting it off," Malaika said, wiggling her eyebrows.

Chen smiled mischievously "You know..."

"Yes, yes, you're that woman," Malaika said.

Chen nodded, clearly very pleased. "What's with Mr. Hawaiian shirt?" she wanted to know.

Malaika shrugged, downplaying what she really thought about him, which was that he was the most beautiful man she'd ever seen in person. "He's friendly. Can't hurt to make friends while we're here."

"Hmmm," Chen narrowed her eyes. She danced away from Malaika backwards with her eyes still trained on her.

Malaika rolled her eyes and shook her head.

"What are you drinking?" Paxon's voice cut in as he tried to speak over the music. Malaika shook her head. "Nothing, thank you."

"Sure?"

She nodded.

He took her hand in his and inclined his head slightly for her to follow. For reasons unknow to her, she did. He guided her to a chair where the music was a little less blaring. There they chatted about global warming, of all things. He told her that the best car for the planet was a Tesla.

"Who can afford a Tesla? It's not helpful."

He laughed.

"Us mere mortals want to do our bit for the planet but literally cannot afford to."

They talked about French politics, which he knew next to nothing about, so it was mainly her babbling and him listening. She realized this and decided to ask him more questions. That was the correct social behavior, you talked and then you had to let the other person talk while you listened. He half-answered in favor of asking her more personal questions. She didn't know how to elude them and steer the conversation back to him.

"Lo?" She nodded; she still hadn't formally told him her name.

"Why is your husband so unlucky?" he asked again.

Malaika gave him what she suspected was a worried look. "There's a lot to unpack there," she finally said.

He looked at a bedazzled watch that, like him, was massive. "I've got some time." His voice was light and encouraging.

Malaika let out an explosive sigh. Where to begin.

She told him all about her marital misadventure or as she thought of it- hell on earth. She told him all the things she had never told her mum or Chen because she didn't want either their judgment or their pity once they understood that her marriage was where hope went to die. She even told him this. She told him she felt trapped, because all her life she was dependent on her parents and then she got married to a narcissistic ego maniac with incomparable small dick energy and basically became his dependent.

"I know because I don't cook or clean well or enjoy them or hosting people, I don't inspire affection, so the sad state of affairs that is my marriage is largely my fault." She sighed again "I want not to feel fear of making mistakes as is human to do because I'll be shouted at and told that I'm useless because of it. I want to know what a peaceful day is like where there isn't any shouting or rigid rules that I have to follow to the letter else I am castigated."

She told him she wanted to be kissed with such passion and desire that it stole her breath away. How she wanted the things that big pop singers talked about in their racy songs and how her husband hadn't touched her since Aila was conceived. At this Paxon's head snapped up, his look incredulous. Now that she had started baring it all she couldn't stop, and went on to tell him how she stayed a virgin until she was 25, thinking marriage was where all the sex, affection, and worshiping was. How wrong she'd been.

"It seems I live in make-believe-land," she said aloud, really wishing she was super drunk to dull the humiliation that was settling over her now that she was telling him. Though, somehow being able to talk about this was like lifting a weight. "I'm drowning and I feel like I don't exist, but I have to keep pretending that I'm waving. I have to pretend I'm flying even when I'm falling." Tears were now pooling in her eyes. Malaika had no knowledge of when they'd appeared.

"Part of my problem is needing someone to save me instead of saving myself." Malaika laughed, but there was no mirth in it. "Sometimes it feels like I don't exist – like I'm human mist. Maybe I never existed and feel this way because I want to or am only now realizing that I don't." Malaika rambled and paid close attention to her fingernails which she was rubbing against each other.

Paxon pinched her shoulder.

"Ouch!" she yelped, rubbing her shoulder.

"You exist," he said in his deep voice. "Do you think he's cheating on you?"

She shook her head, then amended. "Even if he was, I doubt I'd care. I don't know what happened to us. He just has never really wanted to be affectionate with me, you know. I mean, there was a time as a teenager when emotionally unavailable vampires were the sexiest thing to me but..." she trailed off.

She shook her head and began rubbing her nails together again. "Maybe I don't deserve to be worshiped and adored because I'm not super wifey, or because my body has changed, or because I'm difficult, but then why are there all these stories of women who get that?" Her nails paused from the deleterious motion so she could use her hands to gesture wildly in the air without aim.

"Anyway, I must be drunker than I thought," she observed. To her surprise, he was still there next to her - listening after her miserable information dump, looking at her with an expression she didn't recognize.

He shook his head "I asked." He smiled kindly then said, "You should be yourself. Not what someone wants you to be. Honestly, I'm a little disappointed."

Malaika frowned, "In me?"

"Yeah. You're a woman; you shouldn't be trying to find ways to fit into this patriarchal bullshit. You should be trying to smash it. You're gorgeous; you can have any guy you want."

Malaika swallowed a protest and schooled her features into a smile.

"Someone once told me that some people come into your life to show you what love isn't. Your husband sounds like he fits the mold. Maybe he was meant to be a temporary person that has somehow become your forever person."

She heard his words, but it was taking a minute for her brain to decode them and pass on the message.

"You need a fuck off fund," He said

"A what?"

"A fuck off fund. Money for a situation like a job or relationship that's going terribly, you can say..." he showed his enormous, middle finger.

She stared at his hands. They were large and thick. He wore a single, large, silver bracelet on his right hand and the watch on the left. Fine, dark hairs misted them and she thought it odd that she noticed and wanted to touch. As he spoke he kept curling all his fingers except his thumb and little finger, then flicking them outward, thumb first. It was strangely sexy.

"Then you can live for a while while trying to figure your situation out. It's not your job to inspire someone to not treat you like shit," he said with a kind of fierce determination. "I've only just met you, but I can tell some things about you: You're smart, a firecracker who speaks her mind. I can tell you're a great mum. You're a beautiful woman. That your husband thinks you're not good enough as you are and that he needs to mold you into what he thinks you should be or what he wants is fucked up. What are we? In the Stone Age, that you should be limited to cooking and cleaning...You are so much more and deserve more, Polynomic Princess."

Malaika rolled her eyes but smiled. "I don't have a fuck off fund, and I can't fuck off; I have a child. Besides, how can you be so sure about me?"

"You're not the only woman who's had a string of shit men. Just don't start believing their bullshit."

"Which is?"

"That you aren't worth more and only your husband could put up with you."

Malaika wanted to argue that she didn't believe that but didn't have the energy to lie.

As if sensing her thoughts, Paxon said, "It's a fucking lie." He said each word slowly, as if he wanted to make sure she understood.

Malaika burst out laughing. She didn't know why she was laughing. Nothing about this was funny. "Last time I checked no one was queuing up for almost forty women with children."

"You checked? Where?" Paxon nudged her with his shoulder and smiled the crinkly eyes smile. Malaika rolled her eyes. "I'm serious. I think that you are sexy with or without a child. I don't see the link."

Malaika didn't speak-what could she say after that? What was the normal thing to say to all that? She had no idea. So, she shrugged noncommittal and hoped it would suffice.

"Ok, so no fuck off fund?" Paxon said.

Malaika nodded.

"Hmm, maybe you need a night to be worshipped. I can definitely help with that."

Malaika's eyebrows exceeded their usual heights. "Talk dirty to me," she said, to try to make a joke of what he was suggesting.

He didn't laugh. "Oh, I have the full lexicon available." His eyes looked suddenly dark, blacked out by dilated pupils. He took Malaika's hand in his massive one and held her gaze.

Surely, he was joking. He had to be joking, right?

He pointed to the door of the club.

She nodded. Nodded!

He got to his feet pulling her up with him and lead her out of the club.

4

# Four

The Uber back to the hotel felt interminable. Paxon spoke to Malaika but he could see she was only half listening.

He grumbled about the size of the car.

"Mm–hmm," Malaika said faintly.

She could see Paxon had been looking at her skin since they were in the club, was he wondering if it would feel soft ? Before she could second–guess herself, he ran a finger along her arm and leaned down to kiss her shoulder. Malaika was stunned.

"Your skin is remarkably soft!" he exclaimed quietly and then kissed her arm, this time with a quick flick of his tongue, just a taste. Malaika pretended she hadn't noticed the lick, he said, "It smells so nice. It's so soft." He kissed her ear and whispered in her neck, "I want to taste the skin all over your body."

Every time his skin made direct contact with hers, her body thrummed and quieted blaring sirens in her head. Paxon was this strange, engulfing presence and she felt powerless to resist her urge to be tasted by him. She wanted him to gorge himself on her and get deeper into her world and she didn't know why. It scared her but then she told herself to relax. They just met and she lived in Europe. They could have some fun and then she'd be gone, and no one'd be in any danger.

With that, he cupped the back of her neck with an enormous hand and drew her face to his. He kissed her without hesitation. She was surprised at how natural intimacy with him came. She was tentative at first, but then she let herself melt into him under the tenderness of his kisses. He was so wildly sensual and it fueled her desire. She tasted his tongue, sliding into her mouth in quick shallow swipes, then deepening. She broke away to catch her breath and that small space between them felt like a chasm. She was a married woman! She told herself over and over, but she felt his manhood strained against his pants, telling her that it didn't care. Holy shit, being desired felt incredible and this was only kissing, touching. What would it feel like to give him unrestrained access to her body?

The Uber driver cleared his throat loudly and eyed Paxon disapprovingly in the rearview mirror. Paxon nodded apologetically to him and pulled away from Malaika. He wrapped his arm around her shoulder and pulled her close to him. He kissed her temple, repeatedly breathing her in.

Once they arrived at the hotel, they both thanked the driver and Paxon led Malaika to his hotel room. They rode the elevator in silence with their hands tangled together. Paxon leaned against the mirrored walls and stared fixedly at Malaika. She smiled, and surprised herself by not shifting uncomfortably or averting her eyes. "You should know that I'm refraining from picking you up her up and..." He smiled suggestively.

"What's stopping you?"

"I don't think you'd appreciate being manhandled or treated

like a little toy just because you're a little woman." Malaika cocked her eyebrow.

He dragged his gaze over her, and she felt exposed. Why had she agreed to go with him? In his hotel room she blurted out, "I said a little prayer when I agreed to leave with you. I said, Lord, please don't let him be a serial killer."

"The only serial killing I do is to Honey Pops." His joke crashed on the rocks of her unblinking gaze.

"Bad joke. I sometimes say really stupid things. Character flaw."

A small smile broke free on Malaila's face. "I am a little nervous" She confessed, horrified at the admission.

He smiled reassuringly "What can I do to help you feel less nervous?"

"I am not sure," she frowned. "No one's ever asked me that before, so I've never thought about it."

"No one's ever been considerate?" He wasn't asking; it was like he couldn't fathom it.

"You can't believe that?" she asked. "You can't believe it." She chuckled because she'd never thought of it that way until he said it out loud.

"What I can't believe is that you haven't had sex in a decade." He busied himself making something to drink with the hotel supplies.

Malaika sat on the settee adjacent to the entertainment area. "I mean, I'm really tight." She opened her eyes wide and pointed in the general direction of her crotch. "So it's difficult to," she lowered her voice, "get in." She resumed normal speaking volume, "Which I guess is a turn off. There are things that help, like foreplay, but I guess His Lordship has neither the time nor the energy and so..." she trailed off.

He listened silently. When he decided to speak he asked, "So you've never had an orgasm on your own?"

"Of course I have, but it's not the same as ... uhm, you know" She closed her eyes tight and grimaced.

"Yeah, it's not the same experience for sure," he said.

Her eyes snapped up to meet his.

He carried two glasses with ice and clear liquid. He regarded her with a look she didn't understand before offering her a glass.

She took it from him and scrutinized its contents.

"Just water." He took it from her and took a generous gulp before handing it back to her.

"Oh, yeah of course. I didn't think..." She began to ramble from nervousness, which made him break out in a smile and her thoughts drifted to his lips and the dimple in his chin. His lips looked like two soft, plump cherries. She knew what they felt like. She'd felt the full force of their capabilities in the car ride over. Something lurched to life in her stomach and she put a hand to it to still the sensation.

"You're not going to say anything?" she inquired.

"About?"

"People always say something about me being a woman drinking beer."

He made a weird face. "Err, you jump topics very abruptly sometimes. Also, something like what?"

"Like, if it's guys, they're either impressed or disgusted. If it's girls, they're usually shocked and speak about it in hushed tones."

"You know strange people," he said, making a crazy "Do you want beer?"

Malaika shook her head. She found it strange how gentle and caring he seemed. She wondered what it would be like to have him play the lead in her life, then captured the thought and obliterated it. Snap out of it! She chided herself. She downed the water to sober her thoughts. She set the empty glass down and waited for him to speak or move.

He stood and drank slowly, watching her with a slight smile playing at his lips. When he was done, he put his glass down, never breaking eye-contact.

She cleared her throat, for a lack of a better segue. "Well," she began, and rubbed her hands up and down her thighs while preparing to take her leave.

Paxon shook his head slowly in a "No you're not leaving" way.

Malaika furrowed her eyebrows.

"Well?" he repeated in a low, but soothing voice. He dropped to his haunches in front of her. They were eye-to-eye, so close she was sure he could feel her breath on him. Her dark brown eyes twinkled with anxiety.

"If you could be an animal, what would it be?" he asked and ran his hands lightly up and down her thighs. Malaika slipped her hands out from under his.

"Jaguar." Her answer was immediate.

"Why?" he prodded. She wanted desperately for him to touch more of her but didn't want to scare him away by being a keener. She had been preparing to leave seconds ago so he kept stroking her thighs gently. His eyes swept slowly over her body, sending shivers over Malaika's skin. She could see actual goose flesh form.

She swallowed hard, tried to speak, and failed.

His restraint snapped. He leaned forward and kissed her

mouth. "Tell me," he said, impossibly close to her. His hands were roaming slowly up her body and she watched them as they traveled gently on her person before imprisoning her in his gaze once more.

"Apex predator," she managed. "Impervious to weakness. It runs, swims, climbs trees, and eats crocodiles. It's a beast of raw power but it's also rare and beautiful," she said in a breathy voice.

He nodded slowly and his eyes dropped to her mouth. He planted a feather-light kiss there, momentarily stunning her.

His lips felt like what dreams were made of. Malaika was arrested by the fact that she was kissing someone, anyone, after what felt like an eternity. She was kissing someone who was not the man she was married to.

His voice broke through. "I hope it's cuddly too."

Malaika tried to speak but no sound came from her mouth. She cleared her throat and tried again. "Strange that you have a gentle aspect to you." Her voice was small and insubstantial.

He kissed her gently at first, then deeply. When he finally withdrew, releasing her bottom lip slowly, Malaika was breathing like she'd run a marathon.

"Why is that strange?" He rasped against her lips. Good grief! She thought. He cupped her face and stroked the apple of her cheek, tilting his head just so.

Malaika used what little control of her faculties she had left to respond. "Because you exude so much power and 'I don't give a shit-ness'".

He chuckled. "I normally don't but you looked at me and your eyes – something in them made me want to take you in my arms and protect you." For a moment he did nothing but stare at the length of her. "I like transgression, a lot." He said it like it was an invitation.

Malaika did not need that invitation. "Please don't stop." She said in a weird, raspy and croaky voice not her own. Who was she?

"I won't," he assured her, parting her lips and dipping his tongue in her mouth. It coaxed, tasted, and caressed hers, eliciting tortured little moans from Malaika. Those moans soothed an odd caveman need in him, and he unleashed the full force of his affection on her. "I am going to pull every moan out of you if it is the last thing I do."

Malaika squeezed her legs tight in fear of the liquid heat gathering in her underwear seeping out. He released her lips and a small, whimpering protest escaped her mouth. He groaned against them and the deep rumbling cadence of it sent shivers running all over her skin straight to her nipples, tightening them.

He leaned back so that he was sitting. He held her close to him and in his strong arms a wave of sensations wrapped themselves around Malaika, tormenting her, searching for release.

This is not real a little voice in her head whispered. She ignored it and glided her hands up his arms. Her fingers met behind his neck. In one powerful pull he had her on him, straddling him and his thighs splayed around her hips. She was gathered into the contour of his body.

"You're quite beautiful," he said in a low voice. He trailed light kisses down her neck and sucked on her collarbone. He kissed her the way that she'd always wanted to be and all she could do was revel under his touch. He nibbled on her ear. "I like everything I see and feel, and I want to explore all of you," He rasped against her lips, his voice sounding desperate.

Malaika's communication skills were reduced to nods.

Paxon dawned a magnificent smile that erased all her thoughts. His arms roved up and over her back until his fingers found the zip to her jumpsuit. She sucked in a sharp breath at the realization of what was coming next.

She felt cool air against her skin and the jumpsuit slipped off her shoulders, exposing a purple push up bra. Malaika had always been self-conscious about her modest chest size and stifled the urge to cover herself.

He unclasped the bra expertly and panic flooded her mind. Her bra was flung out of sight. Paxon kissed her shoulder, drew a stiffened nipple into his mouth, and sucked gently.

The sensation was so exquisite that a shiver rippled over her body and a breathy moan escaped her lips. She arched her back in fish pose, giving him unrestrained access.

His hand glided across her other breast, stroking and rolling the tight nipple between his fingers.

She watched as he flicked her nipple with his tongue and twirled circles around it, but the feeling was dizzying and her eyes fluttered closed. She threw her head back.

He bit her nipple and she squealed with delight. He growled at the sound and moved his mouth down her belly.

Malaika's breaths came in quick desperate pants.

He began a slow assault, kissing the length of her and sliding the jumpsuit off completely. He teased her through her underwear licking at her most sensitive part through silk panties wetting the material. "I have to taste you." He said, desperation evident in his voice.

Somehow, hearing the words made Malaika clench her thighs. She wanted him to, but she was also terrified. No one ever saw her naked and she honestly didn't know when she'd last shaved.

His fingers skimmed her inner thighs and when he tried to pull her panties down from the side, her hands darted to stop him.

He stopped and kissed her through them with renewed fervor, teasing her by nipping at her inner thighs.

She felt the warm pressure from his efforts start to move from her core and surround her. She relaxed.

His hands slid the panties until they too were gone. "Hmmm" he hummed .

"What?" she whispered.

He didn't answer.

She bucked her hips, wriggling beneath him trying to get more of his mouth on her with no reward.

He blew on her and the sensation of warm air that cooled almost made her succumb to unconsciousness. He began sucking on her, his pace steady, then slipped a finger inside her. She was so tight and feeling the stretch to accommodate his finger was almost too much for her to take. She felt like he was going to rupture. She could see him fighting with himself to take it slow, to savour this incredible moment. He slid another finger inside her, and she whimpered. Her eyes were dazed with pleasure as he licked, and sucked, and stroked her. Her moans and gasps edged him on. Her muscles clamped down hard as his fingers milked them and he moaned.

She came hard. A pained-sounding scream erupted from her throat as the waves of pleasure cascaded and shattered her.

Paxon did not let up and soon she was crashing again, the force of which was so violent and intense that she tried to get away from him. He withdrew his finger and used his strong arms to grasp her thighs, holding them firm and spread open, pinning her in place, making her feel and ride out the pleasure for as long as it dragged out. And did it ever. He watched her face as the pleasure tore through her, crinkles formed between her eyebrows and she let out soundless screams. Shit, all this already and he hadn't even sunk himself inside her yet. How would she last at this rate? She didn't care, she wanted to be at the mercy of this man, him buried inside her, eliciting high-pitched moans all night long.

When Malaika's breathing started to slow and she could stop squirming involuntarily, Paxon withdrew and came to rest beside her, trailing kisses all the way up her body.

"Hi," he said, and kissed her temple.

"Hi," she whispered back, her eyes shut tight, the tremors still ravaging her as they faded. She rolled onto her side.

Paxon, behind her, slipped a hand under her neck, wrapping his other hand around her. He rolled her onto her back and started drawing circles on her abdomen kissing her on the shoulder. "You ok?" he asked her soothingly.

She nodded vigorously. "Yup." How did one accurately describe how they were after that? Elated? Relaxed? Languid? Destroyed?

"You need anything?"

"Like what?"

"Water, the toilet, food?"

"Oh, no. Why?"

A mischievous smile played at his lips. "There's more."

"Oh." She was a apprehensive.

He turned her head to face him and captured her mouth in a passionate kiss. Her hands roamed his body and she unbuttoned his shirt. He shed out of it and threw it off with a force which made his muscles strain.

Malaika stared disbelieving. His hard-muscled torso was a glorious sight. She was both euphoric and saddened. This was what it meant to be kissed, really kissed. Now that she knew how would she ever go back to anything else? To Axel, who rarely kissed her and when he did randomly jabbed his tongue into her mouth with his eyes open looking around to see who was watching. When she tried to gently suggest ways the kiss could be more pleasurable for them both, he dismissed her as being childish or unrealistic. Paxon's eyes gazing appreciatively over her naked form snapped her out of her thoughts.

"Perfect," he said, then bit his lower lip.

The cadence of his voice blanketed Malaika and she breathed into him. She finally plucked up the courage to explore the contents of his pants and stroked his impressive manhood.

He got up and walked to the bathroom.

She admired his backside, taking mental snapshots.

He returned with a small square, which he ripped open.

Before he could slip it on, Malaika sprang to action. She leaned into him and took him into her mouth. She hadn't done this much, even predating the affection drought. She had no idea if Pax would enjoy it, but she couldn't resist the urge. She wanted to taste and feel him.

Pax's body tensed, his breathing came in short spurts and he sucked air in through his teeth. His growling moans assured Malaika she was on the right path. He slid a hand behind her head and cradled it gently.

"Give it to me Malaika," he rasped.

She looked up at him and was surprised to find him gazing down at her.

He smiled at her. As she sucked and caressed his balls his

eyes glazed over completely and he leaned his head back with a deep, gravelly moan. "Ah Ah, yes Malaika." His breaths came in quick desperate gasps. He whisper begged her not to stop and then moaned loudly while his whole body shuddered. Once he was done, he slid out and bent down to thank the mouth that had made him see stars.

"You want to kill me little woman" he whispered.

Malaika giggled.

He slid the sheath on and lifted her up. "The bed," he directed, with a gentle smile, in response to her questioning eyes. His fingers danced across her chest lightly.

She watched the hungry appetite on his face intensify. She was about to climb on top of him when her phone started ringing. She ignored it and continued to get on top of Paxon. The phone stopped ringing, then started again. She had a feeling she knew who it was.

"You should get that. It could be important," Paxon said to her. She wondered if he meant it or if he was trying to sound reasonable. "I'll still be here." He winked at her.

"Ok. Just hang on," she said, irritated. She moved to where she left her bag, close to the door. She fished out the phone and faced the wall.

"Where are you?" Chen's voice demanded.

"I am at the hotel. I told you this."

"Oh really?" she sounded pissed, "because I'm here knock-ing on your door."

Crap. "I'm in the toilet. Is there something you need?"

"Are you lying to me?"

"What do you want?" Malaika said every word in slow, sharp singularity, fighting the urge to raise her voice.

"Is Mr. Skinny Jeans in there with you?"

"No." This was true; he was not in her hotel room. She was going to hell.

"Better not be," Chen warned.

"Bye, Chen."

"Wait, are you sick from too much alcohol?"

"Oh my gosh, Chen, no! I am not drunk. I hardly drank. Now, see you tomorrow."

"Mxm." She tksed and then reminded Malaika "We said we wouldn't split up,"

"Bye!" Malaika hung up and let out a sigh.

"You good?"

"Mmhmm, just my sister checking up on me."

She turned around slowly, wishing she had at least a bed sheet to cover up. The call sobered Malaika right the hell up. She couldn't go through with anymore of this. She took a deep breath.

"I am so sorry. I can't do this. I thought, I don't know what I thought." She closed her eyes, feeling guilt. "I didn't mean to, like, tease you or...shit." The palms of her hands rubbed her eyes and then froze, remembering her eye shadow,

She started collecting her clothes from the floor.

"What are you doing?"

"I was going to get dressed and go?" She would have thought it was fairly obvious. "You know since I, we're not –—." She motioned between him and herself. "It's nothing you did. It's me. I am a royal mess and I shouldn't have roped you into my mess. I'm so sorry."

There was amusement dancing in his eyes. "Stay," he said to her.

"But—"

He crossed the room and closed the space between them. She

wanted to keep speaking, but he put his thumb to her lower lip and stroked it gently before kissing her. "It's ok." He gave her a smile.

Was it amorous or not? She really was terrible with expressions.

"We don't have to do anything if that's what you want."

Huh? She wanted to get more details on this, but he was already guiding her to the bed.

He climbed inside it and gestured for her to do the same.

She slipped in gingerly, unsure of what was going on.

As soon as she was inside, he gathered her to him. "Good?" he asked quietly.

"Um, yes?"

"Is that a question?"

"I don't understand." She admitted. "I don't understand why you want me to stay or why you still want me here."

"Yeah, me wanting to keep a sexy woman in my bed for the rest of the night; I don't understand it either." He cracked a smile.

Malaika turned to him and smiled despite herself. What in the heck was this?

He asked her when she planned to wake up in the morning and whether he should get room service for breakfast or if she would sort herself out on that front. She decided on room service because, heck, if someone was going to wait on her, she might as well enjoy it while she could.

# 5

# Five

Malaika woke up the next day to calloused fingers tracing patterns on her back.

"You awake?"

"I am now." Her voice was croaky. She turned to face him.

"Your skin is like..." he paused, watching his finger trail lightly across her skin. "Mmm," he moaned.

"Mmm?" she repeated.

"I love the feel of it under my fingers. What do you do to it? It's like fucking silk."

"And with those elegant words, my morning has officially begun," Malaika joked "Besides, I'm a girl. All girls have soft skin."

He shook his head. "Let's try something. I give you a compliment and you say 'thank you.'"

She narrowed her eyes at him.

He ignored her. "You look beautiful this morning."

She burst out laughing, then clapped her hand to her mouth before composing herself. "I can't say thank you to lies," She protested. Malaika knew what she looked like in the morning: a shiny, human, blubber fish.

"Fail," he said dryly. "That's okay; you have a few more opportunities to do better." He chuckled. "You have nice hair."

She snorted. Her hair was flat now. She had really thin hair, which made it easy to manage, but difficult to look full-bodied and lush. She'd slept in flexi-rods for the club night. She'd had curls and some bounce then, but in the morning all of that was gone. It was bone straight, thanks to the Botox treatment. Still, she played his game.

"Thank you."

He beamed at her.

Good god, this man was fine!

"Now you're getting it." He leaned in and kissed her on the nose. "You wanna get breakfast?"

"I am ready for my room service?" She said excitedly.

He nodded.

She rubbed her eyes. She desperately needed to brush her teeth and get out of the bed but was painfully aware of the fact that she was stark naked. Whatever brazenness she'd had the night before, which she attributed to copious amounts of alcohol, had fled. Looking around, she tried to figure out a way to get up and go to the bathroom. She scanned the room for her clothes, not that that would be much use. The damn jumpsuit was the most cumbersome thing to get into. She mentally groaned.

"What's up?" he asked.

"Hmm." Malaika looked at him. "Nothing. I don't have a toothbrush." It wasn't a lie. It was partly true; this did bother her immensely. There was literally nothing grosser to her than unbrushed teeth.

He jumped out of bed and knelt down in front of a duffel bag in the corner of the room. After rummaging through it he returned with some sort of plastic casing. He clicked it open. Inside was a solitary brushhead. "You can swap out the head with my toothbrush in the bathroom."

"You always keep a spare in case you're with a girl who doesn't have hers with her?" She had no idea why she was saying this. It was literally none of her business.

He scrunched his brows together. "I like to be prepared." He said without any kind of judegement.

"Thank you," she said taking out the head and slithering out of bed. She attempted to drag the sheet with her so she could wrap it around her body like in the movies. No reason to abandon modesty, altogether. She almost made it when she was suddenly yanked back. As she walked away the sheet had hit some kind of snag. She turned to pull it free only to see that Paxon had fisted a piece of the sheet.

He was shaking his head at her. "No," he said simply.

"What do you mean, no?" She hoped she sounded as irritated as she felt.

He tugged the sheet and she stumbled a little. He used two fingers to indicate that she should keep right on going and she knew the sheet was not going with her.

The hell with it, she'd never see him again. Did she really care? She walked to the bathroom starkers, never looking back, and closed the door behind her with her foot. She found his toothbrush by the sink and swapped out the brush heads. After brushing she decided a shower would help her feel less out of sorts. She chanced a look in the mirror and groan-grumbled out loud. She was right about the blubber fish. "I hate everything," she said morosely motioning to her morning face.

"Everything ok?"

"Aces," she supplied, wondering if he'd heard her.

"What?"

"Fine," she clarified.

Afterward, she dried off, wrapped herself in a towel, and emerged from the steam-filled bathroom feeling human again. She gathered her things from where they were strewn.

"What are your plans today?"

"Well, my flight is at 6 p.m. So I will pack and keep myself busy until 2 p.m., when I head for the airport. You?"

Once she had zipped the jumpsuit halfway up her back she began hopping, leaning, and contorting her arms behind her to try and shimmy the zip up high enough to reach.

He got up, turned her around, and zipped her up. "That's not going to work," he said simply. placing a sweet kiss on the back of her neck and running his hands down the length of her arms.

Butterflies tormented her insides. "I know; it's so annoying trying to zip myself in this."

"I mean your plan for the rest of the day." He turned her to face him. "Change your flight," he said, looking her in the eyes.

She burst out laughing. What a ridiculous suggestion.

He didn't laugh. He just stared fixedly at her. This was not a joke.

She shook her head and closed her eyes. "You're crazy. Why? Never mind. I can't."

"You can't or you won't?"

"Both."

"Why?"

"My time here is up. The clock has struck reality o'clock and I am turning back into … a pumpkin". "I need to get to South Africa and pick up my kid from my mum and go back to France."

"And one more day will destroy all your grand plans?"

"What is this?" she wanted to know. She slid her earrings in their holes and clasped them shut.

There was a knock at the door.

"Hang on," he said, and collected the towel she'd thrown to the floor and wrapped it around his waist.

It was room service with breakfast. Malaika was so relieved to be dressed but surprised at herself. She'd just had a full conversation with a completely naked man.

There was a mumbled exchange from the door, before Paxon darted back in the room to retrieve his wallet. Minutes later, he wheeled the food trolley in, closed the door, and came back to where Malaika still stood.

"I have a 2-hour work thing I have to go to. By the time I get back you'll be leaving. It doesn't work. Can you stay a few more hours, please?" He slid his hands around her waist and pressed his forehead to hers.

"A few more hours wouldn't hurt but changing a ticket the day of—" she laughed. "It's too expensive." What she didn't say was that doing so would put her in financial ruin since teetering on the edge of church mouse was her general state of existence. "And how would I explain it to my sister?"

"You need to explain to your sister?"

This was a good point. It was weird, but whenever she was with Chen she felt like a kid again. "It's too expensive," she repeated.

"Do you want to spend a few more hours with me?" he asked.

He was teasing. She knew, he knew she did.

"Because I really wanna spend some more time with you," he told her.

Malaika gave him an honest smile and nodded wordlessly. There was a seat in hell with her name on it, she knew that now.

He eyed her lips and brushed them lightly with his. "Thank you" he whispered before returning to the duffle bag. A laptop was handed to her. Paxon plonked down on the bed, flipped it open and she watched as his fingers flew across the keys. "What are your flight details?"

"Can I?" she motioned for him to pass the computer over to her. He did without hesitation. It was a strange thing to her. Axel never let her touch his computer, acting as if it contained the secrets of the Holy Grail. She logged in to her email and retrieved the flight confirmation. She couldn't seem to deny him anything, which she didn't understand. He felt so familiar and safe to her. She handed the computer back to him and eyed the food cart longingly.

He still had his wallet in hand and whipped out a card. "There's a flight tomorrow at the same time. Does that work for you?"

"Urm, yeah. Sure."

He regarded Malaika for a lingering moment, then typed in his card details.

Her phone buzzed. She read the email notification of the flight confirmation on the display. She approached the cart and lifted up the lids. There was cereal, warm milk (she didn't drink milk), bread (she didn't eat bread), bacon, sausage, eggs (she didn't eat eggs), coffee, slices of mixed fruit and sugar (she didn't use sugar). She forwent cereal and settled on bacon, sausage and fruit. She poured herself some coffee and wished there was honey on this cart. Oh well. She dug in quietly.

Paxon walked around her shoveled a sausage whole into his mouth, washing it down with the coffee. He ate the eggs, more coffee, and bread which he bathed in butter. More coffee. He popped a fruit in his mouth, put a hand on her shoulder and leaned down to kiss her. He acted like they'd known each other forever.

She was unused to so much affection, let alone from a total stranger. What black magic was this? Perhaps the most unsettling thing was that it felt like they had been together forever when he touched her. She promised she wouldn't deceive herself with these feelings.

When he disappeared into the bathroom, she sat on the bed waiting. He came out with his hair wet and plastered to his head like it had been gelled back.

"I need to go and show my face before my sister calls the police. I need to check out too actually." And change. She desperately needed to change.

"Yeah, let's go. I can bring your things back here. You can keep the key when I go," he suggested.

Malaika wanted to tell him no, but his plan made excellent sense so, once again, she agreed.

They walked to her hotel room talking about film as rhetoric. She told him about the subversive-superhero horror genre. Where the heros conducted themselves however they damn well pleased because who would stop them? He provided all the reasons it had no merit. She argued for.

"We can't just assume everyone who has superpowers will want to save the world. They are allowed to be selfish and just do their own thing."

"If you were a superhero—" he started to ask but she cut

him off.

"All the people who hurt me would be fried cinder heaps thanks to my laser vision."

He laughed hard, the laugh she was inexplicably growing to love, the one that formed the wrinkle lines at his eyes. His dimples were more pronounced. She caught herself staring and course-corrected before he noticed.

"Yup, I am not the take the high road type. I'm not even gonna pretend. It's *dracarys* and pettiness over here." She motioned to herself. "If you had superpowers you would be pulling cats out of trees?" Malaika offered.

He shook his head. "I don't like cats. They get stuck up there, they're on their own."

She laughed. "Harsh," she told him, to which he shrugged. She opened the door to her hotel room and they both stepped purposefully inside.

The bed was unmade, just as she'd left it. Her mother would be ashamed. She had two pairs of shoes on display on the settee and her vanity case on the dresser with all her makeup and face products spilling over. Her bottle of perfume was next to it. Paxon walked over, picked it up, and plucked off the top. He inhaled, For a moment Malaika was concerned he might crush it. The bottle looked miniscule in his big hand. She couldn't stop looking at his hands – their sexy, adjoining arms and thick, muscled and hair-dusted package. He looked over the bottle carefully before capping it and setting it down.

Malaika grabbed clothes from her suitcase and got dressed in the bathroom. She emerged in black yoga pants and a beige, light pullover with little pearls on the shoulders. He stared appreciatively. She completed the outfit with leather loafers.

She called Chen. When she told her that she'd be going back

a day late, Chen had a mini-heart attack audible to Paxon through the receiver. Malaika was still talking to Chen on the phone when there was a loud knock on the hotel door. Paxon opened it and in walked Chen with the phone still to her ear. Chen pushed past Paxon and gave Malaika a look that demanded explanation. She looked back and forth between them again.

"Why exactly are you staying an extra day?"

Malaika shrugged. "Why not?"

"And why is he here?" She pointed to Paxon "Did he sleep here?"

She turned to him. "Did you sleep here?"

Unshaken, he replied, "No ma'am." He spoke quietly and politely but it was clear that he was not afraid of her.

She turned to Malaika and mouthed no ma'am, then spoke in their mother tongue. "You better not be doing what I think you're doing, Lo. Whatever you're thinking, don't."

"What do you think I'm doing?"

"Fucking up your life with some random dude! Axel is—" Chen's words were choked off, "but it's not worth it."

Malaika wanted to laugh because Chen had just admitted she thought Axel was "dramatic pause" worthy and the she wouldn't name the way he was. "It's not like that, I swear. This isn't about that." Malaika tried to assure Chen. "He's just a friend. We're going to a concert tonight. Come on, when will I get the chance to see them in concert again? With Aila's schedule and living in France... never. Calm down."

Chen seemed to be breathing normally again, thank heavens.

Malaika told her she'd be at their parents' condo and that she had nothing to worry about. After much deliberation Chen decided to either believe Malaika or let her make her own mistakes. She told Malaika the SADC Power Rangers already had breakfast and were just hanging out. Of course Malaika would join them to say goodbye. She only saw them once every other year. Chen mumbled a goodbye to Paxon as she left.

"That was dramatic," Malaika said, trying not to sound embarrassed.

"She's a good sister," he said.

Malaika wanted to be snarky but said, "Yeah, she is." She sat on the bed. "So, I don't think I need you taking my stuff over to your room."

"You sure?"

She nodded.

He handed her his room key. "You'll still be here when I get back?"

For the number she could not remember time since meeting him, she nodded and gave a reassuring smile.

He pinched her chin, drew her mouth open, and kissed her earnestly.

Malaika leaned into it, enjoying feeling desired. She pulled away and gave him a warm look. He kissed her on the forehead before he left. Malaika's eyes followed after his strong and sure frame. As soon as he was gone, she joined her people. They were all congregated in Martha's room. She got to hear about everyone's adventure. Chen went home with Vesuvio (big surprise) and she wore a devious smile on her face as proof. When Malaika told them that Paxon saved her from the gropey dude at the bar then took her back to her hotel room before leaving, they all eyed her with identical skepticism. In all the years they'd known her, Malaika was the saint. So while they didn't want to believe her, her scandal-free record forced them to. Malaika wondered when she'd become such a convincing liar.

Time together passed quickly, and they already knew when they'd be meeting again – Delano and Martha's wedding. They had a chat group where they kept up with each other.  They relocated to the hotel waiting area and waited for their car to come and take them to the airport. Delano had Mailaka look at his latest work project, which was looking to turn his city into a smart city over the next five years.  Malaika thought a sponge city – one that would prioritize minimizing water waste - would be best but his company had other ideas.

Delano looked up, then whispered to her. "What did you do? Thor over there is hanging around like a lost puppy."

Malaika looked up too quickly and her heart clenched in her chest. Paxon was back. She knew he saw her watching him. His stare was so intense it felt like his eyes were actually touching her. He didn't smile or approach. It was like there was some unspoken agreement between them. He winked at her and she almost fell over. It made her feel powerful somehow. He didn't know her but there was this invisible tether between them, she tugged and he reacted and vice versa. It felt like anything was possible. Finally, he busied himself on his phone.

"I'm married," Malaika reminded Delano, in response to his question.

"Yes, but does Thor over there know that?"

"He does.  It was the first thing I told him.  We're just friends."

"I don't look at my friends like I'm going to open them up slowly and devour their juicy centers," he said.

She smacked Delano on the shoulder. "Why are you always so gross?"

"Don't lie, you love me."

He was right. Delano and The Vuyo were like the big brothers she always wanted.

"Be careful." Delano warned.

Malaika didn't know if he meant be careful what you're doing, you might ruin your life or be careful he'll hurt you.

About 20 minutes later their car arrived. She hugged them all.

"I'll see you in a few days," Chen told her.

"I love you," Malaika responded.

When they were gone Malaika took a deep, shaky breath and turned to where Paxon sat. He was already putting his phone away and rising to his feet. Their eyes met, the intensity of his stare sending heat straight to her underwear. When there was no distance between them he took her hand in his and tangled their fingers. It scared her how comfortable all these things he did felt. Worst of all was the knowledge that none of it was real, but still she felt like he was hers.

"Have you had lunch?" He asked as they got back to the hotel room.

"Yeah, we broke bread one last time before parting," she said with a smile. "How was the work thing?" she reciprocated.

He raised an eyebrow, with a 'meh' expression.

"That good huh?"

"Let's just say I was there because they have it in writing that I needed to be there." The duffel bag he had slung across his body was tossed to the floor and he collapsed on the bed with his long legs hanging over the edge. He was still holding her hand and she stood looking down at him.

He looked at her. "What do you want to do?"

"I'm not sure. If I said I wanted to catch up on my favorite series what would you say?”

"Do you want a foot massage with that?”

She burst out laughing. “I’m serious.”

"So am I.” He pulled her down so she fell on top of him. He wrapped arms possessing bear-like strength around her back, pressing her flat against his chest. Their faces were inches apart.

"Is that really how you want to spend your final day in the Big Apple?”

"Maybe,” she said. “How do you want to spend my last day here?”

"Buried inside you,” he whispered.

A small sigh escaped her lips. God almighty! Her traitorous face gave away her thoughts.

He smiled triumphantly and his gaze intensified.

She opened her mouth to say something then closed it again.

"Sound good to you?” he asked casually, as if suggesting they have a coffee.

Malaika gave him a nervous little laugh in response. “But then we watch my show?”

"Anything you want” he said, his voice was gravelly, but she could tell there was sincerity in it.

He tilted his head and kissed her deeply, then rolled her onto her back. He straddled her and pulled his sweater and shirt over his head simultaneously.

His marble sculpture-like torso had her speechless and she put her palm to his chest. Anxiety loosened its grip on her stomach. His eyes turned dark. He glided his hands up the sides of her ribs and she shivered. Then her pullover was gone.

He kissed her, every surface, fold...inside and out.

When he did sink into her, it was with a deep and satisfied

groan. She gasped; the sensation was a sharp, biting pain. Paxon drew her hands above her head and entwined their fingers then slowly trailed a hand down her side all the while her eyes remained captured by his, not bothering to keep the smugness from his face.

"Fucking perfect," he whispered, enunciating, clearly.

Before she could settle in her embarrassment his mouth latched onto a nipple and stars exploded in her vision. She sighed her pleasure and he rocked a steady rhythm in and out. She was so ready for the feeling of being filled in the most impossibly, delectably pleasurable way. She tried to focus solely on the feeling, the rhythm, but couldn't. It was a sensory overload.

Paxon eventually rolled his hips against her pelvis, sending shock waves of pleasure straight to the tight bundle of nerves in her sex. Each thrust deeper, more intense, harder, all the while he growled her name and moaned in her ear,

"Malaika, my little woman," and "Fucking perfect, give it to me." He nipped at her earlobe, licked and sucked on her neck. At the peak of the rhythm of their bodies colliding with desperate abandon, he bit into her collar bone.

She broke hard and suddenly.

"Oh my Pa—."A silent scream tore through her throat.

An intense pleasure, designed only to destroy her, ripped through her entire body, causing her to bury her face in his shoulder. With her legs around his waist, she pulled his body closer. She wanted to feel him everywhere on her.

He moaned his pleasure, a deep animal-sounding thing, and continued his assault until he, too, broke, pouring himself into her. Her name, which never seemed to leave his shuddering lips, made her feel powerful. It was as if she could convince him to rip the world in half for her. What a strange thought.

"Holy shit," he panted.

"Holy shit?"

"Yeah. Holy shit. You're—" he swallowed audibly and took in a labored breath. "That was—" he swallowed again. "Intense."

Before she could protest, he pulled her up to him and kissed her. It was a slow and lazy kiss. It felt like he was making love to her mouth now. After a long while, she pulled away from him.

After, he didn't move. He lay staring at her letting his eyes roam all over her body with a smile while he caught his breath.

She wanted to know what he was thinking but didn't want to ruin the moment.

"I'm not too heavy?" He wanted to know

She shook her head. He was heavy but he wasn't crushing or squeezing the life out of her.

He rolled onto his back and pulled her close, cradling her on his chest.

"Are you ok?" he finally asked.

She nodded.

"We're gonna do that again to the point of physical exhaustion before you go." He said to her, wearing a cocky smile.

"The kiss or?"

"Or," Paxon said eyeing her enticingly.

Malaika gave a strange sort of giggle.

He kissed her temple. "What's so funny?"

"You just say this really dirty stuff like, so casually, it's..." she chuckled. "Hot." She surprised herself with that.

He arched an eyebrow. "There's nothing dirty about your vagina." He gave a solitary chuckle.

Malaika was beginning to think he was the most unusual man she'd ever met. When she failed to say anything after that he spoke,

"Let me go take care of this." He pointed to the filled sheath wrapping his length. Malaika nodded.

He nodded too and gave her a tender kiss. He pinched her nipple gently and ignored her huge eyes. "Be right back," he said against her mouth.

While he was in the bathroom Malaika lay there staring sightlessly. What just happened? He just made love to her, completely destroyed her body, turned her mind into senseless mush and he was going to do it again, to the point of physical exhaustion, apparently. Oh, and he was going to feed her too. It had felt so right though, so unbelievably perfect as their bodies locked together, flowing in synch.

"We can order or go out," he said as he sauntered out of the bathroom.

"Order," She answered, unable to tear her eyes away from his enormous manhood swaying from thigh to thigh as he walked toward her.

"Lazy," He teased.

"Yup, and you won't shame me for it," she quipped.

He called room service and had a lengthy discussion about menu options and the extra charge for bringing dinner up, something they didn't normally do for meals other than break-fast. Malaika ordered seafood and he got steak.

"Still want to watch that series of yours?" he asked.

She shook her head. Spending time doing anything other than drinking in every detail of him seemed like a grievous misuse of time.

"Thank God." He said. Malaika thought he sounded too

relieved.

She suspected that he was a man of his word and was ready to do everything possible for her, as per their verbal agreement which could include sitting through a show he might not like. But a part of her was panicking because she knew their time was running out. From the moment she met him, she'd loved every moment with him. It was like time was split open and pouring out. She couldn't spend enough time with him. She wanted to devote the time to figure out a way to keep him in her life.

"But I still want a foot massage while we wait for the food," she told him.

He jumped at the chance to get his hands on her again and Malaika revelled in a quiet satisfaction. She wanted his hands on her, anywhere on her, so long as she could feel his warm touch on her skin. "My liege," he teased.

She tossed a pillow at him.

He sat up against the headboard and took one of her feet and began kneading with his thumbs.

Malaika closed her eyes and exhaled.

He smiled, and Malika knew he was pleased with himself. "What do you *really* do?"

"Like, for a living?"

"Yeah."

"That's sort of a difficult question. You know I live in France but I'm not French. So, getting employment like a normal person has been a challenge. After graduate school I thought employers would be waiting for me with large welcome signs." She sighed.

"Anyway, I started my own freelance business where I hire myself out to companies to supply them with content; basically a glorified researcher. It's okay. It has peak times of the year and quiet times."

"Mmm," she moaned as he kneaded a particular spot on her foot. "My sister and I also have this side project, an app to get women in the SADC region to invest their money and understand how investment works so that when they retire or are widowed they're not left in abject poverty."

"That sounds amazing. How does it work?"

"Well, the app is essentially a chat that opens in whatever social media they're already using and sends them information on things like inflation in short videos clearly explaining the concepts and how they affect them and advising them on next smartmoney steps."

"That's actually pretty incredible!"

"Yeah. We make zero money from it but it's something we're passionate about."

"Where do you get the videos from?"

Malaika smiled at him. "My sister is a programmer, so she does all the technical stuff and I am sort of the talent and video person. I write the script and create each video. It's basically me talking for two minutes."

Paxon looked amused and impressed. "Send me the link."

She shook her head. "Never."

"Your, uh, husband must think it's awesome, huh?"

Her smile immediately evaporated.

She knew he was watching her closely. "No?"

She shook her head once. "My husband thinks it's childish and stupid. Seeing me filming the videos or uploading them puts him in the worst mood so I only work on it when he's not home." She laughed.

"I had an interview with a small British radio station about it, so he had to pick Aila up instead of me. When I told him what the interview was about he said, "Your app'?" She looked at her nails and begun rubbing them together finding the ridges and focusing the motion there, remembering Axel's face "The way he said it, was like, like 'all this effort for this worthless stupid thing that you take so seriously'."

She began to peel nail polish off her nails absent-mindedly. "I hope you don't think I'm telling you this because I want you to feel sorry for me. I'm not downtrodden or whatever. You asked and, I..." Malaika was acutely aware of his eyes still on her as she gave this awkward monologue. He put a hand on hers and stilled them.

"Why'd you tell me?"

"I don't know. I sometimes word vomit. I had a feeling you wouldn't laugh, and I was right."

"Word vomit?" he repeated his curious tone.

"Yeah like my uncurated thoughts that just blurt out because I can't think of another way to articulate them."

"Can I please see a video?" he pleaded and poked his bottom lip out.

Malaika narrowed her eyes, scrutinizing him. Eventually, she reached for her phone on the side table and opened the messenger app and navigated to the messages from the app.

He watched the video in silence. When it was done, he took his phone and asked her how to get the messages from the app. Once she showed him how, he signed up and said, "It's really great. I'm not just saying that. My charity works with widowed women who are a new type of poor in our societies, you know sort of forgotten. This is incredible. Is it only for women in the SADC?"

Malaika shook her head. "We targeted that community

because it's our immediate community, but the content can be adapted for different communities. Wait, your charity? You have a charity?" She made a face. "What exactly do you do?"

"Guess."

"Construction, sports, or security."

He burst into a fit of laughter. "Why construction?"

"Because you're built like a brick wall."

He was still vibrating with laughter when he said, "Sports."

"Which one?" she asked before remembering she was never supposed to see him again. "Never mind, don't tell me."

He raised an eyebrow. "I'm sharing your app with my charity. It's a lot to ask from a virtual stranger, but can you give the content a wider reach so it's relevant for my widows?"

"Hmmm," she pretended to be thinking it over. "Yeah, it's fairly easy. Consider it payment for all the..."

"The, um, you know?" he teased, saving her from having to say the awkward three letter word.

"Hey, I'm allowed to be a prude."

"You are, but you don't have to be with me. Feel free to express yourself fully and explore whatever you want to with me."

"I don't know what to say to that."

"You don't have to say anything. Oh, and I consider your debt paid in full."

Malaika's cheeks heated.

"How many people are there involved with your charity?"

"About 450."

Her eyebrows found new heights.

"Yeah. You don't want to know, but I'm kind of a big deal."

She made a faux impressed face. "If I had any sense, I would get a selfie with you and ride your social capital wave."

"You can if you want."

She shook her head at him. She never wanted him to have any way of contacting her after tonight. She also never wanted him to feel like she used him for his fame, even though she knew nothing of it. What happened in New York stayed in New York and since this was a one-time thing, why not go all out?

There was a knock at the door. Malaika yelped.

Paxon chuckled, delightedly.

"Shhh," he soothed, running his hand up her leg and under her bum "I won't let him in. It's probably room service."

He pulled her to him and placed her on his lap, then gave her a peck on the mouth and her left bum cheek a gentle squeeze. He carried her and put her down gently on the bed before calling to the door. "Coming" he put on his pants, grabbed his wallet and headed to the door.

Malaika crawled under the covers just in case.

Paxon returned with a food cart identical looking to the one from the morning.

"Seafood for the lady." He lifted the metal cover dramatically.

She smiled and wished he was really hers.

"Can you get me a robe from the bathroom?" she asked him.

"Why can't you get it yourself?"

"Whoa, so much for being a queen," she said in annoyance.

"What do you mean? You disinherited yourself of your title?"

She threw another pillow at him.

"I know what you're trying to do and it's not happening. Walk your tight, sexy ass to the bathroom. I wanna see you and chart all the ways I'm going to explore you and make you do that silent scream after dinner." He bit his lower lip and smacked her ass.

She jumped in surprise. Her cheeks were hot, so hot, in fact, that she pressed her palms to them.

He pressed a palm to her cheek too and said in a low voice with a wicked little smile tugging at the corners of his lips, "I'm going to taste you inside and watch as you cum in my mouth and when you beg me to stop and try to wriggle away..." he paused. "I won't let you go anywhere, not until you realize how perfect every inch of you is."

Good grief! Her mouth went dry. She walked off in a daze. Him smiling at her the way one does their favorite treat was picture perfect.

Upon returning, she found he'd moved the little table from the small lounge area to the bedroom and spread the food out over it. There was an unopened can of beer next to her food.

"I didn't hear you order this." It was more a question than a statement.

"It's all you drank at the club."

What the heck? He was paying far more attention than she ever imagined.

"Thank you."

"Eat." He pointed to her plate.

He told her about how he was pro small businesses and how hard it was to find the right fit for what exactly it was he was trying to do with his platform as a public figure.

"What is it like to be successful?" she asked out of nowhere.

He stopped speaking and looked at her like she was an alien. "Uh," he rubbed his beard. "Success doesn't really feel like success."

"What do you mean?"

"It's reaching one point on your plan but by that time your sights are already on the next point. There's still so much to be done that I don't think anyone really sits and thinks, 'I am so successful, pat-pat,'" he patted himself on the shoulder.

This explanation, oddly, made sense to her

"What's it like to be a great parent?" He turned the inquiry to her. She laughed out loud.

"It's terrifying. I feel like I don't know what I'm doing more than half the time but I know I'm doing ok. She's alive, right?" she joked.

He gave a half-smile. He speared a small piece of steak and offered it to Malaika.

When they were done eating and drinking, she yawned loudly and went to brush her teeth.

Paxon lounged on the bed with the TV remote in hand, flipping through channels without enthusiasm.

Malaika searched for her pajamas in her bag and brought them out. She set about trying to put them on when she felt his eyes on her.

"What?"

"Nothing," he said, sounding suspiciously innocent. Rising, he stalked over, took the pajamas from her hands, folded them and put them back in the bag. "You don't learn." Amusement colored his voice and he shook his head like he couldn't believe she had really just tried to pajama him. He led her to the bed and nestled her between his legs

He eyed the space between them and raised an eyebrow.

She scooted closer to him, but not close enough to press her body against his.

"Closer," he said.

His deep voice sent shivers dancing and prickling all over her skin. She shuffled closer.

"Closer," he said, simply.

If she got any closer, she would literally be attempting to burrow into him, but she did what he said.

He wrapped an arm around her body and lowered his head, brushing his lips against her bare color bone. His lips were feather light.

She grabbed onto his broad solid shoulders to anchor herself.

"Hmmm." He kissed her hip bone. "I'm going to need a lot of time to kiss, lick, smell, and touch this part of you." His hands ran down her back, over her backside and hoisted her so that she sat on him.

He did precisely what he promised he would. She silent screamed more than once.

By the end of it, Malaika was too physically exhausted to do anything but lie there trying to catch her breath, head spinning.

"What are you in the mood to watch?" he asked.

"Something funny."

"Like a romcom?"

She heard the hesitation in his voice. "There are funny films that don't involve romance," she said defensively.

"Name one."

She named four.

"Ok. I can't find any of those."

"Then anything is fine."

"Anything?"

"That's what I said, isn't it?"

"So, if I put something on that has multiple explosions, profanity, and gruesome and graphic deaths..."

"Why would you want to watch that?"

"So, not anything then."

She snatched the remote from him, flicked through the channels and stopped on a science fiction movie.

"Good choice," he commented.

She scoffed.

As they lay watching, she ran her fingers over the fine hairs on his chest.

He brought one of his legs over hers, so they were tangled in each other. From time to time, he kissed her temple and the top of her head They watched in a comfortable silence. Malaika fell asleep on his chest, wrapped up in him.

# 6

## Six

She woke up early despite having slept very few hours. How did she manage to sleep soundly like this? He was wrapped around her like a boa constrictor. How she was going to detangle herself from Paxon? She started by moving slowly and stopping. Move. Stop. Move.

He stirred, pulled her closer to him and kissed her forehead, effacing all her progress to detangle herself.

"Trying to escape?" He said in a deep, croaky voice, beyond sexy.

"Morning," Why was she nervous? She rose on her arms and rolled away. She headed to the bathroom and got ready. After collecting all her things, she did several sweeps of the hotel room.

Paxon was sitting up reading something on his phone. "Come here," he said, holding out his hand to her. He wrapped a massive arm around her waist and showed her his phone. It was a message from someone called Ombre who said the app, her app, was brilliant. She was asking how he discovered it.

"I told you I wasn't lying."

Malaika smiled at him. She wondered for a second what she would be like if she was with a man who was this supportive and loving.  A better version of herself?  Then she chided herself because she tried to convince herself that even without validation, celebration, and congratulations, she was great and had value.

An impulse to kiss him overtook her, but she tore her eyes away from his luscious lips.

He turned, as if sensing her desire, picked her up off the floor, and before she knew it his huge body was covering hers. She whispered to him unconvincingly to let her go, that he couldn't keep doing this to her. "Hmmmm. Stop? Why?" He moaned, savoring the way she felt. He knew she didn't mean it.

A mind-numbing kiss later, she was undressed again, her hands pinned to the bed, his lips on her neck and collarbone and his hard length stroking the inside of her exactly where she needed it.

She spread her legs wider for him and kissed him ravenously.

"It's not my fault. You make me greedy for you,"

She accepted her fate. Her morning was going to comprise mind-scrambling orgasms followed by being late for check-in at the airport. It was worth it. She was glad that was how they left each other. No weird goodbyes at the airport or awkward long drives to the airport. She didn't think she could avoid a sappy goodbye there in the hotel room.

"Thank you for everything," she said. He stopped packing things into his duffle bag and turned to face her.

"I don't know how to do this, but you should know that this..." she motioned to the general surroundings. She exhaled roughly and pursed her lips before continuing, "I'll never forget it. It's probably the best thing to happen to me in all my life aside from Aila."

He closed the distance between them with two quick strides and encircled her in his arms. The only thing he said was that he wished they had more time. They lingered in each other's arms before she told him she needed to go. Her cab would be there any minute.

When she got to the door he spoke again,

"If you were mine..."

She stopped and turned to him.

"I'd be a very lucky man."

Tears threatened. She fled, twisting around so fast it was slightly dizzying. She sobbed the entire ride to the airport. She couldn't give the agony a name, it simply overwhelmed her. The plane ride was an interminable haze where she spent her time trying to hide her inner turmoil from the other passengers seated next to her and hoping all the crying wouldn't be evident when she landed and had to interact with humans. When she got to her mother's, she was still numb and speechless.

As the months went by Malaika convinced herself that it was all a dream. There was no way a man as incredible as Paxon would have taken an interest in her and, what's more, done everything he had with her. The only thing she had as proof was the email confirming the flight change he insisted she make so they could have a few more hours together. Daydreaming about him, about how it felt to have someone look at her and not see a girl performing failed adulthood, a girl with no agency and who was so past sad and anxious that she'd just given up altogether was literal torture like running in place. It was eternal thirst and firey yearning with no quenchable respite. Paxon didn't see the way she actually moved in the world and it was freeing–

she could be who she wanted to be.

Somewhere along the line, she found out Paxon was a second-season NFL player. American football always seemed like a watered-down version of rugby to her with all that padding and cheerleading. But he wasn't lying; this dude was a big deal in the States. She had no idea what his position, a tight end, did despite having read several explanations on the net. His social media pages boasted hundreds of thousands of followers. His rookie season was marked by all sorts of broken records. A lot of the comments on his posts were from gorgeous women. Despite knowing that he had access to the crème de la crème of gorgeous beauties she still hoped she had left an indelible mark. That was until a year later, when she saw his engagement to a leggy, busty, shimmering, genetic-lottery-winning sports anchor named Bonnie Mathers.

"I wonder if he calls her BM?" she thought and she stared at picture after picture of his fiancée's perfect smile and large breasts.

"Oh, stop being an idiot," she chastised herself, as she closed the browser. "You're searching out pain. All this does is confirm what you already knew: You're nothing to him."

She willed herself to forget him. Daydreaming about a man that was never hers and never would be wasn't healthy. Real life was much more disappointing and practical. She wished him a happier marriage than hers and shut her heart off as she turned off her laptop.

The morning of the competition, she decided to change Aila's bed sheets while Aila ran around in circles. Running was Aila's stress reliever before any gymnastics meet. She was fitting the comforter in its cover when Axel walked in.

"It's not like that" he started in.

Malaika groaned internally. She said nothing as she knew what would inevitably follow: You don't know how to do that Malaika? No, I don't. That's why all the beds in this house are made and have been for the past thirteen years she screamed in her head. Yes, because Rumple-fucking-stiltzkin drops by in the morning after we leave and makes the beds in our house. The lack of logic in his question pissed her off.

He took the comforter and its cover from her and began inserting one into the other. He expected her to stay and watch, so when she walked away to go and help Aila finish getting her things together he hissed,

"Always like zat with you. You always react like a teenager. You don't want to be teached anything." He compared her to his nephew who was a certified loser chasing pipe dreams.

She knew to keep her mouth shut. The problem was he got angrier when she kept quiet, nuclear-level angry when she answered back, and infuriated if she walked away. He would follow her just so he could continue yelling at her. Once he started it was like a train gaining momentum. There was no stopping it, only waiting for it run out of fuel. If she was lucky, he would think he was done and go away so she had a chance to leave. Otherwise, the yelling would pick up all over again.

She asked Aila quietly if she'd remembered to pack everything.

"Hello!" Axel yelled.

"Yes?" Malaika said. She tried to restrain her own growing anger. Why did he come here? Did he want to wish Aila good luck? Was he looking for something?

"You hear what I say?"

"Yes."

"And?"

"Ok."

"Zat's it? Ok? You always tell me ok."

"What do you want me to say?" Wrong answer.

He launched into a loud rant about how she should say she would make an effort to change.

She zoned out. She'd grown accustomed to his undulating mood swings over the years. Sometimes things would be great for two weeks and then they would revert to this for five months. In the good times he would shower her with gifts and trips on first-class planes in five-star hotels only to remind her of it in the five awful months that followed. She wondered what this situation would look like in her friends' marriages. She wondered if their husbands were yellers.

Aila broke in with a question.

Axel was forced to stop so he could answer her. He finished by telling Aila she would do great and to let him know how it went because he would have his phone with him.

Why wasn't he coming? Malaika thought. Though, honestly, she was glad.

In the lull, she left the room, trying to draw as little attention as possible to herself. Her final preparations were made at warp speed.

"Did you make me a sandwich?" Aila asked as they drove away.

"I did." Malaika pointed to the cooler bag in the backseat.

"Thank goodness," She sighed in relief. "Your sandwiches are the yummiest."

Malaika turned her eyes from the road so she could smile appreciatively at her. She marveled at just how big Aila was getting. They got to the gym hall, where Gracious and Goodness helped them unload all Aila's things.

And now Malaika was standing beside Paxon, a forgotten dream, after watching her daughter be named best overall gymnast and getting two gold medals, that much closer to international competitions. They stood in silence. She felt uncomfortable and broke it awkwardly,

"Your fiancé come with you?"

He shifted, looking as surprised as she felt at the words. He shook his head. "We're not together anymore."

She nodded and continued to say the wrong thing. "What happened?"

He was silent, something at work behind his expression.

She began to think he wouldn't answer, when he murmured, "She isn't you."

The heck?

7

# Seven

Exactly when did he realize that his fianceé was not her? Her amazement transformed to anger over his sudden, and completely uninvited declaration.  Just as she opened her mouth to tell him off, Aila came bouncing up.

Her gold medals swayed from her chest.  She wore sports pants on top of her leotard. "I did it!" Aila squealed joy and rapture uncontainable.

"You did it" Malaika echoed holding back tears.  Malaika wanted to wrap her into a massive bear hug but was unsure. Aila was in that strange phase where she didn't want to many public displays of affection lest she be deemed childish. To Malaika's relief, it was Aila who leaped into her chest. Malaika buried her face in her boisterous daughter's shoulder and Malaika retrieved her phone and took innumerable photos: Aila biting into her medals, with Anaïs, and some with her aunts.

"It's like paparazzi," Paxon commented with a laugh.

"Yup," Malaika said quickly and continued snapping. She took several selfies with Aila until Paxon offered to take them. She offered him her phone and he took over as official photographer.

"Mum, can Karim come to Appleberry with us?" Aila tugged at Malaika's shirt sleeve.

Whenever Aila did well at a competition they went for celebratory desert at Appleberry. Karim, Camille's son, was Aila's best friend. Because he was usually the best in the male category, like Aila in the female portion, they shared a mutual respect and healthy competition in practice. He was an alarmingly muscular kid whose dark eyelashes curtained his light brown eyes. He would be devastating when he grew up.

"Sure," she said. "Anyone else?"

Aila shook her head. Her female gymnast friends hadn't made it into this competition.

"Mum, aren't you going to get your phone back?" Aila attempted to whisper. "He might steal it."

Malaika stifled a laugh. "No sweety, this is an old friend of mine. His name is Paxon. He won't steal my phone."

Aila looked at him skeptically

"At least I don't think he will."

"I'm keeping this," Paxon said, tucking the phone into his pocket with a grin.

Malaika scowled.

Aila frowned at Paxon and looked back at her mother, her apprehension settled. "Hello, my name is Aila."

"I know. Your mum told me a lot about you, plus I saw you crush it on the floor. Congratulations."

Malaika was sure that if Aila's complexion allowed for blushing, she'd be scarlet.

"Thank you. Are you coming with us to Appleberry?" Aila asked innocently.

"Oh no sweety, I think Paxon has—"

"Yeah, definitely!" Paxon cut Malaika off.

Aila seemed pleased.

Goodness and Gracious looked on suspiciously. Karim's mother, Camille, had joined them and looked at Malaika confusedly and at Paxon like he was responsible for the air she breathed.

"Great," Malaika said too enthusiastically hoping to conceal her genuine disappointment at the turn of events. Camille was looking at her like she'd never seen her smile before. It was well within the scope of possibility, she was not a smiler.

"Me, I'm Camille," Camille said, extending a hand to Paxon.

"Paxon," He answered politely.

"Fanny and my sister, Christiane." Goodness stole a page out of Camille's handbook.

"Paxon," he repeated and shook their hands too. He turned to Malaika, "Can Vesuvio and the others come too?"

She nodded like a droid.

"Perfect," He said, sounding too excited about dessert. "You drive ahead and we'll follow."

Malaika nodded as soon as she saw Karim join Aila.

Paxon made the pitch for dessert to his group.

"I mean; I guess," Vesuvio said, not sounding at all happy about it.

Malaika couldn't decipher social behavior but she'd always had a radar for people who weren't fond of her. She ignored the sirens going off but if he rained on Aila's parade she was sure she would end him. He didn't know her well; when it came to Aila she was no-nonsense borderline dangerous.

They drove in a four-car convoy while her guilty conscience wondered what she could do to off set her carbon emissions.

At Appleberry's, Malaika led the way, holding the door open for the now sizeable group that included Paxon's troup.

They put three tables together to accommodate their group. Camille clung to Malaika like flies on a dead dog because Paxon went wherever Malaika did. Aila and Karim headed for the play area.

"No gymnastics," Camille and Malaika yelled after them. They were prone to practicing their routines outside the gym for fun and to show -off regardless of the danger of injury which would surely end their seasons.

They grumbled something unintelligible before disappearing.

Malaika and Camille exchanged a knowing look and shook their heads. She and Malaika had become natural allies after years of shared practice and tournaments.

Orders were taken quickly and small talk ensued. Malaika dreaded small talk. She struggled to be engaging but not too personal. As conversations developed around her, she found herself wishing to be alone with her thoughts. She nearly started when Paxon spoke from beside her,

"How's the app?"

"It's been gaining traction. I think it's because of your charity actually. Anyway, we were accredited as exhibitors at this year's Long Live Technology conference, so thanks for that." She gave him what she hoped was a smile of gratitude.

"What's Long Live-"

"Oh, Long Live Technology?"

He nodded.

"It's a massive tech conference that pertains not only to the technology industry but development, fashion, many different areas where technological innovation is used to advance the industry or better people's lives. Heads of state, billionaires, and CEOs are usually key speakers and debaters. It's really diverse and an excellent place to network."

"Congrats," he sounded impressed.

She smiled uneasily, disused to someone being impressed with her.

"Why you never tell me about this app?" Camille spoke from across the table.

"It's never come up," she shrugged.

"How are the widows?" Paxon was interrupted as his dessert was placed in front of him.

"It's weird 'cause we have to involve therapists and grief counselors in our processes to just kind of see where the widows' heads are at, you know?"

Malaika did know. Her mum was a widow, but she didn't say this.

"Society forgets them and they have to find a new space to occupy; it's not easy," she said quietly.

"Exactly" He pointed to Malaika enthusiastically. "You get it."

"You have windows?" Camille asked, looking between Malaika and Paxon.

"Err, wid-ows," he enunciated slowly. "Yeah, well, it's my charity. We work with widows."

She looked to Malaika, who gave her the French equivalent.

"Ah," she said, then furrowed her eyebrows. "You are a bénévole/ONG?"

Paxon looked to Malaika for help.

"He opened a charity. He's an athlete who has a charity organization," Malaika offered.

"A professional athlete?" Camille asked.

Malaika nodded.

"Which eh, eh, j'ai pas le mot." Camille couldn't think of the English word to express her question and gave up, exasperated

"Football," Malaika provided. "But not our football, American football."

Camille looked to Paxon, Geneva, and Vesuvio. Malaika could see the pieces fitting together; she now understood why they were surrounded by giants.

"Why you gotta say it like that? Not *our* football," Vesuvio asked.

"Because American football is so localized. It's not like football, which we call le foot by the way, where we compete against other countries. Football world champions actually mean champions of the world. Also, it's called football in America, but I feel like you hardly use your feet in the game."

He tossed a hand up at her. "You keep saying we. Who are you, the bench lady? Besides, you're just a hater because we're living the dream and you're not."

Malaika nodded passively. He wasn't wrong. They got paid to do something they enjoyed.

"Vesuvio, come on," Paxon chided.

"No, he's right." Malaika said, undesirous of Paxon's defense. "Your market is so enormous that even local championship equates to global success in the economy of scale."

"I know," Vesuvio said.

Paxon shot him a death glare.

"All these fancy terms," Geneva spoke for the first time. "Paxon said you were smart."

Malaika scoffed at the compliment.

"I see you've forgotten what I taught you about accepting

compliments." Pax teased her. His smiling eyes bore an amused twinkle.

She remembered this smile, the one that brought out the wrinkles at the corners of his eyes. "Oh, thank you Geneva," she said with a smile.

"Happy?" she shot a look to Paxon who merely shrugged, still smiling.

His lips looked as soft as pillows, full and pink, and his bottom lip a little pouty. A flashback of them on her body, his teeth grazing and nipping at her came to mind and she had to look away from him. She squeezed her thighs together and busied herself with the charms on her bracelet. A moment later, her coffee was placed in front of her and she texted Aila. They appeared, panting hard.

"How you know each ozer?" Gracious piped up.

Malaika looked to Paxon and his smile deepened, revealing those damned dimples. No one was going to let Malaika get away with just: he's a friend.

"My sister's birthday party in New York. We were at a club. A guy attacked me and Paxon saved me."

Gracious frowned and Malaika knew she was going to have to go into details. She explained the bar situation and how the dude grabbed her by the neck before Paxon got him off her and flung him into the adjacent wall like a rag doll. "And then we became friends." She said it the way you would 'the end' of a bedtime story.

"Oh, that's such an amazing meet cute," The beautiful woman who introduced herself as Fern exclaimed.

Malaika smiled.

"So strong," Camille said and touched Paxon's arm.

Malaika didn't know who she was more embarrassed for:

Paxon, Camille, or herself.

Paxon looked at Malaika and raised his eyebrows slightly.

She averted her eyes to keep from bursting out laughing.

"So Aila's dad," Vesuvio said unceremoniously, making a gesture like Malaika should fill in the blanks for him. "Where's he at?"

"He usually doesn't come to the competitions."

"Why not?"

"He has stuff to do, I guess."

"You guess?"

"Vesuvio!" This time Geneva said it. To Malaika he said apologetically, "Ignore him. Vesuvio just doesn't have a filter."

"It's cool. I do most of the Aila-related stuff like all mums, or most mums, anyway."

"Yes, but we are here at his place," Goodness interjected.

"Y'all here *in* his place?" Vesuvio smirked. "Ok, I see."

What kind of mess was he trying to start? Malaika had enough practice ignoring her sisters in law' jabs and pretended not to notice.

"No more questions Vesuvio or you're paying for everyone," Paxon warned.

That elicited a laugh from him and then he rang out, in a really good singing voice:

"Man whatever. My black card, they don't decline that."

Paxon rolled his eyes. "So glad you're leaving in three days."

"Please... you lying. You know you gon' miss my sexy self."

"What? I don't think you're sexy."

"I'm sexier than you," Vesuvio retorted.

Paxon shook his head and said facetiously, "Ok."

"I'm sexier than him, right ladies?" Vesuvio polled.

The ladies all laughed at the ridiculous turn the conversation had taken.

"Well, I mean, I know you don't think so," he addressed Malaika. "But the rest of you choose: me or him?"

Camille immediately pointed to Paxon. Gracious forfeited after giving Malaika a strange look because she said she was too classy and serious to be part of such silliness. Goodness said Vesuvio. Fern chose Paxon. Vesuvio looked at Fern and narrowed his eyes accusingly.

"Traitor" he hissed

She shrugged.

"That's it, Vesuvio, you're paying for everyone's desert."

"The hell I am," he protested.

"What happened to your black card, they don't decline that?" Geneva wanted to know.

"Shut up."

Again, the entire table roared with laughter.

Despite his protests to the contrary, Vesuvio made good producing a black card and paying for everything when it was time to go.

# 8

# Eight

When leaving Appleberry's, Paxon lingered behind and gave Mailaika an entreating look. She halted so they were left at the back of the group, walking slowly.

"You gonna give me your number or do I have to keep surprising you and inviting myself like this?"

Malaika smiled despite herself. She held out her hand and he placed his phone in it.

He sent her a text immediately.

"I got it," she told him.

He smiled.

"How long are you here for?"

"Pretty much the entire off-season."

She shook her head. The word "off-season" held no meaning for her.

"Until training camp, actually, so not the entire off-season." He smoothed the hair at the back of his head. "About four months."

Her eyes doubled in size. "That's a while."

He put his hands in his pockets. "Yeah, I know." He smiled

and nudged her shoe with his. Malaika jumped right off the curb in surprise.

She almost fell over and he had to reach out to catch her. His huge hands steadied her as she wobbled precariously.

"Don't know your own strength there, Kent." She joked to hide the fact that she was flustered by his touch.

He laughed.

"Mum!" Aila called.

"Coming Boops." She held up her car keys. "I need to go open the car."

He nodded. "See you soon," He spoke just above a whisper. Malaika heard uncertainty in his voice. Could it be that he wasn't sure how she felt about him?

Still, the feel of his warm skin sent shivers down to her core. She exhaled a shaky breath and watched as he waved to everyone else.

Malaika and Aila drove in silence until Aila broke in

"Your friends are American."

"Yes, they are."

"I want to go to America some day."

"You will."

"When?"

"I don't know. One day."

At home, Malaika got everything for dinner going. Axel was busy working on something in the backyard. Malaika called a greeting to him. He responded by look at her and returning to his task. Maliaka wandered to her bedroom upstairs and lay on her bed. She didn't know how long she lay there just staring at the light in the ceiling.

On impulse, she called Chen. Before giving her a chance to say anything, she launched into a full description of the day's events.

Chen's responses ranged from, "Aila is the best! The best there ever was!" to "They are all there?" She sounded exactly like how Malaika felt: flustered, confused and excited simultaneously. Once Malaika lapsed into strained silence,

"Ok. So that's nice. Your friends from New York are there; what's the problem?"

Malaika knew what Chen was doing; mining for information and didn't know if she was prepared to tell her.

"Chen," she inhaled deeply. "Paxon is—" she couldn't say it.

"Paxon is what?"

"I have feelings for him," is all she managed.

At first Chen said nothing. Then,

"I knew it. I was just waiting for you to pour out the truth."

She sounded so self-satisfied that Malaika wished she hadn't said anything at all.

"Ok, so how can you have feelings for him?"

"It's sort of a long story but something happened between us and I think it's why he's here."

"Something like what?"

"Chen, I don't think I can talk about all of it, but he told me he broke off his engagement recently because his fiancée was not me."

"What did you do?" Her voice took on an ominous quality.

Malaika let out an exasperated sigh. "Never mind Chen. Just forget it."

"No, tell me!"

"It's nothing. I gotta go." She hung up on her.

The phone rang immediately after and she answered it without looking. "I said it's ok. I shouldn't have said anything—"

"Shouldn't have said anything about what?" Paxon asked.

"Pax! Hi." Malaika's heartbeat raced.

"Hi."

"I was talking to my sister. I thought you were her calling back."

"You ok? You sound nervous."

"Fine. Thank you." She tried to sound upbeat.

"What's up?"

"I'm really glad I got to see you today. Can we get coffee tomorrow?"

She told herself to say no, to say she was busy, or it was too short notice. Her mouth refused to comply. "It was great seeing you, Paxon. Tomorrow is good, I think. I have church at 11 but we can meet at 1 p.m. Does that work for you?"

"Perfect. Where's church?"

She gave him the address.

He was silent for a beat before saying, "That's not far from where we're staying, apparently. I can walk over."

"I'll be waiting outside for you," She told him.

"Can't wait."

"Umm, ok. Bye then."

He chuckled and hung up

She hugged the phone to her chest in the hopes of quieting the butterflies that were now riotous there.

The night passed in a foggy haze.

Aila was always buggered after a competition and as expected, opted to sleep instead of joining her for church the next morning. For the first time she didn't mind. Axel was a typical French Catholic, meaning he only entered a church when someone had communion, a baptism, or a wedding.

Malaika waited just in front of the church steps with her eyes glued to her phone.

"Hi." Came Paxon's deep voice by her side.

She jumped. The phone slipped from her hands and she fumbled trying to make sure it didn't drop to the floor. She caught it just in time and glared at him.

"Sorry," he said though he clearly wasn't.

"I hear the words but the tone is wrong," she said to him.

He pulled her to him and hugged her. "Sorry," he said softly.

She felt moisture start to weep from her unmentionables. Get a grip she scolded herself and pulled away.

"That's more like it," she said with a smile. "Now, do you have a café in mind or am I the guide?"

"I'll follow your lead boss lady," He said, putting both hands in his pants pockets.

She led the way to a café around the corner. Once seated and their orders placed, she looked at him expectantly.

"What?"

"What do you mean, what? You insisted we go for coffee so you could explain yourself. "So..." She gestured to him talk.

He gave her a curious look. "You're direct."

She shrugged and took a sip of coffee.

Paxon continued to stare.

She fixed him with a deadpan expression while thinking damn it this man is fine.

"Ok." He twisted his coffee mug on its coaster.

She listened and examined her coffee mug.

He exhaled explosively, freeing his mug and placing his hands on the table as if laying out his cards "I've thought a lot about you since I watched you walk out of my hotel room crying. It makes me sick thinking about it." He took a deep breath. "I wanted to say I'm sorry."

Malaika was confused. "For what?"

"For pursuing you. I know you probably feel guilty, but it's not your fault, it's mine."

Malaika burst out in hysterical laughter.

"Okay," he said, clearly confused by her reaction.

"I'm sorry." She fought back the fits of laughter. When she finally regained control she cleared her throat before speaking. "Are you dying?"

"What? No."

"Did you suffer a concussion recently?"

He was visibly confused.

"I read that in your sport there are all these delayed side effects from concussions."

"I didn't have a concussion recently." He no longer sounded confused or amused. His voice held irritation.

"You have nothing to apologize for." She took a sip from her coffee mug. "You're not the one who vowed to love and hold before God and state. I did that and then I did you. That time with you was literally the best time I've ever had with a man, ever. I didn't feel sad because of it." She looked around while trying to see how to phrase what was in her head so it made sense to him. "Well, yes I was sad because of you but, only because I wished what happened was more than it was. You know?" She was afraid to look over at him. "Real," She said quietly. When she heard no response she forced herself to look at him.

He was staring at her with an inscrutable expression.

In the awkward silence that followed, she cracked a joke. "So, looks like you came all this way for nothing. No apology needed." She laughed nervously.

"I came all this way to see you," he said. "How have things been for you since...?"

"I mean..." She shrugged. "I'm usually really busy with Aila's schedule. I am in a book club which is the highlight of my month, really. I go to visit my mum for a few months of the year."

"What about your husband?"

"Umm, what do you remember about what I told you?"

"Everything," he said.

She assumed he did not want to revisit the torrid facts of her marriage.

"It's not easy," she said. "I mean, I got a toy because after—" She pointed to him. "I couldn't really pretend to be a robot anymore."

He dawned a cocky smile and she smiled too, more out of embarrassment at her admission.

"You wanna get some dessert?" he asked.

What she really wanted was a beer. She remembered he had no qualms about her beer guzzling ways. "Sounds great. I'm going to get a beer with that." She asked for the dessert menu and a Heineken "So you're here for a while. What are you gonna do during all this time?"

"I have an ad campaign with a fashion brand but my involvement there will be done in a couple weeks, tops. Honestly, my plan was to see if you had some time."

"You could have slid into my DMs to find that out." She laughed.

"It's much better seeing you in person." He captured her gaze. "Seeing you yesterday was—"

"I look much different, huh? When I'm not with SADC Power Rangers I forgo African garb for civilian clothes."

"You are so strange. I saw you in "civilian clothes." Remember?"

Malaika couldn't help the huge smile that spread across her face.

"I also saw you without any clothes." He didn't break eye contact.

"Never forgot," she assured him.

"Me neither."

Her stomach leapt. "So, tell me about this brand campaign."

He didn't try to steer the conversation back and acquiesced.. "During the meeting the boss was like this is how we're going to do things and everyone else was all like looking back at each other—" he demonstrated by looking around at imaginary people, "and fucking asking each other are you okay with this? What do you think?"

He laughed. "It's such a strange culture. Like, this guy is your boss. You do what he fucking says. It's not a democracy." He shook his head, clearly amused and baffled.

"WTF," Malaika said.

"Yeah, what the fuck?"

"No. Welcome to France. Everyone has a voice and expects to be heard."

"Yeah?"

Malaika nodded. Her phone chimed: a message from Axel wanting to know when she was coming home.

"You wanna be my official French immersion guide?"

"I'll think about it."

"Fair," he said, sucking on his spoon and dragging it down his bottom lip. Watching him do it was mesmerizing.

"I'm nothing if not fair."

"Really?"

"No. But I'd be happy to show you the ropes. Excuse me." She furrowed her eyebrows and began typing out a response.

"You gotta go?"

"Not right away," she assured him.

"Where are you staying?" she asked when she put the phone down.

"I rented an apartment in the 7th arrondisement."

"Cool." She didn't really know what the point of her question was.

"You live far from here?"

She nodded. "I drove today because public transport rarely runs to where I live on the weekend. Otherwise I would have taken the metro."

"I took the metro here and it's really good and new. It's far more advanced than the one back home."

"Except when they're on strike, which is like 40% of the time," she joked. It wasn't much of an exaggeration.

"That's a lot," He seemed surprised.

She raised her eyebrows in agreement. "Yup, I guess it balances the scales, the price for having a fancy metro system."

He laughed.

She felt like she was talking too much. He was more of a listener which made her ill at ease. ....

# 9

# Nine

Malaika and her family were having dinner. Axel and Aila chatted away while she was left to her thoughts. She still didn't know what Paxon's endgame was. She didn't buy the whole 'she's no you' answer.

He was an NFL star. She might know zero about the sport but one thing she did know for sure was that beautiful, sexy, childless, single women trying to get athletes to put a ring on it were plentiful. He could have nearly any woman on the planet so it made absolutely zero sense why he was giving her any attention. She resolved to get to the bottom of it the next time she saw him.

Her phone chimed. She expected it'd be her mother. She'd been hounding her to come to Paris for Christmas, but her mother had successfully resisted by claiming it was too cold. She lived in Haartenbos, a tiny oceanfront town in South Africa that was always cold. Every time Malaika had been there her hair turned to frizz and she'd gotten a mild form of frost bite called winter fingers. She looked down.

"Looking forward to learning the ropes with you. You looked beautiful today." Malaika was unable to contain the smile that overtook her face.

"Mummy, is that Gogo?" Aila used the Shona word for grandma, her mother tongue.

She looked up and realized both Aila and Axel were staring at her. She shook her head and put the phone down.

"My sister tell me zat zere are some people who come to see Aila at ze competition." He said.

"Yeah, my friends from New York."

He waited for her to elaborate, but she didn't. "Zey come just for zat? To see her?"

Malaika nodded. "I told them about it and since they're here for a while they'll probably come to a few of her meets." Malika laid the track in the event that they did come again.

"My sister say someone attack you in New York and zis people help you?"

Malaika nodded again.

"Why you didn't tell me?"

He never reacted when she told him something horrible happened to her or he blamed her for it. "I don't know, maybe I forgot." She pushed out her chair.

She began clearing the table and asked what they wanted for dessert. After serving them, she loaded the dishwasher and packed away the leftovers. When she was done, she told them to put their bowls and spoons in the machine. She headed up the stairs and started getting ready for bed when she remembered she never replied to Paxon's message. She brushed her teeth as she typed a response.

"Thank you. See you tomorrow." She added a smiley face, so the message didn't seem perfunctory.

"Can't wait," was his rapid reply.

She put her phone away before she started obsessing. She went to Aila's room to check if she'd packed her school things for tomorrow. She had and was now just changing for bed.

"What are we reading tonight?" Malaika asked. Even though Aila was 12, she insisted on reading with her before bed.

Aila pointed to a book on her shelf. The Gruffalo. Aila was definitely too old for it but Malaika still made all the voices. They'd read it so often that they both knew it by heart. Aila always joined in right when the mouse realizes that his monstrous ruse was in fact not a fiction.

Malaika retrieved it and came to join her on the bed. "A mouse took a stroll through the deep dark wood..." She said in her omnipresent narrator voice. When the story ended, Malaika closed the book with a dramatic snap.

"Love you, sweet dreams clever mouse," they said to each other.

Malaika kissed both of Aila's cheeks and pretended to eat her nose. Aila squirmed out of her grasp but came back so Malaika could capture her again.

Malaika left sure to leave the door slightly ajar.

She slept alone ever since Aila was born. Axel had always watched TV on his tablet without earphones and the light and sound kept Malaika awake. When they had Aila, she slept in their room for the first two years, so rather than stop, he began sleeping in her home office downstairs. Initially, it really bothered Malaika but she tried to see the silver lining: without him snoring like a congested bear she got more rest. Over time, though he used their separate sleeping arrangements as part of his withholding affection arsenal, she came to accept and even prefer it.

The next day after taking Aila to school Malaika packed her computer in a bigger purse than she usually carried. Paxon wanted to meet after his work meetings so she'd be working from a café. She wore her reading glasses and hair in a chignon, the trappings of her serious concentration mode.

She was in the middle of an exchange with a client who thought she hadn't changed the text enough. She hated this part of her work. Some clients wanted her to essentially write or re-write the entire text, which was completely different to supplying them with researched content. She offered that service, but because it was more expensive most people chose the research option. Some, like this client, tried to weasel their way into getting her to do both services for the price of research. She was about to respond to another annoying email from him when Paxon pulled up a chair in front of her.

"Hi." He smiled.

Malaika's eyes travelled the length of his gorgeous face until they reached the dimple in his chin. She smiled and waved at him from across the table.

"You wear glasses." He pointed to the frames.

"Only when I'm working," she admitted.

"How'd your appointment go this morning?"

"Alright," he made a gesture with his hand and a miffed expression with his mouth. "We were only at the most amazing private museum in the 17th arrondisement." He shook his head disbelieving "This city is the most amazing backdrop. It's so crazy that people just live here like mieh it's nothing."

"It's alright," she said feigning being unimpressed.

His smile widened.

"You need to stop doing that," she said.

"What?" He frowned.

"The smiling." She tried to imitate his.

"This?" He pointed to his own face, chin dimple fully on display. "Why?"

She wanted to tell him because every time he did it her underwear threatened mutiny. "Because it's infectious and in Paris we don't smile."

He smiled wider. "Yeah, tell me about it. Everyone is so—" He made a face which was either meant to be surly or pompous.

"Perfect," she said of his 'Parisian' face.

He snorted. "You ready?"

She nodded and closed her laptop mid e-mail response and stuffed it into her bag.

"We can leave that at my place if you want."

Say it's not a problem, Lo. You don't need to be anywhere near a bed with him. Nope, curiosity won. "Great!"

They walked the short distance to his building. His apartment was on the 1st floor and he insisted they take the stairs. Malaika was unashamedly lazy. He was, of course right the elevators in Parisian buildings are too small especially since he was not really a regular sized person.

The apartment was palatial, which Malaika expected, so she didn't spend too much time taking it in.

"Where should I put this?" She held up her computer.

He placed it on a coffee table in the lounge.

"Ok, let's get going. I will have to leave at 4 p.m. to fetch Aila."

The day's tour was of the most interesting English bookstores. Most interesting just meant her favorite bookstores. Malaika initially wanted to take him to an obvious tourist magnet but her hatred of crowds and long lines decided for her. Because she frequented the stores so much the owners knew her and talked to Paxon about the history of their stores and lives. Paxon was attentive and indulged them with questions and opportunities for them to sell him on their businesses.

They were thrilled when they found out what he did; some knew exactly who he was. He posed for photos with them to be used on the bookstores' social media pages. He bought a book at each store. Some were on French art history, World War II, Paris and a surprise pick on fashion and design.

Before Malaika knew it, it was time to fetch Aila.

"Where are Vesuvio and Geneva?" Malaika asked as they walked from the last store to the metro.

"They wanted to do more touristy things, but since I'll be here for a while..." He looked over at her.

She smiled back and shot for a glib tone, "You'll just be hanging out with me until you leave, then?"

"That's the plan."

Malaika stopped walking and turned to face him. She looked up to meet his eyes. "Why Paxon?"

His lips pursed. He began to speak but she interrupted.

"I need to understand." She shook her head to clear it. "I've seen on the player social media profiles absolutely stunning models as partners. Real models. Why are you— not that I'm not fabulous, but—" She began to gesticulate "Help me out here..." These things only happened in fairytales and her life wasn't by any stretch of the imagination.

His shaking chest was the only evidence she had of his laughter. She smacked him on the chest, but it was really only an excuse to touch him. He was rock solid like she remembered.

"Stop laughing."

"Are you done?" His deep voice rang out.

"I am."

"I want you to listen carefully." He paused, lifted his hand to the back of his head, and exhaled.

If she was not mistaken, this was nerves. He was nervous... because of her?

"That night when you told me the things you wanted; you weren't asking for too much, you'd just been asking the wrong person." His hand dropped from the back of his head and he pointed at her. "You and I have a connection which has held strong despite time and distance." He placed a hand on his chest. "I haven't been able to get you out of my head despite the not-so-ideal circumstances of timing. I know it'll be better with you."

"What'll be better?"

"Everything. You keep telling me you're a mess as if that's all the information I need. It's like I should run out the door just because you're struggling with life, but sometimes life doesn't treat us right."

He shrugged. "If I wanted easy, I wouldn't be here. I'm not afraid of difficulty. I want real."

"I'm not here to tell you to leave your husband but I do know that you're not a fucking Stepford wife and we don't live in an era where you are forced to stay married to patriarchal bullies. What you told me; that's not a life."

Malaika narrowed her eyes until they were slits, unconvinced.

"You're allowed to be your own person. I want you to be that person- with me."

Malaika popped a piece of gum in her mouth, hoping to look intimidating. She didn't know how to react. What was he offering her?

"Are you glad I'm here?"

"Wow, talk about playing dirty," Malaika said. She offered him some gum, which he took. "First of all, you don't have all the facts." She sighed "The truth is there is merit to why he is this way with me. He makes most of the money and then he comes home and works on the house, fixing stuff. A lot of the time he doesn't like what I cook. It's a lot for one person. I can see why he feels like I do nothing." She turned from Paxon and started walking again. "I mean I try to stay on top of things but I've never really been good at any of it. Growing up my parents always had help for those sorts of things. I fail a lot and..." her voice trailed off into silence.

"The fuck? You can have an equal division of labor," He said in a disgusted voice.

"But that's what I'm saying; it's not equal."

"And so, because he does more and earns more, he can treat you like shit? Is that it?" he asked.

Malaika said nothing.  He was refusing to see her point because he had decided that she was weak. "This is precisely why I never wanted to see you again," she huffed.

"You never wanted to see me again?"

"Correct. Because I didn't want to have you judging me or thinking I'm downtrodden or weak. That's not what I—"

He put both arms on her shoulders and said, so gently, "Malaika."

"Paxon," Malaika answered with as much ferocity as she could muster.

"That's not at all what I'm saying or mean. You know that."

"Do I?" she snapped. "I told you those things at one of my lowest points because you were there and willing to listen. No one is interested in how miserable someone's life is. You made me feel like a queen. I needed that to endure the rest of this shit show of a marriage. I just needed to remember that, yes, *he* thinks I'm his burden dragging him down but that if I wanted, if I really wanted, someone else would want me. Someone else would have me and be fucking happy about it. I slept with you and entertained thoughts of you long after because I needed that to remind myself that I'm a kickass motherfucker, that I'm strong, and worthy and perfect just the way I am. But, I have to call a cat, a cat. That all happened in a time capsule. It wasn't real. I am still broken and you are still you."

He stared at Malaika in silence.

Paxon was looking down at Malaika, as she powered through her emotions, explaining to him that she didn't need his help or validation and didn't want his pity. She didn't understand why he wanted to be there for her, to support her, to bring her only good things. No one had ever shown up for her in that way nor did she expect anything from anyone. It was a difficult thing for her to comprehend because of her marriage and it really was a strange thing for another man to be offering. What was he offering? To shield her from her asshole husband? What right did he have to do that? How did he even plan to do that from across the pond when the season was back on?

"I don't believe you."

Malaika opened her mouth to speak but he disarmed her with a smile.

"You know how I feel for you and I know you feel it too. It sounds arrogant, but let's not pretend, please," He spoke matter-of-factly.

Malaika shook her head incredulously.

"I'm not judging. I won't weigh in if you don't want me to. I didn't come here to make things weird or hard for you."

"Thank you," she said quietly.

"Do you want me to leave?" He watched her.

She went rigid.

She could see he wanted to smile because he suspected that he knew what her physical reaction meant.

She shook her head slowly.

Then he did smile. "Okay, so you're a mess. I know that, so you don't need to keep telling me. I don't scare easily, and I'll at least warn you if I'm about to check out."

This made her laugh.

"quickly make you laugh like this as much as possible. Your laugh is loud and buoyant. I love how your cheeks round, and your mouth opens to reveal cute little teeth." He hadn't heard her laugh much, Malaika thought. She wanted to pull him in for a hug but restrained herself.

They rode the metro together in silence.

When they got to his apartment Malaika said,

"It was really nice hanging out today."

"It always is."

The way he said it made her think he was thinking specifically of the first time they 'hung out'. She smiled in the absence of a proper response.

He pulled Malaika into the circle of his arms and pressed her against his ginormous frame.

Her body remembered the feel of it. It remembered feeling safe, nurtured, and desired. She closed her eyes and allowed herself to indulge in it, even if only for a moment. His scent was intoxicating and she hung on to him to steady herself.

"Even when we battle like we did today, it still is."

She chuckled at how dramatic he sounded. They'd hardly battled.

She thought it felt like her vibrating soothed him. She felt precious in his eyes and had somehow found a place in his heart. "I'll call you later," he said quietly.

When they let go of each other she turned quickly to leave.

"Aren't you forgetting something?" he called to her.

She turned back and saw him waving her laptop in his hand.

"Right, right. Of course. Where's my head at?"

He gave her a knowing smile.

She stuck out her tongue at him.

This made him smile.

It was a smile she'd never seen him wear before. To be fair she didn't know him all that well so it was quite possible that there were many other facial expressions he had that she'd never seen.

He groaned and pulled her to him. He stroked the apple of her cheek and held her gaze. She wanted more than anything to kiss his soft, full lips but somehow managed to keep it together. She didn't want to scare him away. She'd bide her time, and hopefully, he'd wait for her to be ready. He took a step back and slid his hands into his pockets as she slipped out the door.

# 10

## Ten

Later that night Paxon texted Malaika: *Do I get to see you tomorrow?*

Tomorrow was a tricky day. Aila didn't have any classes and would spend most of the day at the gym. Normally, Malaika spent her entire day with her. Instead of texting him all this she called.

"Hi," his voice always sounded persuasive, drawing her in.

She closed her eyes and breathed into the phone. "Hi. Tomorrow I spend almost all day at the gym with Aila. I usually use the time to work. If you want, you could join me whenever you have the time or we can just meet up the day after?"

"Same gym?"

"No, I'll text you the address."

"Perfect."

Malaika bit her bottom lip.

Malaika worked on her computer, feverishly replying to emails and doing keyword searches in order to finish quickly, occasionally looking up to admire Aila's strength and finesse on the balance beam. From the side entrance, Camille's high heels came clicking towards her. She finished the sentence she was writing and snapped the computer shut. There would be no getting anything done with Camille there.

Camille was wonderful and spritely. Malaika thought that odd at first but once she told her that she was not Parisian but actually from a small farming village called Bar Le Duc it all made sense. She was carrying two caramel macchiatos. Malaika was immediately glad for Camille's interruption.

"To what do I owe this?" Malaika asked, pointing to the coffee.

"Tell me about your friends, the big men."

Malaika rolled her eyes. "What do you want to know?"

"They are single?"

Malaika shrugged. She didn't know the details of any of their personal lives.

Despite her halfhearted response, Camille grilled Malaika about how they had known each other, how long the group would be in town, and, finally, her app.

"How come you never tell me about the app?"

"Pffft." Malaika didn't know how to answer. "You know how when you are working on something and you hope it will become monumental but you don't want to jinx it by talking about it before that happens?"

"Quoi?"

Malaika sighed and tried again. "I didn't want you to think it was just a dream that would never become real...which would lead you to think that I labor under delusions of grandeur."

"Afraid. You was afraid."

"I think that's an oversimplification."

"We're friends. I am excited even if you fail. All ze timez

you listen when I cry about Mounir. You make me half-burned apple pie."

"It was not half-burned!" Malaika protested.

"You keep Karim so I can be miserable alone and he don't see."

"Karim is family now, as you may have no doubt divined," Malaika attempted to steer the conversation away from pain fuelled emotional territory.

Camille gave Malaika the side-eye, utterly unconvinced by her performance.

"Camille, you're my friend and I'd do all those things over again."

Camille smiled earnestly. "Just not burned apple—"

Malaika cut her off, "The apple pie wasn't burnt. Ungrateful cow." She arched an eyebrow.

Camille dissolved into loud, infectious laughter.

"So, how is our boy looking for the next competition?" This is what Malaika called Camille's son, Karim.

The boy was really intense when it came to his regime and competitions. She supposed that was why he was a good companion for Aila, who was also fiercely competitive. She didn't have many friends, even at school, preferring to concentrate on school work and gymnastics. Malaika loved that about Aila and wanted to believe she had something to do with her admirable work ethic. She also secretly worried that Aila was missing out on her youth. She sometimes seemed lonely and reminded Malaika of her childhood self.

"He iz having a hard time with bullies at ze school," Camille said, and Malaika heard the absence of hope in her voice.

"They are only picking on him because he's exceptional. That newspaper article last month called him a boy wonder and soon-to-be the most decorated French male gymnast in decades," Malaika tried to sooth her friend. "I hope he knows that."

Camille nodded and gave Malaika a grateful smile. "I tell him all the time but..." she sighed, "...zey call him names like terrorist and tell him to go back home to his origines."

Malaika was well versed in this barely veiled xenophobic term 'origine'. Like Camille and her son, she and Aila didn't look French. Axel and Malaika had spoken to Aila about this on many occasions. They told her to ignore it and that it was not a reflection on her but on the fear and ignorance of people who did this. A distraction. It was actually one of the few things they were united on.

"I hope his young spirit uses it as fuel to be a beast in everything. Let them keep talking." She looked at Malaika and gave her an appreciative smile before taking a sip of her coffee.

The two women created a sort of bond stemming from their shared home continent. Camille was a very successful real estate agent and absolutely fit the part. She always looked so polished and shiny. Malaika remembered the first time she saw her pull up at the gym, in a shiny Jaguar. She wore heels, with manicured nails, perfectly bronzed skin, and highlighted hair fluttering around her like a silk scarf. Her wardrobe boasted some of the biggest names in fashion. She sashayed down the hall like Beyonce in the "Crazy in Love" music video. Malaika felt like she needed to shield her eyes from Camille's glam. Despite all her success she had a husband who resented her for it and took on another wife in Morocco. Camille divorced him but sometimes when she spoke Malaika could hear longing, not necessarily for him, but a partner. Camille's husband made sure she never realized how beautiful she was through years of bullying and belittling. Camille was the only person other than Paxon whom Malaika ever said something to about her marriage. Malaika refrained from telling her the kinds of details she told Paxon, but Camille had an inkling that all was not greener on her side of the fence. About a year ago Malaika was so close to telling her about Paxon but her spidey sense told her that the parallels between what Camille's husband had done and how she'd stepped out of her marriage, were too close.

Many times, Malaika wished she could trade places. She would take agency over a partner any day. Malaika was kind of a loner and enjoyed her own company, anyway.

Camille told her about a cultural event she attended last night. Then, she revealed the other reason she had come bearing caffeine, bribery. She had a date Friday night and wanted to know if Karim could come over.

"Of course. Is he sleeping over or will you come get him after?"

"Can he stay ze night?"

Malaika nodded and smiled conspiratorially.

Camille blushed. "What?"

"I didn't say anything."

"Zen you can wipe zat stupid smile from your face."

Malaika did exactly that though inwardly she did her "famous" silly dance.

Aila loved having Karim over. They played video games and came up with new gymnastics routines together. They fought sometimes, which Malaika guessed was normal for their age. Overall, Karim was an easy addition to their family.

Malaika wanted to ask about who her date was but didn't.

"Will you send me outfits before?"

Camille agreed. Whenever Camille went on a date she sent Malaika photos of prospective outfits for her to weigh in on. She kept in excellent shape so most everything looked incredible on her.

Malaika always reminded her not to come off as a keener and hoped she took heed. Malaika would hate to see her with someone who took advantage of her because they could sense her desperation.

They stared in silence at the floor where the kids were following coach commands and dusting the air as they practiced. She once asked her what getting a divorce was like. Camille had said if it could be avoided, it should and Malaika remembered the look that clouded Camille's eyes when she told her how men got mean during divorce. She wore a haunted look Malaika would never forget.

Malaika sipped her caffeine and felt a hand on her shoulder.

"Mind if I join?" Paxon asked.

Malaika turned and smiled up at him. "Oh, hey. Not at all."

"Hello again. Camille?"

Camille radiated her kilowatt smile. When she smiled her hazel eyes shone and Malaika felt like she had to squint just to be able to take in the full glory of her beauty.

"How was your morning?"

"Spent it with Vesuvio, Geneva, and Fern. They are going to Brittany and then Normandy tonight."

Malaika nodded, being sure to show how interested she was. Chen had always said it was important to not only be invested in what was being said in conversation but in Malaika's case, show it since, according to Chen, Malaika's face was permanently set in an indirect gaze which gave people the impression she wasn't interested.

"What are you having?" Paxon pointed to Malaika's coffee.

"Macchiato." She raised the cup a little.

He took it from her and sipped it. "It's good," he said, looking over to Camille and sounding surprised.

Malaika was still a little taken aback. Drinking from her cup wasn't that personal considering he'd kissed her before. She had to stop thinking about that she yelled at herself mentally. Yet very time she saw him she thought about the way he had stroked her and kissed her. The ghost of his lips on her skin gnawed at her with dogged persistence. She shook her head to jog her thoughts back to the present. He gave her a quizzical look and she pretended not to notice. She grabbed her cup back.

"What are you ladies talking about?"

"Camille has a hot date on Friday, and I'll be watching Karim for her."

"Not zat hot," Camille said, sounding a little embarrassed "Iz just a first date, you know." She shrugged.

"Well, you are hot so the date will be hot because of your presence," Malaika said with a smile. "Paxon should give you a pep talk about that. He is really good at pep talks. He gave me one at a particularly low point in my life."

"I don't even remember what I said. All I know is that I was fired up that day. It was a good one though," Paxon said, winking at Malaika.

"Yeah, I had tears in my eyes." Malaika wiped away an imaginary tear.

Camille laughed at the pair of them.

"It was good," He repeated enthusiastically "Speaking of dates, I need a date to the launch for this brand project I told you about."

Malaika was silent. She assumed he wasn't talking about her.

"Lo?"

"Hmmm?" Her eyes roamed the gym floor.

"Could you accompany me?"

"Oh. When is it?"

He smiled, shaking his head. "I'll text you all the details when I have my official invitation."

The three of them sat in labored silence momentarily before Malaika resumed teasing Camille about her upcoming date as a distraction.

When the kids were dismissed by their coaches Aila seemed happy to see Paxon.

"I told my mum Coolcome to the USA one day." She told him Malaika made a disapproving face.

"You should," he said. "Where would you go?"

"Where do you live?"

"Minnesota. Do you know where that is?"

"In the USA," she answered.

He laughed then pinpointed it geographically to her.

"Well, if I come I will go to your town. Will you pick me up from the airport?"

Paxon looked to Malaika. She shrugged and rolled her eyes at him, indicating that she had nothing to do with their imaginary plans.

"If you get your mum to send me your flight details, I'll be there with a big welcome sign and a glitter horn like she has at your competitions."

Aila raised her eyebrows. "No glitter!" she begged.

"Hey!" Malaika protested indignantly.

"Ok, no glitter. French flag?"

Aila laughed but agreed.

Karim added that he wanted to come too and Camille and Malaika exchanged amused looks and rolled their eyes. Paxon was clearly a child amateur.

They all made their way out of the gymnasium still talking before Malaika paused and looked at Paxon "You should not encourage them. These are kids; they will force their way and then you'll be stuck babysitting all summer," she warned.

"I don't mind. That'd be great."

Malaika supposed he must mean it. So naïve. Aila was already ahead, getting into the car, so she turned to go. On impulse, she mentioned it was Aila's birthday in two weeks.

"If you're in town, you can come to the BBQ Axel is throwing at our house. She nearly bit her tongue off with regret as she tried to achieve a noncommittal tone.

"Definitely! What should I get her?"

Her heart leaped inwardly though she only shrugged. "Don't ask her because she'll have you maxing out your credit card," she said in a whisper.

"Ok," he chuckled and whispered back.

"Talk later?"

"Definitely," she said, trying to imitate the quality of his voice.

He rapped on the car window and waved at Aila. She lifted her head from her tablet for a second and waved once before diving back into her game. He gave her a quick hug and dropped a kiss in her hair.

She pretended it was perfectly normal but knew at some point she was going to have to broach the subject of touching. Not today, though. Everything seemed so right, peaceful, and easy with him and she hated to ruin it.

That night Paxon called.  She told him she was trying on a new collagen acai berry face mask. After spending time with Camille she always felt like she should take better care of her appearance. Also, if she was going to be Paxon's date to this fancy function, she wanted to put her best face forward. She mentioned the face mask to explain why she couldn't hold the phone up to hear ear properly. He asked to see it.

"Absolutely not."

"C'mon , I bet it looks amazing."

She switched on the camera.

As soon as he saw her, he started to laugh. "Do you actually feel it doing anything?"

"Not sure. I still have 2 minutes left. Usually I feel it after when I'm washing off all the slime."

He grimaced. "Hey, is it okay to talk? I mean—"

"Oh Yeah.  Aila is asleep and once Axel finishes dinner he usually watches movies downstairs until after midnight."

"Is he not curious about your life?"

Her answer was a slight shoulder rise.

"That's pretty late to stay up watching movies."  Paxon observed. "What does he do? I mean his career."

"He's in tech investment."

He didn't comment, abandoning that line of questioning in favor of asking what tomorrow would look like. "At this rate, it might be easier for me to send you my weekly schedule so you could let me know when and where you could meet me," she joked

"That sounds really efficient. When can you send it to me?"

"Ugh," she feigned annoyance, though it did sound much easier than the back and forth they'd been doing. "Text me your email address I'll do it before I go to sleep."

"Any excuse to get my email address," Paxon teased.

"Says the guy who flew half way around the world to hang out with me."

"Pretty full of yourself, I see. Just where do you think the United States is? It's not half-way around the world from France." He laughed.

"Whatever." she answered, laughing. "Alright, I'm out. It's late. I have to be up at ridiculous o'clock."

"I like that: ridiculous o'clock."

"Bye," She said.

"Good night, Princess. Or should I say Queen because Aila is the princess?"

The way he spoke sent shivers dancing up Malaika's spine. Still she managed a snort so he would know she thought it was silly. She washed off her face. Her skin felt like a baby's bum. She made a mental note to tell Paxon. She popped into Aila's room to see how she was. Fast asleep. She was about to close the door when Aila made a cooing sound. It was so adorable despite the fact that she was not a baby anymore. She tiptoed inside and tucked the duvet into her neck before kissing a soft, warm cheek. She headed downstairs to take meat out of the freezer so that it would be defrosted by the time she woke up. Malaika cut all the peppers, onions, tomatoes, celery, potatoes and garlic she was going to put in the pyrex casserole dish along with the meat then and put it all into a lunch box ready for the morning. She got a bottle of water to take upstairs with her and checked to see that the front door to the house was locked. She was about to go upstairs when Axel called her.

"Malaika?" Malaika jumped in surprise.

"Yeah?"

"For Aila's birzday I order one cake and the bouteilles of

champommie and champagne. How many bouteilles you sink we need?"

Champommie, the beloved kids champagne that tasted like apple cider, was a big hit even with adults. She suggested 20 champommies and 5 champagnes.

Axel spoke to Malaika about logistics stuff a lot. She was terrible with numbers and estimations but she gave her opinion all the same, else there would be hell to pay. He would blow a fuse and scream at her for not making any effort and call her too stupid to figure something as simple as this out.

"Ok," he said.

"Goodnight," she told him to prevent him from calling her out for rudeness. Axel always demanded respect for inconsequential things but he didn't value it coming from Malaika.

He grunted.

# 11

## Eleven

A good morning for Malaika was one where she didn't have to interact with Axel. This was a good morning. Malaika rose early to put the roast in the oven. She spent five minutes praying, then cleaned up the kitchen. After, she went upstairs and got ready. She tried different eyeshadow looks before settling on something understated and more au naturel than she had imagined last night. She got Aila up and helped her get her morning started. After her bath, she went down to make Aila's breakfast while she got dressed. She came down with her school bag and her gymnastics bag. Malaika gave her fruit and muesli. She ate it all while Malaika made orange juice.

Axel was up and in the downstairs shower. Because he spent most of his time downstairs, he used their guest bathroom to get ready. Malaika didn't mind because he moved around like a drunk rhino on the days when she didn't have to be up early. Aila and Malaika were heading out the door when Axel came into the kitchen for his breakfast.

After dropping Aila off, she headed to a café near her school. When Paxon arrived, she was sufficiently distracted by the internet.

He looked like a man on a mission. "Come for a drive with me?"

"Yup," she said, sans hesitation, packing away her things.

He was telling her that he rented a car for the duration of his stay and was told to get something small because parking in Paris was extremely difficult.

"It's true parking is tough. I've found people's cars literally kissing my car's ass— that's how tight the space was."

"Yeah?" he looked at her as spoke.

One of the things she really appreciated about Paxon was that he listened to even the drab things she said. But she also hated how closely he observed her. It made her feel both self-conscious and seen.

"Small is definitely the smart way to go," she confirmed.

He smiled, pleased with himself. "Glad I made a wise choice."

They walked a short distance and stopped. She looked around, waiting for him to show the small car to her. There weren't any in sight. Paxon walked up to mini cooper and Malaika stopped, expecting him to unlock it. Paxon walked on and stopped two cars down at a sports car. Malaika's eyes could see the car he was standing next to but her brain was slow to catch up to the reality. Paxon used his finger to unlock the space gray Aston Martin. She glared at him sarcastically.

"What?" He asked, faux innocence all over his gorgeous face.

Malaika shook her head.

"You're judging me."

"No. I'm just—"

"Bullshit.,"

"You said you got something small."

"It *is* small," he said in protest "I barely fit in it." He pointed at the arresting sports car on the side of the street.

She pursed her lips. "We all have our cross to bear," she said, rolling her eyes at him.

He laughed. "You're really funny, you know that Princess?"

She flicked him off with her helpful finger. "Chen always says," she said dryly. "You might want to consider underground parking. I don't know how much of a difference it will make but I suspect you'll get fewer scratches that way."

"Got it," he said with a wink before walking around to her side to open the door for her.

She laughed out loud. No one had opened a door for her in...had anyone ever opened a door for her?

He smiled at her. "What?"

She just shook her head.

She directed him to the autoroute because she could tell he was itching to speed with minimal interference from other cars. When he accelerated, she felt like a cartoon being forced backward into her seat and imagined her face distorted by the speed and wind. The windows were closed, though, so chances were she just looked constipated.

Paxon turned the radio on and occasionally sang along to the R&B songs coming from the car's speakers.

"What are you into?" he asked her.

"What do you mean?"

"Music."

"All sorts, honestly. I really like when orchestras mix with Dubstep or House music. This is fine too. I listen to it sometimes. I guess it depends on my mood. This is you, then?" Malaika said in reference to the music.

"Yeah, I like other stuff too. No orchestras, though." He

stopped singing, bit his bottom lip and danced in his seat.

Was he trying to impress her or get her to jump him?

"So, I was thinking it would be nice if you came with me to one of these meetings with the brand." He took his eyes off the road to look at her.

She furrowed her eyebrows. "Sure," she said, feeling anything but.

"Yeah?"

"It'll probably be my only chance to have a close encounter with fame," she joked.

He smiled and Malaika was sure she detected relief.

"Now that's sorted I can share my findings about my face-mask last night." she said changing the subject

"So, it turns out I wasn't meant to wipe anything off. I was just to let it sit and let my face absorb it."

"Uhh..." he was nodding like he understood. "The face mask!" he exclaimed "Did it work?"

"The truth is, I don't really know what it was supposed to do because the packaging was mostly written in Korean. I saw acai berries and was like yasss because I know they are healthy."

"Hmm." He shook his head amused.

"So, your work situation? You say you're a housewife, but I always find you working. What's that about?"

"After graduate school I couldn't find work first because I didn't have working papers but even after I got them the protectionist laws here, well I guess like everywhere. So, before a company can employ me they need to prove that they can't find a French person who's not qualified to do the job. If they can't find one, they have to prove that they can't find an EU citizen who can do the job and only then does my candidacy become real."

"What are you qualified to do?"

Malaika sighed, "I studied at a liberal arts university so here in France they don't know where to slot me because I can do many things and their system requires you to be a jack of one trade. A master of one." She slapped her hands on her thighs "It's just very—"

She looked out the window. "I mean I get that employment is a mess all over the world right now and it's not really a reflection on me, but people think I'm just copping out and a lazy millennial."

"But you work as a freelancer?" he sounded so encouraging.

"Yes, but the work is seasonal and I get the impression that once people know that I'm from Africa, they doubt my capabilities. Like, they suddenly want to know what exactly I am trained in and where I got my training, which are things I know they don't worry about with people who look like they're from here or the U.S., you know?" She looked at him. "I had an Australian woman ask me when I am going back home and when Camille turned the question back on her it startled her. She couldn't understand why anyone would ask her that even though she's a foreigner here too."

"That's fucked up," he said.

She shrugged. "It could be worse. It could also be better, but voila! There it is. What about you?"

"Me?" He took a hand off of the steering wheel and placed it on his chest.

"How did you become the NFL legend-in-the-making you are?" He chuckled.

"I was always into sports. I took 13 sports credits in high school and I did a lot of sports in university: volleyball, swimming, basketball, high jump, martial arts, but my favorite was ultimate."

"Ultimate?"

"It's like football, our football, with a Frisbee. So, I gave football a shot too and ended up getting drafted right in college and voila!" he said just like Malaika had.

"Were you good at all these sports you did?"

"Pretty much. I've always known sports would be my path but I didn't know which sport in the beginning. Once I started playing football it became increasingly obvious for many reasons. If you can make it, it's a stable career choice."

Malaika nodded and wondered what that was like, having a stable career.

"What made you get Aila into gymnastics?"

She inhaled deep before answering "It was either that or ballet, but gymnastics has a better chance of giving her a viable career option. She enjoys it." What she didn't say was how she always wished she could be a gymnast.

"Ok, do you have a destination in mind? We've been driving around for a while."

"No, I just got you to the highway so you could speed in peace. You don't get a speed demon machine like this one and not actually test the zero to a hundred time."

"Aw," he teased "You did that just for me? I'm touched."
He laughed.

She scoffed but smiled. She checked her phone. Technically she could spend all day doing nothing with Paxon but that seemed weird. She also did have work to do.

"What else do you have planned for the day?" she asked him.

He turned and aimed a smile her way. "Nothing. I am trying to do something different each day with you or before or after I see you. I have a fitting in the evening and then there's a social thing for all the brand partners, but I won't go. I was thinking Netflix."

"You're really just spending a summer in Paris chilling, huh? Paris and chill."

"And getting to know you."

"I think you're trouble," Malaika said without thinking.

He looked at Malaika and cocked an eyebrow while smiling. She promised herself she wasn't going to smile—shit.


"Eyes on the road mister." She put her hand to his cheek and turned his face back to the road. Before her hand slipped from his face, he grabbed it and tangled their fingers, lowering their hands to the gearshift. His hand was warm and strong, yet gentle.

"You can't do that," she said. She wanted her voice to sound forceful, a little indignant even, but it was breathy and completely lacking conviction.

"Why?" he said, not letting go.

She wanted to say you know why but couldn't muster the courage. She didn't really think he shouldn't do it, she loved that he did. So, she shook her head once and kept her mouth shut. He lifted her hand and dropped a sweet kiss on her knuckles. She'd never encountered a man of such beautiful opposites. It was captivating.

Paxon firmed his grip on her hand and rested their joined hands on his lap, occasionally stroking the base of Malaika's hand with his thumb. They drove back to the city without talking. When they got to town, he parked close to where they met earlier that day.

"I don't want to be terrible, but I have work to do," Malaika told him.

He kept his eyes locked on their hands and nodded. "I'll call you later."

"You don't have to message everyday if you are busy," she told him with a bright smile.

"Babe, understand that I enjoy communicating with you. You are with me all the time. It's not an obligation." he said capturing her eyes in his gaze.

She took a deep breath. "The car is awesome. You're driving not so much," she teased him. He loved how she tried to lessen the tension with awkward effort.

"You all drive like crazy people here."

"Sure, sure. Blame the French," she said, still teasing.

"Lo?"

"Yup?"  She unbuckled herself and began collecting her things.  He looked to Malaika's eye like there were words unspoken longing to leave his lips. They never did.

"I really do have work to do." She justified "I'm glad you're here. I'm glad I get to see you as often as I do." She wore an uncertain look. "I'm just cautious because I mean, how long will you still want to show up every day for someone whose time is so limited? You know, before you just forget about me."

"You don't have to worry about keeping my attention.  I didn't see or hear from you in two years and still needed to find you. It really fucked me up actually." His nervous laughter filled the car. "Do you plan to forget me?" She wondered if he knew she could sense his uncertainty.

"No," she shook her head resolutely.

"Good," he said with a smile.

"It messed you up, that time we spent together?" she looked worried.

Paxon smiled reassuringly and the dimple made an appearance. "You're pretty unforgettable," he told her in a low voice. "Pretty and unforgettable," he amended.

She stared at him open mouthed.

"That didn't stop you from trying," was all she managed.

She was referring to his engagement to Bonnie. Her words were sharp. Malaika was aiming for sugar and spice and not always so nice.

"Ok," he sounded amused at her response. Yes, she was jealous. That knowledge seemed new to her. Her mind kept making these stray observations about feelings. Was she starting to understand human behavior and emotions? She wanted him. Before he could answer she spoke,

"I've gotta—"

"Go, yeah."

Neither of them moved for a moment. He shifted in the leather seat. She knew she should feel like a terrible person for wanting him, as a married woman but the feelings he had were so strong and completely beyond her understanding. She hated doing the wrong thing, but she loved spending time with him. She loved being seen by him no matter how short-lived this all turned out to be. She felt excited, for the first time, about something other than the next contemporary fiction novel on her Audible shelf. She went to her car and sat there in a daze as he watched her. Finally he gave her a solitary wave- probably a polite signal to get gone. Engine roared to life and she drove away.

Malaika was early so she didn't have to fight for the parking under the tree. It was the best spot because it was slightly bigger than all the others. Malaika laughed maniacally in her head over the small victory. While she waited, Malaika worked.

Not having internet was wonderful for her productivity. The internet was where her attention went to die or get high switching from window to window at the speed of white light. She was no longer beating herself up for cutting her time with Paxon short today because she'd gotten a lot done. She congratulated herself.

Aila filled Malaika in on 5eme gossip when she got in the car and Malaika listened with keen interest.

During her gym practice, Malaika resisted the urge to check Paxon's social media.  Camille was not there to keep her company. Her mind drifted to Aila's upcoming birthday party. It was on Sunday afternoon. Karim was sleeping over on Friday and Malaika thought it made sense to just have him stay till Sunday, since he would be back then anyway. She suspected Camille would enjoy some time to herself. Malaika texted her and she was in total agreement. Malaika knew Camille would make every effort to ingratiate herself when she saw her next.

When it was time to leave the gym Malaika drove home listening to all Aila's favorite songs.

Axel was lounging in track pants on the couch flipping through channels when they arrived home. They pecked each other on the mouth and then he and Aila hugged. Aila headed straight for the shower before doing her homework. Malaika sorted through laundry and had a pot of mixed vegetables on the stove and asparagus soup brewing in her Thermomix. She got her earphones and plugged them into her phone so she could talk handsfree and called Paxon so she didn't forget.

"Hi." He sounded out of breath.

"What are you doing?" she asked, forgetting her manners.

"I was in the shower. Hopped out to get the phone."

"I can call back later," she offered.

"No, it's fine. I'll put you on speaker."

"You getting ready to chill or have you changed your mind and decided to go to the function?"

"Turns out I actually do have to show up for a short while for photo ops."

"That's cool."

"It'd be cooler if you were coming along."

Malaika laughed.

"I'm serious."

"I haven't been out to anything in—Besides being home is the best. Comfortable, toilet, ice-cream."

"I don't disagree; home with you does sound like a good time." He was not going to be deterred from flirting, it seemed.

"You are impossible," she told him, not meaning a word of it.

"That's why you love me. What are you doing?"

"Laundry and cooking dinner."

"What's for dinner?"

"Turkey in white sauce, mixed vegetables with asparagus soup and rice. It sounds like a weird mix, but it's actually really good."

"I hope I get to try it soon. You can cook for me."

"If you promise to stop being so impossible."

"I can't promise you that. I plan on being as impossible as I can get away with." Malaika burst out laughing. "You have told me your evil plan. Now it won't work."

"Nuh uh, I have a secret weapon. I'll hug you while you cook."

"To make the experience less patriarchal?"

"I take it back. Your detective skills are really bad."

Malaika gasped in mock offense.

"Malaika!" Axel's voice boomed. "Can you stop it? You're not a teenager to laugh so loud. I try to watch somesing."

Malaika sighed.

"What's wrong?"

"His Lordship requests that I keep my laughter down."

"Ah." Was all Paxon said.

"Papa?" Aila called to Axel.

"Oui poupette." he answered. She couldn't hear what they were saying. "I guess I should let you finish getting ready" she said to Paxon.

"Sure."

And then, because she was so used to saying this to Camille and Chen when they were getting ready with her on the phone or Skype she said, "Text me a picture of your outfit." As soon as she realized she'd said it, she slapped a hand over her mouth.

He laughed into the receiver. "Ok Lo, but only because it's you."

"Great!" she tried to mask her faux pas.

"Call you later?"

"Yes, please." Somebody needed to stop her, seriously.

"Later, Lo."

"Hmmhmmm." She didn't trust herself to say actual words at the moment.

After dinner, Malaika went over homework with Aila. She did so with the enthusiasm of a cat waiting to be bathed and felt guilt about being more excited about something other than Aila's homework. Was she being irrational? She had no idea. Her phone buzzed and a small spark caught in her chest. She had to catch herself from jumping and reading the message immediately. She played back Aila's latest routine in her mind so there was sufficient -I wasn't waiting for your message- time between receipt and opening of the message. She opened it to reveal a photo of Paxon in a full-length mirror wearing a black suit over a crisp black shirt with the top two buttons open. His shoes were black too and his hair was gelled back. He was clean shaven, like the world's sexiest secret agent.

*Looking sharp* she texted him. He didn't reply and she was a little deflated. She continued going over homework with Aila. When they were done, she was ready to collapse. She got a bottle of water to take upstairs to bed with her before switching off the lights in the kitchen, dining room, and corridor. Cleaning up the kitchen would have to wait until morning. Sure, she'd have to wake up an hour earlier than normal but at this point she was too tired. After her evening ritual and reading Aila's bedtime story, she collapsed into her bed. Her phone rang.

"Hi," she said groggily.

"And then?" Chen sounded both expectant and irritated.

"And then what?"

"You didn't finish telling me the story about Hotel Guy-Thor."

"I told you to forget it."

"N'kay," Chen said. Malaika knew it is anything but. "Anyway, do you have everything prepared for the press session you are going to next week?"

"Huh?"

"The Live Long Conference. Next week's the press sessions."

Shit, she groaned internally. She'd forgotten. The conference was not until the middle of next month, but a month before there were press sessions for exhibitors, like her, to hold press conferences to get some traction before the actual event. She had organized everything months ago and set the automatic emails to be sent, but then blanked on it being next week. All the stuff with Aila and the national team and now with Paxon being here had her spinning too many balls at once.

"I am ready," she lied. She was going to have to go through the press packets. Maybe she could get Aila to help her put them together. Everything arrived in the mail months ago and she just left them in the boxes in her home office. Chen herself would be coming to town for the actual conference next month but this build-up Press Sessions event Malaika had to do alone. Monday was the first session and she needed to be at the exposition park by 7 a.m. Aila's party was Sunday, which meant Malaika would be prepping for that all of Friday and Saturday. When would she have time to get the press packets done? Maybe she could call Camille to help. It was such short notice, though.

"Very good," Chen said. "Are you, Aila, and Axel okay?"

"Always," said Malaika dryly. She asked how Maika, Chen's daughter, was.

"You know she is always good. Getting so big. There is talk of a boyfriend. Her father came here hyperventilating about it. Fool helped himself to my expensive alcohol, pacing in my lounge. Can you imagine?! Nx." Chen kissed her teeth either in disgust at her estranged husband's antics or disbelief.

Malaika laughed because only Chen could make a six-foot-four criminal defense lawyer sound like a clown. "Don't worry. Everything will be fine with the boyfriend. I'll get to the bottom of it. You know Maika thinks I'm that cool aunt she can talk to."

"Oh please, look at you!" Malaika knew Chen was frowning and rolling her eyes. "Cool aunt..." she muttered. "Anyway,

I'm sorry I was so, you know, the last time we spoke. Tell me about Thor."

"That is an in-person kind of conversation." Malaika said. "You'll have to wait until next month."

"Stop trying to be suspenseful."

"Stop being a story lorry," she retorted.

Chen kissed her teeth then added, "Keep me posted about next week."

"Definitely. Night."

"Bye, dude." Malaika closed her eyes, still trying to find a solution to how she was going to get everything ready for Live Long Press Sessions. She had to take Aila to school. Axel wouldn't do it, especially if he knew it was for the app he thought was total rubbish. Malaika's buzzing phone interrupted her thoughts. She checked it lazily. It was a text message from Paxon.

*Good night, beautiful.*

Her heart skipped. She was about to text him back when something dawned on her so she called him.

"Hey," he answered on the first ring.

"Call to wish me sweet dreams?"

"Kind of" she giggled. She couldn't stop giggling. He probably thought she was so corny. In fairness, she was. "I was wondering— well I have a scheduling issue—I forgot about..." She exhaled. Her brain was mush.

"Let's have that again."

"Remember the Live Long Technology conference I told you about?"

"Yeah."

"The press sessions are next week, Monday and Tuesday. As an exhibitor I have to be there for our app and there are press packets to assemble and cart over there by 7 a.m. Aila's party is on Sunday."

"What's your question?" He cut through her bush of obfuscation.

"Is there any way you can help me pack the press packs or maybe take them to the venue while I take Aila to school and then I'll figure the rest out as I go?" She stopped talking and realized that he was probably still out. "I'm sorry. You're probably not back yet. This could have waited till tomorrow. I'll call back then."

"I'm not still out, Lo. I'd love to help you. Just tell me what to do. I'll follow your lead."

"Erm, okay? Why?"

"Because Cool lighten your burden if I can."

Malaika loved how calm he always seemed and how he seemed to want to make her his everything. She tried not to think too much about the fact that she wanted to love him. She was aware though that she was falling for this man who was only meant to be a temporary escape.

"You can explain all about how you will use me for free labor tomorrow."

Malaika laughed nervously. "So rude of me. How was tonight?" she said.

"It was okay. I got the mandatory photo ops. There were some nice cocktails. The location was like a living piece of art. The building was amazing, like everything else in this city." His bored tone belied his admiring descriptions.

"Good. I'm glad you had fun?"

"Mieh, thanks," he said with a chuckle. "See you tomorrow, babe."

When did he start calling her babe? "Paxon, I, I don't want

you thinking—" Why was she finding it so hard to express herself?

Paxon remained silent, patiently waiting for her to finish what she was trying to tell him.

"that I'm using you or taking advantage of your feelings. I think you're great but I'm also figuring things out."

"Er, ok." his voice was laced with uncertainty. "I think you're…" he took a breath, "…incredible."

Malaika didn't know what to say to that. She really wished there was a book she could read on appropriate responses to compliments that fell in the supererogation category. She made a mental note to search for such a book.

"I'll see you tomorrow, babe." He finally said after he lack of response.

"Ok," Malaika breathed into the phone.

Every time he called her babe, something in her came undone. She wanted to belong to him. Somehow, unbelievably, she saw he was bewitched by her. She felt more like a woman, and powerful.

# 12

# Twelve

She blinked and time had flown past. She explained everything to Paxon and he'd said he was coming over a little bit earlier to help set up for Aila's party and then with packing for the Live Long Press Sessions. Aila was visibly vibrating with excitement. Most of her gymnastics acquaintances were here and one or two friends from school. Karim had been with her since Friday and the pair were playing video games. Malaika, an avid gamer herself, played with them often despite the ridicule Axel bestowed on her for it.

Camille was bringing an elaborate desert she said she made but Malaika was willing to bet it was bought. Camille's manicured nails couldn't withstand what was required to make a dessert from scratch. Malaika was excited to hear how the date went in graphic detail last week but couldn't tell from Camille's mood. Camille had sent a picture of the dude on the sly but because she was such a drama queen she withheld all photos and juice about the date for their in person DMC as Camille called the deep meaningful conversations. Malaika was glad she had waited for it because it was dripping with sexy salacious escapades. In a way, Malaika lived vicariously through Camille's dating life.

As Malaika got dressed she made extra effort with her eye shadow, mascara, and maroon eyeliner. It made her eyes pop but also looked understated, just the way she liked it. She decided on a pale orange maxi dress with loafers. She clipped the top part of her hair back with two small purple crocodiles. She made a mental note to remember to suck in her stomach after wiggling under the perfume she spritzed into the air above her to maximize perfume exposure.

The doorbell rang. She went to see who it was on the intercom screen. Paxon. He was early, just like he promised.

"The gate is open," Malaika said into the intercom.

He showed her a thumbs up and Malaika heard the ancient wooden gate creak open. She unlocked the door and looked up into his square-jawed face. He obliterated her with a smile.

"Hey," she managed and commended herself on her level tone.

"Hi," he said with a wave then leaned in to hug her and whispered in her ear, "Beautiful."

She had to place her hand on her stomach to quell all the riotous butterflies. Behind him stood Geneva and his girlfriend. Malaika hugged them both; it only seemed appropriate given she was the host. They were all carrying gift bags. Malaika stepped aside and motioned for them to come in. She purposefully didn't pay attention to their reactions as they took in her home. It was tasteful but far from lavish as she supposed theirs were.

"This is so wonderful," Fern cooed. "To live in a nice house in the country."

"Thanks," Malaika said, not sure if she believed her. "It has its perks and its drawbacks."

"Like every place," Fern assured.

"It's really great of you to come. I thought you were visiting Normandy."

"We are back from the South and have a little over a week left here."

Malaika nodded from the other side of the kitchen island as she sorted things according to what should go out first.

"Hello," Axel said. Malaika hadn't heard him enter the kitchen. "I am Axel, the husband of Malaika." He stood notedly apart from Malaika and smiled without any other physical motion.

"Good to meet you," Geneva said, leaning forward and giving Axel a firm handshake. Fern followed suit. Paxon gave Axel his hand and said what Malaika thought was a rather frosty, "Paxon."

"Oh, you are ze friends from New York," Axel said, looking to Malaika for confirmation and squinting slightly.

She gave him a weak smile and an even weaker nod.

"Actually, we're from Minnesota," Geneva corrected, and Axel looked at Malaika with a confusion-strewn face. Malaika squirmed internally. She knew she would have to explain in explicit detail lest Axel call her a liar.

"We met in New York, but they live in Minnesota," Malaika clarified.

Axel nodded. "Cool. Can I give you somefing to drink?" Axel ran them through the list of beverages they had on offer. "Malaika, can you get cups?"

Malaika stopped what she was doing and moved to the cabinet above the sink to get cups for them. She brought them to the island, thinking Axel would take them and pour the drinks while she continued arranging dips, cold cuts and saltines. He did not.

"You are early," he commented.

"We came to help Lo set up and pack the press packets for her app press conferences next week," Paxon clarified.

Axel turned to Malaika and she busied herself pouring out drinks.

"Where do we put these?" Geneva asked of the gift bags. There was a table for gifts which Malaika pointed to while thanking him profusely for the effort and thoughtfulness. Geneva took the bags from Paxon and Fern and placed them on the table.

"Where's the birthday girl?" Fern peered around in search of Aila.

"She and Karim are playing games upstairs." Malaika grabbed her phone and sent Aila a message. Seconds later, the door upstairs creaked open and Aila and Karim came thundering down the stairs. They spilled into the kitchen looking feral

"Aila you are not dressed yet!" Malaika's voice was shrill even to her own ears. She feared the scolding she'd get from Axel for not having organized things properly and making sure the birthday girl was ready.

"But mummy..." she whined "It's not time yet."

"But guests are already here, see. You shouldn't wait until the last minute." Malaika gestured to the three guests.

"Hmm," Axel sneered. "You say her that but she see you always doing things at the last time."

Malaika pretended not to have heard and hoped her tutting would drown him out.

"Hello Paxon," Aila said and hopped over to give him bisous.

She rose on her toes as much as possible but Paxon still needed to do a fair bit of bending to reach her. She greeted everyone and Karim followed after.

"Va changer," Malaika ordered in her sternest voice and pointed upstairs. Aila complied willingly because there were people around. Karim stayed behind and offered to help take things outside. Axel went to start up the barbeque while Geneva stood close by, paper cup in hand. They seemed to be in a discussion. Malaika wondered what about.

"She is so precious," Fern said.

Malaika couldn't tell if she was being genuine or not. Aila was past the cheek-pinching age; few people referred to pre-teen middle-schoolers as precious. However, she smiled politely in response.

"Looks like you don't need much help setting up," Fern observed.

"Yeah, what I really need help are the press packages. Would you like to do that now or later?" Malaika turned to Paxon who was silently acquiesced.

"Okay. Come with me." She called them to follow her with a wave of her hand. She led them into her home office, which was varying shades of green. A leather office chair had boxes piled on it.

"Each box has a number written on it. 1 is messenger bags, 2 pens, 3 keychains, 4 the mini notebook, 5 memory stick, 6 sticker, and 7 the brochure/pamphlet," Malaika said. "Numbers 2 through 7 get packed in number 1. Make sense?"

"Yeah, I think we got it." Fern clapped her hands together. "You did the first half of the work for us.

"So, the pens you have to slide into the penholder." Malaika stopped and stared in wide-eyed horror. She hadn't numbered the penholders and slapped her forehead. "Oh no! I forgot to number them." Her head dropped. "This ruins the whole order."

Paxon waved it off. "It's a small oversight. Not to worry. We can just stick it inside the books and then put the pens in them. Just show us how or where you want it stuck in the book."

Malaika smiled in relief. She took out a mini book and the penholder and showed them where she wanted it.

"Got it," Paxon said, giving her a thumbs up. He was full of them today.

She smiled nervously at him. "Thank you both so much for doing this. I'm not just leaving you like minions. I'll set up really quickly out there and be back to help. There are 1000, so..."

They both nodded.

"Let me know if there's anything I can do to facilitate the work."

"Don't worry. Go, we got this," Paxon said with a warm smile. "Get Geneva to help out there."

"Ok. I'm already less stressed."

Back outside Malaika took everything out. She checked on the cake in the fridge and was tempted to stick a finger in it and taste the cream. Her pigs in a blanket were done so she transferred them from the oven to a serving tray. She had mozzarella balls, Italian ham, and cherry tomatoes on sticks still to assemble. Geneva and Axel came inside. She looked out the window and saw that the barbeque fire was in full blaze. She left the assembly line and got the meats out of the fridge just as Axel entered the kitchen.

"Can I have the meat?"

She showed him the trays of meat lined up ready for him to

take out, hoping he'd be pleased but he barely noticed.

"Where are the ozer people?"

"In the study making press packets."

"You think it's correct to invite people to come and do zis for zis fing?" He said sounding incredulous. He said "thing" flippantly.

Malaika ignored the insult and tried to change the subject. "Did you need their help for something?"

"No, no. Do I need nofing! It's not good to tell people to come and work on this stupid fing…I dunno press mechant."

"Why does it bother you? I didn't ask your friends or family. They're my friends and they offered to help."

"It's not because they offered to help that—"he was interrupted.

"Lo."

Malaika swiveled around to Paxon and pasted on her most convincing smile

"I wanted to know if I can take a press packet for my organization. They have such cool stuff."

"Of course," She said in a voice high enough to summon bats. "But, uhm, maybe you want to come out and join us. I think you can finish it after everyone's gone."

"No way!" He acted like the suggestion was insanity. "I promised I'd help. I only came to support you." He looked Axel dead in the eyes as he spoke.

She looked to Axel and waited for him to say something. His silence grudgingly abandoned the issue.

"Ok, can I have the—"

Malaika pointed to the trays before Axel could finish his request.

"What iz zat?" he said, referring to the fact that Malaika

had pointed to the trays. Malaika looked at him, not believing that he was finding another reason to pick a fight. She said nothing and Paxon said nothing. Malaika wondered what he was thinking. She wished he'd leave and not witness all this.

"Hello?" he raised his voice. It was a question that demanded an answer.

"Yes, there is everything you need." She hoped he would leave it alone.

"But why you point ze fing like zis?"

Malaika did a mental sigh and closed her eyes.

Paxon moved and came to stand in front of Malaika. Malaika was surprised but thankful for the intrusion. His enormous frame blocked her from Axel's view. Axel was tall and slim. Malaika held her breath. He took a tray and handed it to Axel.

"Here you go man." His voice contained a sort of forced cheer.

Axel took it reluctantly. Paxon handed him another tray and Axel left without another word

Malaika looked to Paxon with eyes the size of lightbulbs. She was about to ask him what the heck he was doing but he tutted. Before she could protest the doorbell rang. More guests.

"So, it begins," Paxon said ominously. He chuckled and Malaika gave him a look that managed to both thankful and condemning. He motioned for her to get the door.

She was met by her sister-in-law, Goodness. Goodness greeted Malaika with as much enthusiasm as Malaika felt at seeing her. She motioned her in. Goodness always came with tons of stuff so Malaika went to Goodness's car to help her husband bring in bags, boxes, or suitcases. She didn't know what it would be this time. When they were done, she came and found her in the kitchen making something. She brought something to eat but needed to use Malaika's kitchen to get it ready. Malaika hated this about Goodness. She always came with food that she prepared special for Axel. She then left the food in freezer bags in the fridge. It created clutter and made it so that the kitchen was an unnecessary hive of activity.

Malaika talked with Goodness's husband, Jean-Yves who was generally nice despite being what the French called a Monsieur Je Sais Tout, a know it all. He was telling her about an author Malaika was only discovering through a video game.

Fern and Paxon came to join them.

"You are here again," Goodness said when she saw them. Fern exchanged a look with Paxon.

"This is our first time here," Paxon said and looked at her with a blank expression.

"Yes, but I see you again."

"Yeah, we came to see Lo."

"C'est qui Lo?" Goodness asked Axel, who had just returned from putting the meat on.

"Why he call you Lo?" Axel asked Malaika. "And why you wear zis? Are you going to change?"

"It's something he heard Delano and Vuyo call me." Malaika answered his first question and pointedly ignored the second. Seriously? He wanted to attack her appearance in public.

Her answer irritated Axel. He huffed and narrowed his eyes as though he was thinking. Malaika suspected he only did the narrowing eyes thing to make her anxious, to send her mind spinning wondering what he was thinking.

"I meant to tell you earlier; I love your dress," Fern said, making a fuss and insisting Malaika turn a full circle so she could inspect it.

"Thanks. I'm trying to channel summer because it just won't

come." Both women laughed.

"I have wide leg pants in that color, but the color doesn't pop on me the way it does on you."

"You're too kind," Malaika said, feeling embarrassed.

Paxon cleared his throat and looked at Malaika expectantly. "What was that?" he asked and Malaika laughed.

"Mind your own business," she told him playfully.

"Just for that, I'm on strike."

Malaika rolled her eyes. "So French."

"When in Rome," he quipped with a shrug.

"What's he on about?" Fern wanted to know.

"Paxon has this thing where he tries to make me uncomfortable whenever I don't accept a compliment."

"Fern, can you get your fiancé to sub for me?" Paxon moaned.

"Get him yourself," she said and winked at Malaika.

Malaika's brother-in-law introduced himself to everyone new and went in search of the birthday girl.

There was a knock at the door and Axel went to get it looking surly as ever. "Malaika!" he yelled.

Malaika jumped. "Yes." She hurried over to Axel and joined him in greeting the new guests. Aila and Karim planted themselves on the sofa in the lounge, playing a game with a tablet shared between them.

Some of Malaika's friends from church came. Everyone seemed to be mixing well. There were some more kids, mainly Aila's cousins. She and Karim finally abandoned the cyber world for reality. They were all running around in the garden.

Malaika couldn't find the new serving dish so, she just took an old one. She put the fancily sliced cantaloupe on it. She spent 30 minutes watching how to do it on YouTube last night, so she hoped people were impressed. She put it out and returned to the kitchen to get the little starter plates. She was counting forks and knives when Axel walked into the kitchen holding the serving dish with the cantaloupe.

"Malaika, is this the new dish?" It obviously wasn't; he knew that but he was trying to prove a point. Malaika had already lost before his tirade began.

"No, I don't know where it is, so I just put it in that one."

"And you say I talk a lot and I'm always upset. I always have somesing to tell you." He was angry. She didn't know why. "How can you put zis out for people?"

"What's wrong with it?"

"What's wrong wiz it? Are you serious Malaika?!" he narrowed his eyes at her and then distorted his face in a way that made him look both disgusted and disgusting. "I always find something, some mistake you do." His voice was raised and rising. Malaika was thankful everyone was outside where there was plenty of noise. He angrily slammed the dish on the island and stomped around the kitchen in search of the new one. He found it. "How I do zat? I am ze smartest person in the world?" He pointed to his head and then gestured about himself. He was glaring at her, nostrils flared "You always make me upset."

"It's not a big deal, Axel." She was careful to keep her voice low.

"Si, it iz a big deal!" He was getting angrier, his mouth snarling and Malaika knew things would only get worse. She should have kept her mouth shut.

"Everything okay, Lo?" Malaika turned to the doorway leading to the corridor. Paxon's massive body occupied the space. He looked either disbelieving or angry. Axel stopped in what Malaika thought was surprise or annoyance but then recovered quickly masking his facial expression.

"Fine. Did you need anything from the kitchen?" Malaika tried to sound normal.

"No," he said far too quietly for Malaika to know what his tone and answer meant. He stared at her and his jaw tightened. He didn't leave, so Axel was forced to put his rant on hold. Axel transferred the cantaloupe into his appropriate serving dish and stormed out. Malaika watched him in silence and hoped she could just ignore Paxon's presence.

"Are you ok?"

"Yes. Why wouldn't I be?"

He tilted his head at her. "What was that about?"

"Oh," she waved her hand dismissively. "Nothing."

"It's not nothing, Lo."

"I didn't use the right serving dish is all."

"And that's why he was that angry? Questioning your intelligence? I don't like the way he talks to you."

She shook her head. "You weren't supposed to hear any of that."

"But I did."

"Paxon—" She let out an exasperated sigh. "How far are you guys with the packing? Do you need more snacks? A break?"

"Almost halfway through."

"You guys deserve a break." She smiled at him.

"I think I will take a break and join you. But seriously, where is Geneva?! Dude has been dodging work like he's running from Fern's mum." They both laughed at this.

"Is she like a monster-in-law?"

Paxon grimaced and nodded vigorously. Then he put a finger to his lips.

"Oh," she whispered, and they snickered conspiratorially.

"Malaika!" Axel's booming voice interrupted.

"Yup."

"Can you come?"

She walked slowly in the direction of his voice. Paxon followed. She found Axel on the terrace looking intently at the settings.

"Where are the big spoon to dish?"

"I'll go get them."

"You need me to tell you to bring—" his eyes bored into her and then he stopped speaking when he saw Paxon beside her.

She turned to go and get the spoons. Again, Paxon came with her. He was like an annoyingly large shadow she couldn't shake. Not that she wanted to, she just didn't understand why he was glued to her. Once she was back in the kitchen, she pulled open the drawer where the serving spoons were and got them out. Paxon took them from her.

"Why are you shadowing me Paxon?"

"You want me to go away?"

She rolled her eyes at him, but he disarmed her with his ridiculous smile and said, "You wound me."

She laughed. They returned and delivered the serving spoons. Malaika called Geneva over. He left the circle of men hanging out by the grill not doing anything useful but looking very busy all the same. It was so strange to her how men managed this, looking busy while doing nothing.

"Get your ass in the office and pack bags man!" Paxon commanded.

"I was coming right after this beer."

"Bullshit," Paxon said, matter of fact.

Geneva went with his beer, looking very sorry for himself.

Malaika laughed quietly. She was allowed to laugh; she was not the one forcing him to work.

Paxon shook his head disapprovingly at him. "Making me ashamed to call you my friend," he called after him.

Malaika smacked Paxon on the shoulder.

He shrugged. They sat on the terrace double chair.

Malaika observed everyone present to celebrate her little girl's birthday. It warmed her heart. The birthday girl zoomed past, curly pigtails bouncing as she did.

Gracious came to sit on the adjacent chair. She was the more abrasive one of Axel's sisters. She was munching on a pretzel. "How you like France?" She pointed to Paxon.

"It's as amazing as all the adverts say it is."

"Where have you been?"

Paxon rattled off the things he'd seen and where he'd been.

"You should see the Abbaye Saint Michel."

"I'll make a note to do so before I go back."

Just then Malaika remembered she needed to bring out the salad. She moved to leave and said quietly, "I need to go and get the potato salad out."

"You need help?" Paxon asked, looking at her as she rose.

Malaika shook her head. She got inside and took the potatoes out of the pot. They had boiled earlier and she added them to the bowl along with some celery and radish. Then, she drowned everything in mayonnaise. After the mayonnaise was in the bowl, she used a wooden spoon to mix the concoction. She tasted a mayonnaise sodden potato. It was delicious and still slightly warm. She took the bowl back outside, placed it on the table, and returned to her seat. Lots more people had come to take up residence on the terrace furniture. Fern was out of Malaika's office and sipping wine happily. Axel was heading into the kitchen and she asked him if he could bring out a beer for her.

"Stop it wis zat," he said. "I don't want you start to ask me to do a lot of fing."

She kept quiet and waited for her embarrassment to pass.

Paxon rose to his feet. "I'm going to the kitchen. Can I get you something?" he said looking directly at Malaika. He towered over everybody.

"That's okay. I'll get one later."

"No. You're running around all the time; I got you. It's in the fridge?"

"Yeah. You can't miss it. It's big and grey."

"Very funny. Keep my seat warm," he said.

"'Kay."

And he was gone. Gracious eyed him with puzzlement as he left. Malaika had no idea what was going through her sister-in-law's head. Axel's obnoxious friend Blaise was in attendance and he, too, stopped his loud banter to scrutinize Paxon going to get Malaika's beer.

"Yeah, I am really impressed. You organized all this and the press packs, talking to all the guests, and mumming all at once," Fern piped up.

"Thanks." Malaika thought she might want to get to know Fern better if she had the time.

A few minutes later Paxon reappeared carrying a Heineken bottle in one hand and a bowl of crisps in another. He sat back down and handed Malaika the bottle.

"Thanks," she said quietly.

"Don't mention it"

After she was done with her beer she was on a nice buzz.

Axel called to her from the kitchen window and instructed

her to gather everyone for the cake cutting. She did. Everyone sang for Aila, who blew out her candles with formidable gusto. She then cut the cake into slices for everyone. Her aunt Goodness danced enthusiastically which was both entertaining and helped Aila feel less self-conscious.

When they were not being micro-aggressive and giving Malaika thinly veiled insults, her sisters-in-law weren't awful humans. One thing she did credit them for is that they were good to her little girl and for that she would put up with whatever nonsense they threw her way.

When all was said and done, she had gotten to talk more to Fern. They'd exchanged numbers and agreed to meet in the week before she headed back to the US. She came with Malaika to help serving people and packing up at the same time so that there wasn't too much cleaning up. Paxon went to help Geneva finish the press packs. Everyone was gone except for Paxon, Geneva, and Fern.

"This place is really nice. It's like what we in America imagine escaping to the French countryside to be like. It would be great to do a French country wedding, so picturesque." Fern cooed wistfully and then her eyes tripled in size. "Oh my God, do you know any places that would be good setting for a wedding here?"

Malaika surprised herself with her answer "I do, actually. Out here there are all sorts of journées for everything imaginable in France. Like, days dedicated to specific French special activities. A day dedicated to rose enthusiasts, a day for apple enthusiasts, etc. They are always held at these gorgeous venues like old castles, abbeys, or botanical gardens. I actually think I might have one in mind now that you mention it. I'll shoot an email to the city tomorrow during my breaks and let you know. Maybe we can go see it on Tuesday? You're still here, right?"

"Yeah! Definitely!" Fern squealed in excitement.

Malaika gave her a thumbs up.

"What, definitely?" Geneva asked, emerging from the corridor.

"Lo is taking me to see a potential wedding venue."

He looked confused.

"Just think how amazing it would be if we got married right here in the French countryside, sort of!" She was looking at him like it was a no-brainer.

He looked like he'd seen death and its scythe was held to his throat.

"Maybe," Malaika said tentatively. "If it's open to the public."

Geneva rubbed his temple like he was massaging an oncoming headache but said nothing.

Paxon looked at him amusedly but with a hint of pity.

Axel appeared from outside where he was chatting to the village gossip who was also their neighbor.

"We better get going," Paxon said. "I have to be up super early tomorrow to be at the expo place on time."

Malaika remembered she ordered passes for extra members of her "team" when she first applied for the Long Live Tech conference. She didn't know if she'd get anyone to help but she had intended to try Camille, though it would be like pulling teeth. Thankfully, it hadn't come to that since Paxon and Fern agreed to help.

"Just hang on," she said, holding up a finger to them. She dashed to her home office and returned with the printed passes. "When you get there, they'll give you plastic slips attached to lanyards for you to hang the passes from your necks."

Fern took them from her.

Malaika insisted on giving them leftover cake to take with them, which Geneva took with glee.

They said goodbye to Aila and Axel. Fern gave him a quick wave, Geneva shook his hand, and Paxon just said, "Bye."

Malaika walked them out and helped loading the packages in the trunk of their rented SUV. She hugged everyone and Paxon whispered in her ear,

"Thanks for inviting us."

She shook her head at him.

"Of course. I should be thanking you."

He flashed his beautiful smile revealing two rows of perfect white teeth.

"I'll call you later."

An even wider smile tore across his face. "I'll hold you to that."

"Promise by the hair on my chinny-chin-chin."

He lifted his hand and brought it to her chin. He stroked a finger under her it. Then ran his hand through his hair like he was catching himself.

She didn't know if it was because she was starved for affection, but her thighs clenched of their own accord. The heat of his gaze was unsteadying, and she stepped back before embarrassing herself.

"Bye, guys," she said a final time and waved. She watched until the SUV rounded the corner and disappeared from sight taking with it the Paxon's peace and possibility. She sighed, and turned toward the house and walked back into anxiety, fear and fatigue.

# 13

# Thirteen

Malaika was up at 4 a.m. She was up at ridiculous o'clock: miserable and thinking about all the sleep she could be getting instead of trying to will her brain to fall back asleep. It did not comply. So, she got out of bed and dragged her legs that felt like lead to the couch where she retrieved her computer and started working.

She needed to get more organized. She spent so much time telling Aila to get organized and practically chanted daily how it was the key to life but didn't follow her own advice. Now that Paxon and Fern were going to help her tomorrow she was less stressed but deeply rethinking her own organization. She couldn't really blame her memory loss of such a big event on Paxon's surprise appearance and yet... he was all she could think about. He had whispered in her ear yesterday and she couldn't stop thinking about his voice, deep, low, and steady, and his warm breath and soft lips that grazed her ear lobe with featherlight softness. Thinking about it was driving her to the edges of her sanity.

What was happening to her? She wanted to call him right

then and talk to him. About what? She didn't know, but she had a suspicion that hearing him would calm her and make the crazy stop. Her parents had drilled into her that you didn't call people after 7 p.m. 7 p.m. was the border line between decent and no manners. She texted instead.

*You're probably asleep. I can't sleep. I am nervous about the sessions, I guess.*

She hit send. She had spent minutes laboring over whether or not to write asleep or sleeping and now that she couldn't change it, she regretted sending it. He would wake up in the morning and think she was desperate. She sighed and was about to get up in search of water when her phone vibrated. Malaika held her breath and unlocked the screen to read the message.

*Can I call?*

Malaika couldn't help the enormous smile that overtook her face.

*Call.*

Her phone rang almost immediately.

"Hi."

"Why can't you sleep?"

"You're awake!"

"Yeah, I am. So, why can't you sleep?"

Malaika said nothing while she contemplated telling Paxon that it was him. He was the reason she couldn't sleep. More specifically, his voice and warm breath and his damned soft lips.

"Lo?"

"Yeah," She replied and thought the appropriate thing to do was lie. Tell him she was worried about the sessions where she'd be speaking in front of large groups of people and simultaneously promoting and defending her app. "I'm thinking about how to give you a socially acceptable answer."

He chuckled. "Let's hear it," he prompted.

Malaika cleared her throat once and before she could answer he said,

"Don't do that with me. You don't ever have to filter yourself with me."

Malaika could tell he was sincere. "I was thinking about you and you being here yesterday."

"Yeah?"

"Yeah."

"Good, I hope."

"That's the problem, I think."

"That your thoughts about me from yesterday are good?"

"No. Well, yes..."

"No? Well, yes? It seems really difficult if you can't really say it. I'm sorry I—"

She cut him off, "You whispered in my ear and I can't stop feeling it and thinking about it."

"Baby," he said quietly and the affection in his voice made her yearn to be near him.

"I love hearing you. Your voice or maybe the way you say things to me—it calms me." She was terrified to be saying it out loud but relieved to be able to say it without consequence. Without fear that he'd bolt at her admission or laugh at her or like Axel, tell her she was acting like a child and that life wasn't a movie.

"Really?"

"Yes," she whispered. For some reason when she started speaking to him, she'd gotten up off the leather couch and relocated to the floor, braving the mammoth spiders that were no doubt lurking. She had her knees pulled up to her chest.

"Good," he said. "I'm here for you."

Malaika didn't miss the double entendre.

"I want to be with you right now. Next to you, skin on skin, holding your little hand with long nimble fingers in mine." He sounded like she felt.

Malaika closed her eyes. She wanted to question why he felt the need to point out that her fingers were long. They were long, and her violin teachers always cooed over them like they were the most beautiful things they'd ever beheld. "Do you ever think about that time we spent together in the hotel?"

Paxon sighed. "Every day."

"Me too." After a pleasant silence, she sighed audibly. "I'm sorry to have disturbed you this late, or early. I just wanted to hear you."

"Disturb me whenever you want."

Malaika laughed. He made her feel like she was perfect, like everything she did was absolutely the right thing. She was addicted to that feeling, the feeling of not being a total and utter fuck up. She needed to figure out a way to create that for herself. "I'll see you later, Pax."

"Bye, babe."

After the call, Malaika closed her computer and attempted sleep. This time her brain was cooperative and when she woke up again it was to get Aila to school on time.

She sped to Porte de Versailles exposition park and walked as fast as she could in her black wedges. She had opted for blue high-waisted pants, with a crisp white button up shirt and a black blazer. She had really wanted to wear her beige heels because then the outfit looked incredible. Realistically though, she'd be standing and walking for hours, so she sacrificed looks for practicality. She knew French women did it, rode bicycles in 5-inch heels, walked on cobble stone streets in 9-inch heels and shoved it with the best of them in the metro in needle-thin stilettos, but Malaika accepted defeat. She just wasn't Parisian enough.

When she got to her stand, Paxon and Fern were lounging with coffee cups in hand. Everything was laid out neatly, perfectly. All she had to do was walk around and take her place.

"Morning, you two," she said, catching her breath a little.

Fern beamed. Paxon was in the process of smiling but stopped. His eyes took in Malaika's appearance slowly. His look went from pleased to see her to appraising to something else she couldn't quite understand.

"Hi." He managed and pulled her into him for a hug. "You are a very beautiful woman." He whispered in her ear.

Her heart squeezed. Before realizing what she was doing, she gave him a peck on the neck. He moaned low and Malaika pried herself back from him. She averted her eyes and busied herself with taking photos of the stand. She hoped Fern was oblivious to the strange magnetic pull Paxon had on her.

Paxon had to go because of his brand commitments leaving Fern alone with Malaika. Malaika liked what little she knew of Fern and the two spent the morning in pleasant chatter about anything and everything. Whenever Malaika had to do actual sessions Fern volunteered to take photos for Malaika to use for events and marketing. Malaika had gotten a call from Camille to check in on how the event was going. Malaika had used it as an opportunity to enquire about the abbey as a possible location for Fern's wedding.

Mid-afternoon Paxon called. "Hi."

"What's up?" Malaika said.

"I'll be done here soon and head back to help pack up." He told her.

"Oh, don't worry about it. Most of the packs have been handed out and Fern is still here. There's very little to pack up. We got it."

"Are you telling me you don't want me to come back?"

Malaika laughed. "You play so dirty Pax."

"No, I play to win," he said.

Malaika was about to answer when she spied Fern's eyes on her and temporarily lost her wording.

"Lo?"

"Yes. I'll see you later." She said in her most casual sounding voice and hoped it was convincing.

Fern smiled a wry smile. "So..."

"So," Malaika repeated, gathering leftover bags and placing them in a carton

"What are you going to do about him?"

"Do about who?"

"How did it start?" she asked point blank.

Malaika blinked in surprise.

Fern just stared at her.

"I'm not sure what you me—"

"When did the two of you fall for each other?" Fern asked in slow, clear words.

"We haven't fallen for each other," Malaika tried to protest, but knew her unconvincing efforts were falling on knowing ears.

Fern stayed silent, waiting.

Malaika's shoulders sagged.

"At my sister's birthday celebration in New York."

She didn't raise her eyebrows in surprise or slut-shaming

disgust; she just waited.

"He was just so easy to talk to and then there's the unfortunate fact that he's—" she motioned to her whole body.

"Unacceptably attractive?" Fern supplied.

Malaika laughed and nodded with her. "He's a great guy with an enormous heart. He feels like a brother-in-law because he and Geneva are close."

"Are you going to tell me not to hurt him or you'll break my legs?" Malaika asked with a hint of snark.

"I'm going to tell you that I hope you don't hurt each other."

Malaika looked sightlessly at the poster of her app standing beside her stall table. She wanted to say so many things about how she felt about Paxon but all she finally did say was, "Such bad timing, that I would meet him when I did." She laughed derisively "He's perfect."

"No, no, no, perfect he is not. Don't go all fangirl, groupie, on me or him." Fern laughed warningly "He's a great guy but let's not put anyone but ourselves on pedestals. He cares a lot about you, and I can see you care about him too. He fills you with a joy that you can't hide. I'm assuming you can't talk about it."

Malaika gave Fern a curious look and revaluated her initial assumptions about Fern's intelligence. "I met him at an especially low point in my life, my marriage. He was so kind and gentle towards me. He just listened to me ramble on about what a shitshow everything was for me and still kept the same enthusiasm to be around me. I knew he wanted me and, like you hinted, there isn't a sane straight woman who doesn't want him I let him and I enjoyed every moment of it. Then, I came back to the real world. He went back to his. I never ever in all my days thought I'd ever see him again or that he'd even remember me."

Fern took in a deep breath before speaking "He remembered you. He said your story touched him. He never told us what your story was, but he was in a funk for a while after your encounter. Then Bonnie made sure she was everywhere he looked, and you know men..." she shrugged. "But I swear I could tell when he was thinking about you. When he used to talk about you, he'd get this look on his face and sometimes when he was back with Bonnie and we'd be out, that look would return."

Malaika was staring at Fern openmouthed. "What look?"

"He'd stare sightlessly, like he was longing, and sad, and defeated."

Malaika resumed her work packing up because she didn't know what to say.

"So, what is your story?" Fern finally said while helping demount the stand and all its paraphernalia.

"I married a bully," Malaika said flatly.

"You a whiner?"

Malaika furrowed her eyebrows in question.

"Maya Angelou's mother told her never to whine because it lets the bullies know a victim is in the neighborhood."

Malaika smiled wide and stopped what she was doing to look Fern in the eyes, a trial considering Fern was taller than her. "You've read *Letter to My Daughter*."

"I have." Fern's response wasn't pride or offense at Malaika's surprise. It was matter of fact. "So have you." Fern pointed at Malaika.

"I have." The two women smiled at each other, a mutual understanding permeating the space between them.

Malaika was first to break their moment. "I'm not a whiner."

"Well then, I'm sure you know that you are treated the way

you accept being treated," Fern said.

Malaika wanted to be offended, but she knew this. She also knew that she didn't find the way Axel treated her acceptable but had, over time, for the sake of peace, stopped fighting or defending herself. She just swam below the current and hoped that at some point, someday, things would change. "Yeah, I know" was all she said.

"But also, he's a gaslighting turd!"

Malaika couldn't help it; she burst into laughter. "What? Where'd that come from?"

"You looked great yesterday, and modest, and he was trying to make it seem like you were indecently dressed. I wanted to say look here Dolce & Gabbana but I didn't want to start something, especially since I didn't have all the facts."

Malaika just shook her head. The fact that other people could see how he treated her made her feel shame and disgust. She tried to change the subject. "What will you do after this?" She looked up at Fern.

"Dinner with the boys, then an early night. I wanna do some shopping tomorrow really early and then go to gym in our hotel. I have been slacking and my waistbands have been resisting in response."

"What's your hotel?"

"The Royal Monceau."

"Oh, I hear they have a super fancy designer gym. You must tell me how it is when you go, or have you been already?"

"Not yet but I will keep you appraised." She lifted a box full of posters and other things and waited for Malaika to finish collecting the rest before they walked out to the car together. When it was all loaded into the car Malaika called Aila.

"Everything went fine, Mummy. Camille picked me up and

took me to the gym. We're at her house playing now."

Malaika was so grateful for her friendship with a person she could entrust her child to. "That's great. I'll come and get you in a bit," she told Aila.

Fern was leaning up against Malaika's car listening and inspecting her perfectly manicured nails. When the phone conversation was over, she pushed herself off the car and turned to face Malaika.

"Let's you and I get a drink."

Malaika agreed even though she knew Axel would not be pleased at her going out. She would deal with that later.

14

Fourteen

"What would you like?" Fern asked as they opened their drinks menus. They were at the restaurant on the corner looking out at the golden flame above the tunnel opposite the metro Alma Marceau.

"A Kir," was Malaika's automatic response. She loved Kirs.

Fern ordered a mimosa; something sexy and chic, like her. Once the waiter had taken their order, Fern slapped her hands on the table and spoke.

"What would you do if I told you the story of my life?"

Malaika inclined her head, surprised. "Listen, I guess."

Fern nodded and began. "I come from Newark, New York. My parents were, are, narcissists where they took credit for all my accomplishments. They refuse to accept any accountability for not being able to parent me or give me what I needed. When I was a child their words to me were "learn to be a phony and just do what you're asked". They got divorced and I had to live with Dad. He remarried a woman who had no interest in me at all. She only cared about the fact that Dad was a surgeon and she could spend her days going to pottery class and having coffee with friends in cafés and had a cook. They had a child, my brother.

One day when I was 16, I came home to an empty house. My stepmother had taken my brother and split. Dad was cheating on her, but he blamed me that she left and told me I no longer had a home.  I found myself on the streets.  My guidance counselor and his girlfriend took me in, and I slept on their couch until I graduated high school. Then I got government loans so I could go to college. I'm smart. I thought if I could get an education, I could make something of my life.

After getting my degree I couldn't get a job—big surprise. Companies wanted interns because then they didn't have to pay. They told us there was no position and sent us on our way after having worked us to the bone for free. I remember sitting on a bench outside the building I had worked in for 6 months and thinking to myself what is the point of all this? Now that I had all this debt, I had no way of paying back. I just couldn't see a way out.

I took a job at a bar that only hired me because they wanted to get more male customers and I am a pretty girl with big tits. I hated it and the fact that the only value I seemed to have was my looks. I met Vesuvio there. He would always hit on me and I would always politely decline. One day, Geneva came with him during pre-season. He seemed so out of place and just plain uncomfortable. I wanted to rescue him, to be honest. I started talking to him and we just kind of hit it off." Fern paused.

"That's quite the story." Malaika leaned back to get a good look at Fern. "Girl with a difficult past and all the odds stacked against her meets Prince Charming and lives happily ever after." I don't think I'm that kind of girl," Malaika said bitterly.

"Geneva isn't a charming prince. He's more of a burly, gentle lumberjack." Fern giggled "My story isn't finished. Because I have all this shit, this trauma, I look for ways to fuck up good things with people who want to be good to me.  Even with Geneva, I just couldn't understand why he wanted to take care of me when my own parents didn't want to. I've had to be responsible for myself all my life and all these feelings were holding me back inside. Geneva just kept on being there and loving me even at my worst when I would be hurtful to him to push him away.  I couldn't love him because I didn't love myself." Fern's eyes were glassy as she looked past Malaika.

Malaika couldn't tell if it was because of their brilliant blue color or emotion. "Why are you telling me this?"

"Because I see it in you. The self-conflict, the lie, that no one else will put up with you because you're not worth anything or because you're inherently flawed. Geneva put his foot down. He told me that he loved me more than he could ever love any woman but out of love for himself, if I didn't stop treating him the way I was, like shit basically, he would have to let me go. He said it would break his heart and he would never love anyone the same again, but he would move on. I was so scared to let him love me. I had to recognize what he brought to me was a need I'd been fighting my whole life. He was just there telling me I didn't need to be so scared or self-preserving anymore because he had me. It felt like he was giving me an ultimatum so obviously I didn't take that lying down, but later on I started to see my future without him in it and I realized that I couldn't live without him." She shrugged her shoulders once like that was it.

Malaika looked at Fern and sighed. "I wish I knew what that felt like to have someone need me or care for me like that."

"I think you do know what it feels like and freaking out is

understandable given your situation."

The waiter brought their drinks and Fern sipped from her straw while looking Malaika directly in the eyes. "What would you do if you knew that Paxon would love, and care for you, and adore you to death?"

Malaika opened her mouth to speak and then closed it.

"I'll answer that for you. You'd ditch your gaslighting, emotionally and verbally abusive husband and be with Paxon."

Malaika furrowed her eyebrows. She wasn't being abused. Axel'd never physically hit her. Malaika didn't look at Fern. She'd heard these terms and read about emotional abuse as domestic violence laws changed. She wrapped her fingers around her wine glass instead and sipped from her Kir. She began to feel anger and sadness for all the times she just assumed she was living through what was described as marriage being difficult when in fact it was cruelty. God almighty, she was one of those women she had read about in her sociology of gender class at university. She'd been subjected mental torture day in and out for years and somehow she'd just gotten accustomed to it. Somewhere along the lines, she'd started hiding it for Axel so that people didn't see his viciousness. The thing that was puzzling was why? Why had she let it get this far? She didn't understand herself.

"Forgive me for being insensitive. I know you guys have a child and other attachments, but you are miserable. Like, visibly miserable, and I don't even know you that well."

"So, what? I just switch Axel out for Paxon like lightbulbs?" Malaika said with a little too much frustration in her voice.

"Choose you. Do what is good for you. And I mean all of you: your sanity, your body, your health, the whole you."

Malaika laughed and shook her head in response.

"Ok, I'm not going to bring this up again, but I've said it and I know you heard me." She raised her glass up to Malaika's. "Cheers."

Malaika clinked her glass with Fern's. They stayed silent for a moment before Malaika asked, "So you really want to do your wedding here?"

"Oh, definitely!" Fern nodded. "It's France." She gestured to their surroundings

Malaika laughed and shook her head again.

"You're such a tourist. You poor, deluded tourist," Fern inserted mockingly, to which Malaika nodded and laughed.

"Hey, I didn't say it." Malaika put up her hands in faux surrender.

"But I have a secret weapon: you. No one will pull the wool over my eyes because you'll know."

Malaika frowned. "I think you overestimate my ability to haggle," she cautioned.

Fern just winked.

# 15

# Fifteen

Malaika and Aila were back home going over the pictures Fern had taken from the Long Live Technology event. Aila was putting the ones she liked best in a favorites folder.

Axel came in the room and asked what they were doing. Aila showed him the pictures. He made a humph sound and pointedly quashed any enthusiasm in the room.

"So zis is what you spent your day doing?" You don't have something better to do zan zis? Shouldn't you be looking after your shild instead?"

Malaika swallowed the anger that rose like lava in her throat. She had to organize that someone else take care of their child, his child, because he thought it preposterous that he be expected or even asked to do it. Malaika had to drive an hour one way to Camille's in order for this to be possible. She said nothing, knowing that giving a response was like looking down the barrel of a gun.

"Huh?" he prodded.

She asked Aila to go upstairs and get ready for bed. She didn't want her to witness what she knew was coming next. Aila did as she was told without protest.

Just as Axel began to speak again, Malaika's phone rang. It was Chen. Malaika loved Chen but Chen had a way of always teasing Malaika that made her feel like a silly person. Right now though, she 'd never been so pleased to get a call from Chen. Malaika grabbed her phone and spoke loudly for Axel to hear,

"Chen!" She turned her back to him and exited the room, leaving Axel to himself.

"How'd they go?" Chen enquired.

"It went well. No one asked anything I couldn't answer. They seemed genuinely interested in the concept and wanted to know about its inception and reach."

"Very good. I see we have some new subscribers to the service which I assume is directly because of the sessions. Good work!"

Malaika snorted "Sure, ok."

"What is it?"

"Nothing, it's nothing."

Chen tsked annoyed "Ok, don't tell me. Did Camille end up helping you?"

"Oh, no. Paxon and Fern did."

"Thor again?"

"Why do you call him that?"

"Oh please, because he looks like Thor."

"He does not. His hair is only long at the top now and shorn really short on the sides and back. He looks nothing like Thor."

"How long is that fool staying there anyway?"

"A while, apparently. He has a partnership with a brand, so he needs to be here to see the campaign through."

"Hmmm mmmh," was all Chen said. "If I ask, are you going to tell me about all this in detail?"

"All what?"

"Fine." Chen answered and didn't press any further. "Well, guess what?"

"What?"

"Maika's dad is taking her to Disneyland for Christmas."

"Wow, that's great. I'm sure she's really excited! That's so good of him."

"Mmmm, father of the year," Chen said snarkily.

Malaika cracked up. "You are so mean," she scolded, but Chen ignored her.

"Whatever, so, you people must come and see me for Christmas since my child is abandoning me."

Malaika shook her head. She missed her big sister's shenanigans. "We'll come."

"Yay."

Malaika rolled her eyes, thankful Chen couldn't see her. "Alright Chen, let's talk tomorrow."

Malaika was getting ready for bed and she was anxious. She so badly wanted to hear Paxon's voice. She knew something was wrong. She was becoming dependent on what he made her feel. He was like a drug. He made her world seem less chaotic. He stilled it, and in the stillness she could think clearly. She knew it was wrong and unhealthy, but still called him just to hear his beautiful, deep, rich voice. It was as if she went too long without contact with him, she went into anxiety.

"Lo."

"Hi" she said into her phone.

"You guys managed without me." He sounded a little disappointed.

"Yes, thank you. We went for drinks and girl talk after. You wouldn't have wanted to sit through that." She said. "Fern is a really cool person, I think."

"I'd be happy to sit through anything with you," he said. "And yeah, she's great, really great.

"Paxon don't do that."

"Do what?"

"Say those kinds of things. Act like you'd do anything for me. It's not real. It's just not."

"I would. What do you think I'm doing here?"

"Paxon," Malaika said sternly. She was about to launch into a logical and rehearsed lecture.

"Baby, I want you to know that every moment with you is a moment I want to renew. I wanted to see you again tonight. I hoped maybe after packing up we could do something together."

"Something like what?" Malaika was disarmed. Too easily, she chided internally.

"Anything. Whatever you want. I'm here for you."

"Do you think you could meet tomorrow?"

"I'll free up my time for you if you can meet."

"Please do," she heard herself say.

"Ok," he said. "I'll call you in the morning. I'll push back the meetings and cancel the things that can be canceled."

It was so stupid, but she melted because he was rearranging his day, his plans, for her. He was making her his priority.

"Ok," she repeated. "Goodnight Pax."

"Sleep tight."


The next morning, Malaika was up early humming and making pancakes for Axel and Aila. Axel was always up before her. He would certainly inform her of the time he woke up and how hard he'd been working at some point in the day as a way to show her how little she did. Still, that didn't annoy or bother her today. She felt oddly supported and cared for.

When Aila was ready to go, Malaika drove her to school and was prepared to go to the store for a few things before heading back home but Paxon called and told her he'd come and pick her up. She drove straight home. To her dismay, Axel hadn't left for work. When she asked, he said he wasn't going in for the day.

Malaika panicked briefly and sent Paxon a text.

He called her. "Don't worry about it. I'll come in and say hello before we go. You're the only person I know in this city. It'll be fine, babe."

Malaika didn't say anything.

"Lo? Are you thinking about not coming out with me today?"

"No, it's fine. Come. I'll be ready."

"Sure?"

"Yes, see you soon."

Malaika told Axel she would be spending the day out with Paxon. Axel didn't say anything at first but then as he saw her collecting all the things she'd need for the day he started in on all the things that needed to be done in the house. Malaika said nothing. When that didn't work, he asked about Aila.

"Who will take care of her while you are wiz your friend?"

"I will," Malaika said simply.

"You will, how?"

"Paxon is driving; he has a car. We'll fetch her. Nothing changes for Aila. I'll be there to take her everywhere she needs to be."

"He has a car? What kind of car? Where you see zis?"

Malaika shrugged.

"What mean zis?" He imitated her gesture. "I don't know how you finking in your brain Malaika. You don't know ze car but you are going to take our child in it. Do you know if he will agree to drive everywhere like zis?"

"Look, I agreed to help him out today, I can't say no when he's 15 minutes from the house, Axel."

"Life is so easy for you." He waved his hands at his sides. "Axel works and Malaika just spends her day going out wiz friends to take a coffee or I don't know. You sink life iz like zat? I hope you don't educate Aila like zis."

Malaika endured Axel's barrage and prayed that Paxon would arrive soon. She looked at her phone and debated calling him mid-Axel meltdown. That would make things worse. Instead, she typed a one-word message.

*Call.*

Her phone rang.

"Hey, how far are you?"

"Waze says 18 minutes. Why? Everything ok?"

"Erm, yeah of course. I just wanted to know." Malaika walked away slowly hoping Axel would drop it. As far as she could tell he didn't have anything more to say. What rotten luck that this would be the day he didn't go to work. Maybe it was a sign that she shouldn't be doing this. But what was she doing? Nothing. She was innocently hanging out with someone she knew.

When Paxon arrived, Malaika knew it. She heard the powerful engine of his car presumably maneuvering into a parking spot across from their house. A few minutes later, there was a knock at the door. Axel got it.

"Hey," Paxon said to Axel.

Axel greeted him.

"Great, you're here." Malaika said, flitting by like a breeze. She wanted to get out of the house as quickly as possible.

"Where are you going exactly and when are you coming back?" Axel began. Malaika hated this. He always did this. She had given him all the information he needed before and yet here he was making it hard for her to leave with questions to which he already knew the answers.

"I already told you." She said through gritted teeth. "Now I don't want to be rude and keep Paxon waiting." Mercifully Paxon spoke cutting off any further questioning from Axel.

"Yeah. Thanks for taking the time to help me with getting oriented," he said for Axel's benefit.

"You are going to take our daughter from school and the gym?" Axel interrogated.

Paxon was unaware of this but was quick on his feet. "Yeah, sure," he said, looking at Malaika "Good thing I changed the car," he joked.

Malaika smiled but didn't laugh. "Okay, let's go then." She said and turned to exit the door.

"Bye," Paxon said to Axel.

Axel followed them out to the gate. Malaika knew it was so he could see the car.

"It's the same car," Malaika commented when she saw it.

"But this one sits 4 people." Paxon smiled at her.

Malaika shook her head. They got in and drove away. Malaika didn't look at Axel but she would bet he was seething. She took comfort in the fact that she wasn't sneaking around.

Over the weeks that followed, Paxon and Malaika settled into a comfortable routine of spending their days together. Meanwhile, at home, Axel made it a point to make Malaika's life as difficult as possible. He griped about everything and pointed out what she did wrong or that he didn't like. It wasn't that she was letting any housework slide, it was that she wasn't slavishly doing it all the time. It was as if not seeing her yoked and constantly doing his will was the real problem. He reminded her daily of how he paid for everything. He was usually like this, but somehow the fact that it didn't bother Malaika like it usually did made him renew his efforts in this regard. Her growing regard for herself, clarity on the fact that he was human trash and her blooming happiness did not sit well with AXEL.

On a day when Malaika had spent the entire time cleaning without taking a break, Axel sent her a message. It read: *I love you when you clean.* Malaika didn't have the tools to deconstruct what his message actually meant. While chatting with Fern concerning the wedding party Malaika decided to slip it in there.

"Sometimes I think maybe it's not so bad. Axel sent me a message. He told me he loves me when I clean."

Fern answered without missing a beat. "Nothing like conditional love to make you nauseous on a busy morning."

Malaika often forgot about the time difference when she spoke to Fern. It was 7 p.m. Paris time, which meant that it was noon in Minneapolis. She sighed because she had suspected that that was what it was but it didn't help make it any less disappointing. She was caught in a trap, taught to believe that marriage was tough but no matter how tough, you stuck it through. Now, she was having a hard time perceiving a future on her own, outside the physical comforts Axel provided as well as seeing her future with Axel's continued abuse.

Spending time with Paxon was so liberating. She wasn't

afraid to speak because of the possible consequences her words would procure or let her face express itself for fear that he might find offense in it. She wasn't afraid to talk about her work without being informed of how meaningless and worthless it was. It wasn't so much that he showered her with compliments and praise, it was that he wasn't stripping her worth and confidence.

She drew in a sharp breath as the word, the meaning, the force of all of it overwhelmed her. It was respect. He respected her.

# 16

## Sixteen

Paxon's partnership campaign launch finally arrived and Malaika was dressed in workout clothes because Paxon had told her he got the dress and that someone would be at his apartment to do her makeup and hair. She felt spoiled and worried.

Axel hadn't really made much of a fuss but Malaika suspected it was because he never paid attention to what was actually going on in her life. A week from today Chen would be arriving and she did pay close attention to Malaika and her life. She would notice that Malaika was in love but not with her husband. Chen and Axel got along really well. While she didn't agree with how he treated Malaika, when Malaika would tell her Chen always minimized the situation and chalked it up to her blowing things out of proportion.

Malaika always felt somewhat alone because the people closest to her, her family, didn't take her plight seriously. He doesn't beat you, she'd heard people say. He buys you all this expensive stuff; he is so generous with your mother. So few men are good to their mothers-in-law. Somehow these things meant it was okay for Malaika to put up with his interminable emotional bullying. How did you even go about proving it was as bad as it was without physical markers?

These were the turnings of her thoughts as she got in her car and began the drive to Paris central, to Paxon's apartment. She was able to make a peaceful exit because Camille was keeping Aila and Axel wasn't home from work yet. Lord knows he would have held her up with useless questions designed to lure her into a long exchange if he'd been home and witnessed her leaving.

When she got to Paxon's he opened the door in tuxedo trousers and a crisp white shirt that hadn't been buttoned. She stared at his torso through the gauntlet made by his unbuttoned shirt. Her eyes got to his navel and she followed the trail of hair leading south before catching herself.

"You gonna come in or...?" he teased.

"Yeah," she said and brushed past under his arm which was holding the door open.

Paxon shook his head and smiled to himself. She wanted him. She was always so distant and guarded that it was little moments like these when her walls fell unexpectedly that she relied on to tell him she wasn't going to disappear because of how she felt about him.

"Were you exercising?" he wanted to know, referring to her clothes.

"No, but they're comfortable."

He lifted his head once and opened his mouth to express a silent ahh.

"So?" she asked expectantly.

"So?" he said, furrowing his brows.

"Where's the dress?"

"Oh," he said, apprehension taking over his entire posture. He cocked his head to the side, telling her to follow. He did it the exact same way he had done that night when they met in the club.

She smiled and he smiled back.

He led her into the lounge where a beautiful dress lay sprawled out on the long leather sofa. It was still on a hanger, covered in a glossy plastic with the designer name scrolled along it in bold white letters. He had asked for her measurements a while ago and now looking at the dress, she really hoped it fit because it was quite possibly the most beautiful dress she'd seen up close. She stared and fingered the material in mute awe.

"I take it you like it," he said.

She smiled wide at him. "Correct."

"Try it on."

"Yes sir." Malaika picked it up and folded the bottom so it wouldn't drag on the floor as she carried it. She changed in his bedroom and stared at herself in the mirror. The dress was flattering to her figure but modest. The feature she loved most was that it was flowy and there was a thigh-high slit on her left leg. When she walked it bellowed and danced and the slit revealed her leg. The dress came with a nude pump which had a moderate heel so she hoped her feet wouldn't feel like they were bleeding from being raked across a broken glass floor when they were well into the night. When she walked out in the dress, Paxon stared.

"I knew it," he said quietly.

"You knew what?"

"I knew you would look perfect in it." He seemed particularly pleased with his astute powers of judgment.

"There's a compliment in there for me somewhere so I'm going to say thank you."

"You're more than welcome," he said with a chuckle. "Come here." He beckoned her to him.

She walked to him hesitantly. When she was right in front of him, he leaned down and dropped a kiss on her shoulder. She fixed her gaze on his chest and refused to look up. All this time they'd been spending together they had not done anything to cross the line. They hugged and held hands and Paxon often caressed her back or her knee in the car but nothing more.

Paxon took her chin between his thumb and index finger and tilted her head so she was looking up at him. She thought he would say something, but he didn't. He was just looking at her, at her eyes and her lips. She was suddenly aware of her breathing.

"Thank you for being my date tonight," he said softly.

She smiled. "Thank you for inviting me."

He moved an inch closer to her and their noses were touching. He closed his eyes and rubbed his nose on hers from left to right. The action seemed like it was in slow motion. She inhaled sharply and before she could finish the breath his lips were covering hers. He kissed her slow and soft for a second and then he broke the kiss. Their lips were a fraction of a millimeter apart, but he might as well have been on another continent as far as Malaika was concerned. Their lips not touching felt wrong and was sending her into withdrawal so she did the only thing she could to remedy that. She kissed him. He gave a soft, little moan which made Malaika desperate to feel him, to be even closer to him. They came apart for air, Paxon's nose still connected to the tip of hers breathed against her lips.

She'd been dying to get a chance to feel him again, really feel him, and now she had it, but she was overtaken by fear. Fear that he might not want her or that she would feel guilty because of Axel. So, she waited with her eyes closed wishing, hoping, and sending up prayers to every God she could think of. Please let him want me, let him take me, and give it to me, because the truth was, she'd give up all- ok maybe not all, but definitely many- of her tomorrows for this, for him. From the moment she first met him, his boisterous sincere laugh, his eyes warm with a little bit of devil, and the toned hard lines of his frame, something about that combination had ensnared her and she belonged to him. And to think he felt something even remotely similar made her want to run circles around something- she didn't know what. It was why, he told her, he couldn't say I do to Bonnie and why he chose this endorsement deal with a smaller brand for less money in a European country, to be here with her, to let her be his.

"Pax," she whispered.

"Hmm-mm."

"How much time do we have before people come to get us ready?"

"Hour and a half."

"Ok," she said in a breathy voice.

"Ok?"

She nodded and slid her hands down his arms and underneath his open shirt. She drew the shirt off slowly and Paxon didn't move, not a muscle. He seemed afraid to even breathe. Could this really be happening?

Once his shirt was on the floor and Malaika's hands locked behind his neck, he wrapped his arms around her tiny waist. "I love how compact you are; you fit right into me perfectly, like you belong in the circle of my arms or your waist was made to be held between my hands." Malaika reveled in his words.

He pressed her body flat against his and ravaged her mouth, neck, collarbone and then turned her around so he stood behind her. She sighed and squealed and gave delighted little moans which drove him to the edge of his control.

"I love it when you smile because of me, baby," he whispered in her ear before nipping at its fleshy part and then trailing kisses down her neck. She cradled his head with one arm as his hands worked quickly to unclasp the hooks locking Malaika in the dress. Once they were all unhooked, he freed her from the beautiful material which pooled at her feet. His hands glided over smooth stomach and hooked themselves in her underwear. He licked and kissed her back working his way down her spine while pulling the underwear down as he made his descent. She stepped out of it once it reached the bottom. Paxon flipped her around and knelt before her. He looked up at her and smiled, then focused on her dark curls.

"I haven't shaved, I wasn't expecting anyone to see—" Malaika blurted out.

She was worried he wouldn't want her and that made him ache to tell her how much he needed her, to show her how far from the truth that was.

"This too has its charm, baby," he said and kissed her right where the triangle of curls began. Then he dove into her core mouth first, kissing, licking, and lapping. Soon Malaika was shaking. He wrapped his arms around her legs just under her butt and picked her up. He walked her to his bedroom and set her on the bed standing, then knelt and picked up where he left off. She collapsed and he didn't stop. She crashed from pleasure with a cry that ruptured the silence of his apartment. He kissed her from her sex all the way back to her neck.

"Get inside me," Malaika commanded.

He gave her a wolfish grin. "Beg."

Malaika did as she was told. "Please get inside me, please take me." He got up and leaned over, reaching for the drawer. Malaika sat up and began fiddling with his belt buckle. She got it open then got to work on the pants button and zipper. Once those two were released, she slid his trousers down his thick hard thighs and legs. Oh, how she loved his legs. She licked her lips and took him into her mouth. He let out a surprised but pleased groan as she slid her mouth up and down his hard length. Paxon closed his eyes tight in an effort not to shout. He didn't want to startle her, her mouth around him felt excellent and he grabbed a fistful of her hair. He then guided her rhythm until he thought he might explode. He tugged at her hair to stop her then bit into the foil which was in his other hand and spat the corner out. He bent down and kissed Malaika's beautiful mouth while his hand worked at sliding the sheath on his length. Malaika lay back down and he covered her with his enormous body. He sank into her. She still felt like the most perfect thing, even after all this time. Malaika gasped and he rocked his hips and began his assault.

"You are so warm," he whispered in her ear.

"You are not allowed to stop," she told him.

He sucked and bit into her shoulder before answering her. "We have a lot of things to do before I stop," he assured her. Then his mouth latched onto a pointy nipple while his hips continued grinding into Malaika.

Malaika moaned and gasped and grasped onto his back, pulling him deeper. "Sit back," she said softly.

Paxon stopped and did as he was told. He sat on his knees.

Malaika sat on him and rode him.

Paxon held her by the hips to anchor himself and bit into his lower lip. She felt more than amazing but he had to stop her, or he'd finish before she did.

"You have to stop; I'm going to come," he said panting.

"Come," she said. "Come for me."

Paxon moaned and growled as she rode him relentlessly and then pulled her to him. He needed to taste her skin. He suckled a small breast and then told her in a hoarse and desperate voice. "I'll come for you baby." He put her on her back in the service of finishing and when he was done and they were both trying to catch their breath he said, "It's not enough. I need more."

"More what?"

"More of you, more condoms, more..." he trailed off and kissed her chest. Shudders still ravaged his body in little intervals, and he moaned and caressed the sides of her abdomen.

When they were both calm and quiet, he got up and disposed of the condom in the bathroom. He returned and wrapped his arms around her. They lay next to each other while he kissed and caressed her. He rubbed his nose against her shoulder and then nipped playfully.

Malaika traced the angles of his face lightly with her fingers. She felt content and sated. She couldn't explain to herself why she wanted more too. She didn't tell Paxon her thoughts out of fear.

"Our bodies love each other," Paxon whispered.

Not just our bodies, Malaika thought.

# 17


# Seventeen


The stylist arrived 20 minutes later.  Malaika had taken a shower and was back in the dress. The stylist was trailed by a makeup artist carrying a small suitcase. The makeup artist fussed over Malaika's 'look' and the hair stylist teased and sprayed and tutted when Malaika tried to make suggestions.

"You ok?" Paxon asked her.

"Fine" she told him.

He winked at her.

When it was all done and the professionals were apparently satisfied with their work, they left the apartment in the same whirlwind manner they had blown in.

"We better get going," Paxon said to Malaika.

She nodded in agreement and gestured for him to lead the way.

When they got to the door Paxon turned unexpectedly and drew her into him for a gentle kiss.  When they managed to pull apart, he stared at her.  Malaika thought he would say something, but he didn't.  He just looked at her and then took her hand in his and they left.  There was a car waiting downstairs for them. They got in the backseat and sipped on the refreshments waiting for them in relative silence. Malaika fussed with her dress out of nervousness.

Paxon observed her in silence. He wanted to tell her she was very beautiful but was afraid he might be pushing his luck. She was still married and he had just taken her to bed. She might be spinning from guilt; he had no way to know so he maintained his silence. She finally looked up from her dress. Paxon gave her a reassuring smile. To his relief, she smiled wide at him.

"It's so stupid," she said. "It's not even about me and yet I am nervous." She shook her head at the preposterousness of it.

"Relax," he said and squeezed her hand gently.

She closed her eyes momentarily and attempted to take his advice.


The event was held in a private museum. The tapis rouge welcomed them like a giant tongue flanked by two gargantuan statues of regal-looking lions. The affair was grandiose but tasteful. Malaika was relieved to have a place to cower from the actual limelight- the bar- while Paxon fulfilled his duties as brand ambassador. Whenever he had a minute, he would come to her and ask if she was okay or if she needed anything. Her answer was the same every time and she wondered when he would tire of asking. It was a strange feeling.

Whenever she had gone out with Axel, he immediately left her and went in search of attention from other women. She always felt like he didn't want people to know that they were out together. In fact, this was the result of his behavior. People were stunned to discover that they had come together when they happened to find out. She had told him several times how his behavior made her feel. She initially thought it was because he didn't know how to treat a lady. When he responded by calling her childish and saying, "Malaika always wants all the attention to be on her," Malaika stopped going out with him all together.

When the night was over, Paxon surprised Malaika by telling her the dress was hers to keep. Malaika tried to decline but he all but forcibly put it in her car when she was leaving, after changing out of it. He claimed it was the least he could do after she'd agreed to being on the red carpet as his date.

When Malaika got home, she sat in her car staring at the closed wooden gate. Chen would be there soon. How would she explain all this to her? Would Chen judge her or would she understand and cheer her on? Malaika was having a hard time explaining it to herself but it felt so good and so conscience and moral upbringing aside, she was going with it.

She finally left the comfort of her car and entered her house, which was beginning to feel like a place from which she needed to escape. Upstairs, she got changed and ready for bed.

The next morning Axel had surprisingly little to say to her. She was relieved. He grumbled about how the eggs she'd made him for breakfast lacked joy, how he didn't feel like she had made them joyfully- whatever that meant. She wanted to ask him what exactly she was supposed to be joyful about? Constantly being chastised and ridiculed or the constant state of clutter their home existed in because of his incessant buying? She swallowed both questions down. They tasted like bile. That night she was going to sit through a dinner with Axel and his friend, whom Axel had asked Malaika to set up with one of her friends. Aila and Karim were at a competition and Camille had them all weekend. When Malaika called Aila to find out how she was feeling before the competition, she was met with Aila's insistent questions about the event and Paxon.

"It was fine. I'll tell you about it later. How do you feel?" Malaika tried to steer the conversation around.

"Same as always Mummy. I'll call you after and let you know how I place."

"You'll do great, I know it."

"Thanks, Mummy."

"Mummy loves you Poompoom," she said to Aila.

"Mummy!" Aila whispered hoarsely.

"I know, I know, but no one heard me say it over the phone, surely."

"I did," Malaika heard Karim tease.

"Sorry," Malaika said.

Aila sighed. "Love you mummy. I have to go."


Malaika spent the rest of the day trying to put the house in order, which was always a mammoth task because anytime she did, Axel would go shopping and fill every open space with things. Malaika no longer had space to pack things away, let alone space to pack the storage things she had to buy in order to pack things away. It was an endless cycle of clutter with little room to breathe. Her life felt like that, like she was caught in an endless tease of clutter and hostility and it made her angry because she tried so hard to break the cycle to bring order. All her work was always undone seemingly with the snap of a finger whenever Axel went shopping. Malaika remembered Goodness telling her that she didn't condone Axel's behavior but that Malaika didn't do her part as a woman, that she never packed things away and that because of this it was understandable that Axel could get 'angry'. Still, she tried before she was compared to women who were the reason behind their husbands' and families' meteoric success through organization and being good wives, something she had failed to be throughout her entire marriage.

Evening came. She and Axel were at dinner with his friend Xavier and her friend Noam. Malaika felt a little queasy but thought the feeling would pass. They were all French. She spoke almost fluent French but still felt excluded. Perhaps she was being too sensitive. She interjected whenever she could but couldn't quite get into the conversation. Axel always cut her off and then took control of what she wanted to say. It was exhausting for her. Axel and Xavier both seemed to be having the liveliest conversation with Noam.

The queasy feeling from earlier appeared to be intensifying. She narrowed her eyes as she tasted something bitter in her mouth. Then she checked the time on her phone and found several messages from Paxon. She messaged him explaining everything and where she was.

Malaika whispered into Axel's ear that she wasn't feeling well and asked if they leave soon since the date was for their friends anyway. His response surprised her even when she thought nothing he did could anymore.

"Stop it with zat. You always want to leave early."

Malaika looked away and answered Paxon's message, saying she felt ill but would still be out for a while longer because Axel didn't want to go home. Her phone rang. She didn't understand why Paxon was calling. She excused herself to take it.

"What do you mean he doesn't want to leave?" He sounded calm, eerily calm.

"Well, I usually want to leave early and I guess he's enjoying himself…" she trailed off.

"I see," he said coolly. "How much longer do you think you'll be there?"

"A while. Our food hasn't arrived. I don't think I'll be able to eat though; I'm starting to feel nauseous."

"Leave," he said.

"What do you mean, leave?"

"Go back to the table and tell them you're leaving."

"I can't. Axel would explode and…"

"Who gives a shit if he explodes?! You're not feeling well!"

Malaika just laughed him off. "It's not that serious." She hoped to play down the fact that she really did feel terrible. "It's fine."

"Sure?"

"Yeah."

She could hear in his voice that he wasn't convinced.

When Malaika returned to the table. Axel leaned to talk to her for the first time since they'd sat down in the restaurant. "You think it's normal to go away to talk on the phone for so long?"

Malaika pretended to be trying to flag down a passing waiter. The waiter told her he'd be with her in a moment.

Twenty minutes later Malaika's phone buzzed.

*I'm here.*

She didn't understand the message and chalked it up to the fact that now, in addition to feeling nauseous, she felt dizzy. She had told Axel that she was feeling worse and he had scolded her for ruining the night with her theatrics while still making no effort to budge. Her stomach roiled as the smell of various foods assaulted her senses. It felt like her stomach was clenching and unclenching. Remaining seated upright became a trial. She was desperate for a bed or a toilet. She felt a warm hand on her shoulder. Thinking it was the waiter, she began placing an order for water.

He bent down on one knee and spoke quietly to her. "Get your things."

"What?" She turned and looked into Paxon's eyes, filled with a steely determination.

"What are you doing here?"

He lifted her jacket hanging from her chair back. "Getting you out of here."

"I can't just go. We're in the middle of – "

"You're not well baby." He said like that was the only thing that mattered. There was no point in her attempting to keep up the fiction of normalcy. She realized he wasn't backing down.

"I'm leaving," Malaika announced without conviction. The words came out weak. There was no response from the people at her table. They probably hadn't heard her, which suited her just fine. She didn't want to put on a big production of her exit. She picked up her bag, got to her feet, and turned to leave. When she was two steps away, Axel noticed what was happening.

"Hello?" he demanded in a stern voice.

Malaika froze.

Ignoring Axel, Paxon stopped walking and leaned into her. "Are you ok?"

She said nothing. She was afraid. Afraid of the consequences this action would incur. Paxon palmed the back of her head and Malaika warmed at the tenderness of his touch.

He put his hand on her shoulder. "What do you need me to do?" he asked her.

She shook her head. "I'm okay. Just a little dizzy."

"Malaika!" Axel growled, which made her jump.

This forced Paxon to acknowledge him and Paxon glared directly at Axel. Malaika turned to face Axel, who was now walking towards them.

"What are you doing?!"

"I'm going. I don't feel well and—"

"I don't feel well nofing! Where you see zat? I, I, don't feel—zen you leave? You see zat on TV?" Axel's hand was making the universal sign for you're crazy with his hand pointed at his head. He opened his mouth to continue berating her when Paxon stepped in front of Malaika.

"Are you kidding me?" His voice was a growl. It seemed a perfectly normal question but Malaika could tell that there was nothing normal about Paxon's temperament. "Your wife tells you she's unwell and needs to go home and you tell her not to ruin your night with your friend on his date and now you're shouting because your sick wife is leaving to rest or get medical attention. Are you *fucking* kidding me?" Paxon's eyes narrowed and his body radiated fire, the fire of boundless physical confidence that only a professional athlete possessed.

Axel was stunned and for the first time in Malaika's memory, she saw him give himself over to silence. She was sure no one had ever spoken to him this way. A silence descended their surroundings but for the two men.

For a minute he said nothing, vainly seeking a way to save face. When he recovered, he said, "She is my wife."

"Exactly, she is more important than a fucking date your friend is on and how you look to anyone. She is sick and it's still more important to you to stay and do fuck knows what, seeing as you're not the one on the date here. So, go back to your date Mr. Third Wheel. I'm taking Lo to see a doctor." Paxon turned, dismissing Axel, and taking Malaika with him.

She wanted to protest because she knew this could only yield bad results.

"Ey! Who do you think you are? She's my wife!" Axel shouted and took a step and grabbed Malaika. The minute he wrapped his hand around Malaika's arm Paxon spun around and yanked his hand off. Axel shoved Paxon and, without warning, Paxon grabbed Axel by the throat with one hand and lifted him slightly so Axel, who was almost as tall as Paxon, was forced to stand on his tiptoes. Paxon's other hand shielded Malaika from Axel. Malaika watched in wonderment as Paxon's body harnessed the strength of his athleticism. Axel stared with what can only be described as complete and utter horror with a mix of surprise and fear.

"I. Will. Break. You," Paxon seethed quietly. "I'm here because you don't know how to be a husband to your wife." He stressed the words, filling them with disgust. "You didn't give a shit when she told you she was sick so back the fuck off and let someone who actually cares about her deal with your inconvenience."

Malaika wretched, which drew Paxon back to her. "Lo, are you ok?" he said to the side, still not letting go of Axel.

"Put him down. I think I'm going to puke."

Paxon discarded Axel like he was tossing off a used tissue and leaned in to Malaika. "We gotta go; the car is just across the street." Without warning, he lifted Malaika and all but ran to the car. Once they got there, he opened the passenger door for her and made her sit with her feet out. She heard her phone ring from her bag. He took a plastic bag from the back seat and handed it to her. He kneeled in front of her, looking up at her and rubbing small circles on her back. "You can puke."

"Thanks for the permission," Malaika chirped.

He smiled but she could see it was forced. He was worried.

"It's probably not that serious. A 24-hour stomach bug, I guess. I used to get them a lot from Aila when she was a toddler." Malaika explained. Her phone rang but she ignored it.

Paxon nodded and Malaika couldn't decide if it was because he understood or he was in agreement. Then, she wretched so hard she was forced to lurch forward. She emptied the contents of her stomach into the bag Paxon had given her. Her phone was ringing non-stop and Paxon answered it.

"Here," he said into the phone and then held it in the air so the person on the other end could hear Malaika. "Still think she's being dramatic, asshole?" Paxon hung up.

She wretched one last time, getting rid of the last dregs of bile curdling her stomach. Malaika's eyes and nose were runny and her throat felt like she had swallowed glass shards. She leaned back in the seat and shut her eyes tightly.

Paxon opened the dash and pulled out a bottle of water. "Drink this."

Malaika laughed once but there was no mirth in it and then she sniffed... "What a mess," she said to herself.

Paxon said nothing. When she opened her eyes, he was looking at her. She burst into tears.

Paxon scooped her into his arms and pressed her to him. He held her tight. Malaika realized that she couldn't let him go. He told her he couldn't let go of her to marry Bonnie because somehow the special stolen time they'd spent together had him in a vice-like grip. He had tried to explain how he'd begun to fall in love with her in a hotel room mere hours after meeting her. He wasn't expecting it and he didn't want it he'd said. Sitting with him now as she got sick and cried made her feel both privileged to be able to be with him and also made her feel like she was made of glass and her sadness was pressure cracking her slowly. There was nothing he could do to help her. How could she fix the shit going on in her life? She couldn't banish the edge of desperation to or at least try. She wanted to be the reason he smiled and bloomed. She didn't want to be the person she made small in order not to take up too much space, to make her asshole husband Axel feel comfortable anymore.

When she finally stopped sobbing, she rummaged through her purse for tissue. She apologized for blowing her nose before doing so. He'd confessed that part of the reason he was so enraptured was because of how unusual she was. She apologized before blowing their nose and it tickled him. He offered her the water again and made a joke about how both the vomiting and crying meant she was withering from dehydration. She gave him a weak smile.

"Should I take you to my place or the hospital?"

Malaika thought for a moment before answering. "Can you take me to Camille's?"

"You sure? I really think a medical practice is where you need to be," Paxon said with concern and desperation to stay with her a little longer.

Malaika nodded firmly. "I'll be fine," she croaked. "I just want to see Aila and sleep."

Paxon agreed reluctantly. He didn't like it but he had to respect it. They drove in silence and Malaika struggled to stifle the need to wretch. Her main fear was that she would do so and lose all control of her orifice faculties and fart. She knew it was illogical, but farting was more embarrassing in her mind than emptying the contents of her stomach all over Pax's leather interior.

When they got to Camille's, he cut off the engine and turned to her.

"You shouldn't have come." Malaika said. The words rushed out of her "This— he's going to know. He's going to be so angry. It's going to be really bad. He's unstable like a bomb. The only thing predictable about him is his unpredictability." She stared in front as she said it, not daring to look at him. She heard him take a breath as if preparing to say something. She couldn't bear it, to hear him say sweet things to her to hear him give her hope of a better future with him. She unbuckled herself attempted to flee. She mumbled a wooden thank you, but Pax held her hand. He didn't speak. She was forced to look at him to figure out what he was doing, what he wanted. He just looked at her with an inscrutable expression. She wanted so badly to curl up into him and cry for all the years of neglect and emotional cruelty she'd endured. But she didn't. She knew better. If she let him see her vulnerability he would think her weak and she'd likely never hear from him again or worse yet, he'd start to treat her like shit because he would know how to break her. So, she schooled her features and waited.

"Do you wanna talk about it?" He asked.

She said nothing.

"Sometimes talking about it helps. I don't want to leave you here tonight while you feel..." he trailed off, not sure how to finish his sentence.

Still she sat quiet.

"It's not good to keep things to yourself."

Malaika sighed. There was nothing she could do or say that would make this end the way she wanted. Her mother had once told her that life didn't work the way she thought it did. Those words had haunted her after meeting Pax. The sadness of her discovery of his engagement always lingered in her depths as a reminder. What she really wanted was to take Aila and run as far away from Axel as humanly possible. The two of them could start over somewhere else and live a peaceful existence and maybe one day, if she was lucky, she would meet someone who wouldn't take advantage of her naiveté or cœur d'artichaut and be good to her. That person could never be Pax. His life was a hurricane. Their meeting and connection were too strange. She suspected that love was something that made more sense than this. For as long as they'd known each other, she'd been lost. How were they supposed to have a love or life when she was so needy and her life so messy? There was so much she wanted to say to him. He was a shock to her system in the best way imaginable which was why she knew it wouldn't last. Nothing this good ever did in her life.

"You touched my heart Lo. I can accept almost anything from you. If you need a year or two to figure out divorcing him, I can wait."

"I'm afraid. I divorce him and then what? We have a long-distance relationship? I don't know if you've been paying attention but I—" she sighed. How was she to say she depended on him financially, largely his doing by refusing to let her work but also her fault for accepting it in favor of pleasing him? She shook her head. "Pax, thank you for coming to get me tonight but I have to go."

"Will I see you tomorrow?"

She didn't answer. The fact was that Axel always got his way. No matter what she tried, he would force her to do what he wanted in the end. She thought of the time she packed her suitcases for a short visit to her mum's and he literally unlocked her suitcases at the airport check-in and packed the things he wanted her to take as he yelled and called her too lazy to do it. Or the time she told him not to pick her up from the station after work because she wanted to walk after he had screamed all morning. He showed up at the station anyway. Whatever tomorrow would be, Malaika knew it would require mental fortitude she wasn't sure she could muster when her head was full of thoughts of Paxon.

"Pax, I need to figure things out. I'll call you." This was the truth, but she also knew that she was hiding from having to face him. She suspected he knew it too. He didn't push her, though.

He opened his door and walked to her side.

Malaika was already out of the car by the time he got there.

He looked down at her and closed the space between them. He took one of her hands in his and looked at it. There was something there that Malaika couldn't put her finger on. Was he saying bye or was he saying *goodbye*?

"I don't know a lot about anything, but I know that you're in my bones," he said and then he kissed her slow and tender.

She pulled away from him, eyes frantic.

"What?" he was alarmed.

"I was puking!"

He smiled and shrugged. He kissed her again.

She wanted to stay right there in that moment with him but she pulled away. They were both breathing heavily. She turned to leave but he held her hand and they stared at each other in the dim night light for a moment before he let her go. She darted away into the dark.

# 18

## Eighteen

Once inside Camille's apartment, she collapsed into tears. There in the dark with her back against the door, she sobbed until her tear ducts hurt and dried into crusty flakes. After checking on Aila, she snuggled into Camille's bed with her.

"What happened?" Camille asked groggily.

Malaika told her in a flat voice.

Camille rolled over and put an arm around her. "He never loved you." she said, matter-of-fact. "He chose you because you are ze perfect person to live out a dark fairytale with; he prey on your empathy and use your forgiveness as ammuni-tion." She sighed, "I 'ave never saw at the two of you together and thought oh zey are in love. In ze beginning you looked like yes to be but he 'as always been, how I can say? Like actor in cinema. Like bad actor."

Malaika sniffed once. "You've never said anything." Malaika felt betrayed. If Camille knew, why had she never said anything, done anything?

"What would you say if I told you?" The question was rhetorical "You would 'ate me or think I am jealous or trying to make you lonely like me."

Malaika looked at her friend in surprise. She'd never thought of her as lonely. Guilt overwhelmed her. She'd never really considered what Camille's personal struggles were like. She just always thought Camille had it all worked out because she was age-defyingly beautiful and well put together. "Are you lonely?" Malaika asked in earnest.

Camille gave her an incredulous side glance as if to say what do you think? "I made my choice but it's not for everyone. Life doesn't work ze way I 'ave been sinking. I am not so young and I 'ave a child." She shrugged as if that explained everything.

"That's just crazy!" Malaika said, not wanting to believe Camille "You're gorgeous and—"

Camille cut her off. "Grow up Malaika." She shook her head. "Live in the real world." She sighed, sounding defeated. "Sometimes I sink, I should 'ave stayed. He was much older zan me. Ze strength was already leaving him and I could 'ave ended by being ze ruler." She patted Malaika on the shoulder. "I don't say you should not walk away from that awful man but sink carefully."

Malaika heard her. She wanted to say something, ask a question perhaps, but her mouth worked soundlessly until she resigned to the fact that she didn't know what to think, or say, or ask. Malaika was just waiting for the curtains to crash. She'd been living a life for her husband to display how wonderful he was. He neglected her, disrespected her, hurt her, humiliated her in front of other people, financially controlled and made her doubt herself for years. Malaika had become a coward over the years, afraid to upset her husband, afraid to fail at marriage, afraid of what kind of life she would be taking Aila to if she left. And now thinking about it, she was amazed at how long it had taken her to see the chinks in the Axel's rage-fueled, macho man armor. He was deeply insecure and used external things for validation and emotional regulation. She was one of those things. He thought intimidation and tyranny was being a man. Somehow Malaika had learned to live with it and even hide it from others when he acted up in public. Wasn't that what strong women did? After all, he wasn't hitting her and he provided a roof over their heads and money for food. She marveled disbelievingly at herself because here her friend was telling her that she regretted leaving a man who disrespected her openly and hurt her too.

The next day she woke with a strange feeling which grew over the course of the day. She was relatively young and could no longer imagine the 40ish year remaining of her life playing out like they had until now. There had to be better. At the very least, there had to be peace and she knew she'd never know peace or stability if she stayed with Axel. Though her faculties hadn't stretched to formulating a proper plan she knew that she was ready to change the direction of her life.

She expected the worst once they arrived home but was met with a bizarrely agreeable Axel. He made no mention of the previous night's events and walked around the house silently, even cheerfully. Malaika wondered if she had crossed into the twilight zone. She stayed out of sight as often as possible but that didn't stop him from coming upstairs while she was editing a short review for a smartwatch company.

"How you feel?" he said standing at the door.

Malaika looked at him disbelievingly. This was the first time in years he'd ever bothered to find out how she was feeling when she was ill. "Much better." Malaika wanted to elaborate about the medication she had taken and the doctor she had seen in the morning before returning home but he began again.

"Ok," he said, clearly done with the formality of concern. He threw a large bag with large red lettering on it. VALENTINO. She opened the bag reluctantly, knowing that not acknowledging it would be a grave mistake. Inside she found a beautiful tawny-colored suede shoulder bag in it. She hated suede. She also had no use for a bag this size since she carried a slender backpack for her computer. She stared at it silently.

"And?" he demanded. She took a breath, but he spoke before she could answer. "Are you not happy?"

Malaika was terrified of saying the wrong thing. "It's beautiful," she said in a whisper.

"I know," he said, matter-of-fact and took a breath as if closing off that part of the conversation and moving on to the next point. "Ok, I never want to see that guy in this house again." He made a hand gesture that indicated this was non-negotiable and final. Malaika said nothing. Then Axel began counting off points on his fingers struggling to maintain a level voice. Ordinarily he would have gone into a cataclysmic shouting tirade, but something was keeping him leashed today. Axel never showed fear but right now he was behaving with a semblance of normalcy and she thought it was because Paxon, had put the fear of God in him. He claimed he didn't realize how serious her not feeling well was. He said he didn't remember her telling him that she wanted to leave ...

Malaika zoned out. As always, he was not going to take responsibility for his actions; he was going to justify and eventually turn it around on Malaika if he could manage it. Malaika had learned long ago to just agree and not engage him.

When he was done, he turned to leave but stopped himself.

"How long zis guy is still here in France?"

Malaika knew that what she answered mattered. She shrugged. "I'm not sure."

He looked at her unconvinced but didn't challenge her or call her bluff. He left without another word.

Malaika looked at the bag, wanting to jettison it into a fire. Malaika knew at some point he would explode and a spiral of unease bloomed in her gut at the thought. She spent the next few days anxious overthinking every little thing she did. Making sure everything in the house was just so, the way Axel liked.

Paxon had called every day and she'd called him back promising him everything was fine.

"You don't have to worry about me Pax"

"I know I don't, but I do. You being alone with him," he had told her.

Malaika cleared her throat and changed the subject. "How is it going at the posh gym?"

Pax chuckled "Good. I honestly think the trainer is having a hard time keeping up with me most of the time, but never tell Vesuvio. He'll just use it as further argument for why 'Murica is so much better than everywhere else."

Malaika imagined Pax rolling his eyes and shaking his head. "Pfft," she scoffed.

"I miss you, Lo," his voice dropped to that gentle tone he reserved for her, the one that contained a tenderness that both melted and frightened her.

She took a shaky breath. "I miss you too, Pax."

"When am I seeing you?" He asked, an edge of desperation in his whisper.

Malaika agreed to meet him the next day after dropping Aila

off at school. The truth was she had crossed into this uncertain space. Axel wasn't being a maniacal raging monster and she would catch herself thinking that maybe this wasn't all so bad. That all this time spent with him wasn't so bad. The truth was she had been mulling over Camille's words.

She woke up early one morning three weeks later, moving around wordlessly to get things ready for everyone. Aila came down for her breakfast and Malaika quizzed her for her chemistry test that day. When Axel joined them, he didn't greet Malaika which suited her fine. He kissed Aila on the forehead and began making his hot chocolate and warming his baguette, which he kept stored in the freezer in small pieces.

Malaika finished her coffee and put the empty cup in the sink.

"The cup 'ave no water inside to make soft the coffee rest."

"Sorry" Malaika acknowledged his complaint so he couldn't claim she was ignoring him.

He turned on the tap with unnecessary force. "I have to tell you that every time?" he asked rhetorically his voice starting to rise.

Malaika took a deep breath and began hurrying Aila so they could get out the door as fast as possible. Whenever he started like this it meant he would find any and every little thing she hadn't done exactly the way he wanted and add it to the list of things to use as verbal ammunition.

"How Aila is gonna learn when she see you do wrong fing every time?" he continued.

Malaika held her tongue, making sure not to actually run out of the house. When she got to the door with Aila in tow, she changed out of her house shoes and got her boots from the small shoe rack at the door.

"Zis fing" he yelled pointing at the rack "It's like zis you fink the sings must be?"

Malaika didn't understand what he was getting at. She looked at the rack and saw that one of her slippers had fallen off and was lying on the floor.

"What you want me to do?" He was full blown shouting now. "You want me to beg you to not keep a mess Malaika?!"

Malaika was stunned by his sudden fury and pushed Aila behind her. She backed up, slowly moving away from him and stumbling into Aila. She was afraid that in his rage he might strike her.

"How am I supposed to go to work like zis in zis mood putain?! Aaargh!" he screamed and punched the wall attached to the staircase several times.

Still, Malaika stayed silent and she didn't move. She just watched in horror.

"C'est pas possible, putain! And then that your friend say I don't pay attention of you." He spat in disgust "Pay attention of you when you can't do the simple fing a wife do. Putain! I do my man job! Are you not ashamed at your age you are not able to do zis? Ten years we are married and I have to teach you zat? I suppose I also should teach you how to walk." He was raging and every word inflicted hemorrhaging damage. He grabbed his briefcase and stormed out, banging the door behind him.

Once she was sure that he was actually gone, she let out a relieved breath. She hadn't realized she'd been holding it.

When they got in the car, Malaika put the keys in the ignition but couldn't open the remote-controlled gate. Her fingers kept fumbling and slipping off the remote button or missing it entirely. She tried for what felt like a full minute before yanking out the key and purposely looking at the remote, then stabbing the button with unnecessary force.

"Fuckssake," she hissed, forgetting for a moment that Aila was sitting next to her. What the hell was wrong with the stupid remote? She glared at it and it looked back innocently. It wasn't the problem; the problem was her hands—they were shaking. She closed her eyes and took a deep breath. Then she did everything slowly and with purposeful, if not forced, calm. She managed to nose the car out of their yard without incident.

As they drove Aila broke the silence. "I'm sorry mummy." Her voice sounded smaller than she was.

"Sweety, you have nothing to apologize for." Malaika took her eyes off the road and gave her a reassuring smile.

"I'm sorry. I was just so tired this morning and I couldn't distract him this time," Aila continued.

"Distract him?" Malaika heard the words Aila was saying but it took a second for her brain to interpret them.

"I was studying late last night after gym and I am just too tired today."

Malaika was rendered speechless. Her daughter, whom Malaika thought she had done an excellent job of shielding from Axel's verbal and psychological attacks, was telling her that she understood what was going on. Not only understood but had been acting as a membrane between her parents, shielding Malaika from Axel's aggression.

Malaika let out a nervous and mirthless laugh. "Aila, my angel, you don't have to distract him. It's not your job to protect me from—" Malaika couldn't even finish the sentence because she didn't know how. "Whatever you've been doing, distracting or— stop, baby girl. You just concentrate on school and gymnastics and being happy, Aila. Don't worry about

Mummy; Mummy takes care of herself. It's not your job to take care of me. I take care of you, okay my angel?"

Malaika managed another weak smile.

Aila didn't respond.

After leaving Aila at school Malaika sat in the car at first staring at her feet, not knowing what to do. She called the one person who never let her down. Camille answered on the fourth ring.

"Go to le police," came her immediate response. "When you are there you need to tell them zat you want to make a plainte, zen they will note everything and go and see him."

"Like pressing charges?"

"Bah yes. Iz wat you want non?"

"No. I'm not ready to do that yet."

"Zen you can depose un main courant. You tell zem what 'appen and they take a copy of your ID and zey keep on a file. If somesing 'appen again, you go and make zis fing again and zey add to ze first one. Is like an official diary of ze events when zey 'appen, like a proof."

"Ok, yes. I want to do that."

"Ok. So, you tell zem and they do and you don't 'ave to worry, they won't tell him that you 'ave done it. But you shouldn't expect zem to be happy or warm wiz you uh. Zey are not very all good trained in zis domestic issues and normally are very cold. Sometimes ze one who is trained specially for zat could not be zere. Just don't expect a warm welcome."

# 19

# Nineteen

Malaika had majored in sociology of gender in undergrad. She knew about abused women and now she was one, one of the sad desperate women she'd read about but didn't understand. Technically she'd been one for the last decade but only now was she realizing it. She didn't want to walk away but she couldn't stay because of what it was doing to Aila. She could live a life on a stage and be Axel's display thing, but she wouldn't ruin Aila, not for Axel's show and not for her own comfort. She was finally getting off Axel's highway. She finally realized that no matter what she did, she would never be able to bend far enough to please him no matter how much she watched every move she made to ensure everything was just as he wanted, the curtains were always going to crash. No matter what she did, she would never be enough for him, she'd always be outnumbered by his wants and insecurities.

After leaving Aila's school, Malaika drove to Paxon's apartment. When she walked in, she hugged him for longer than she felt comfortable with. Once she felt him an onslaught of tears threatened. Holding on to him was the only thing keeping

214

the agony at bay. It occurred to her that she shouldn't have come. In her current condition she was perilously low on self-confidence and really, really didn't want Paxon to see her in that way.

As soon as he saw her, he wrapped her in a bear hug and he got that feeling, the one that told him he'd been counting down the days to see her and be near her. He released her, with a gentle forehead kiss.

She smiled weakly and was about to launch into some cheerful small talk but he got the jump on her.

"What's wrong?"

She looked at him in surprise and was paralyzed by what the question meant. She couldn't fool him with the smiles she tricked everyone else with. He paid attention to her, he could see her, and she hated herself for feeling like she needed that.

"Ok," she said, deciding to forgo the pretense. She told him about what happened that morning. She told him she had gone to the police to depose a main courant. She then explained what the difference was between that and a plainte.

"Shit," is all he said and sank into a dining room chair. He ran his hands down his face.

Malaika laughed and once she started, she couldn't stop. Pax looked at her like she was losing it. Maybe she was.

"What's funny?" he finally interrupted.

"I tell you about my day but now I feel like it's you that needs consoling. You look like my news...obliterated you. It's just strange, that's all."

"Yeah. Your news is...you have to get away from him," he said resolutely. "I don't want to pressure you but Lo...come with me." He said it like it was the most logical thing. The easiest thing. "I am leaving in three weeks and you, you come with me."

Malaika shook her head. "Pax," she said as gently as she could, "I can't and not because I don't want to. I want to but there's a lot—" What was she going to say? She could hardly say they were moving too fast because technically they'd been in and out of each other's lives for years now. "I need to focus on what's best for Aila even when I leave Axel; it needs to be just me and her first for a while. It will be hard on her, disorienting, and I don't even know what to expect from the process. It will take time to leave; I don't have anything or anywhere to go so it will take time," she finished.

Paxon looked at her and she thought she could see sadness infiltrate his features.

She turned away from his gaze, fighting off the damned tears. "God, where can I run to escape from myself?" she said in a whisper. She shook her head.

Paxon reached for her and took her in his arms. He didn't say anything. Malaika didn't say anything. They stayed like that in silence for what felt like an interminable moment. Malaika knew she had to go; there was a long bucket list of things to do. First was finding out how she could get help.

She got home with two hours to spare before getting Aila. In her inbox she found that Camille had already sent her the contact information of a woman who ran a group for abused women. Malaika contacted her immediately and found out about resources available to her and how to access them. Next, Malaika contacted the lawyer Camille had sent her details for. She needed to prove Axel was toxic and potentially dangerous in order to get the court to compel Axel to give her a "meaningful" sum in addition to the obligatory child support. Malaika didn't want to have to need the sum in question but the fact was she hadn't held a job with gainful income during her time with him. Whether or not that was Axel's doing was irrelevant. He always insisted that he made enough for the entire family and that Malaika would lack nothing. He didn't mention that "enough for the family" would be used and decided on by a judiciary of one: him. All the information the lawyer gave her yielded frightening truths: she wouldn't be able to get access to housing for vulnerable women easily because it turned out psychological and emotional abuse was a hard thing to prove. Then, based on the information Malaika had given him, he thought it wise to conduct all her business cloak and dagger. He was concerned that Axel would do something or react poorly to having a heads up on being left. Malaika knew this was true of course. It wasn't going to be hard to secret her business from Axel since he pretty much lived a separate life from her. She was relying on his inattention.

It was hard trying to slice through this mire she'd become unwittingly embroiled in. It seemed like the more she tried to wriggle out, the stickier everything became.


Malaika spent twenty minutes perusing the internet for apartments close to Malaika's school and gym. She sent a few emails to real estate agents for the apartments that she thought she could make work. The miserable part of it was that her price range was extremely limited. Leaving Axel would mean her lifestyle would have to make a serious reduction. She was scared but fully prepared to do it. Next, she made a list of all the superfluous things she owned which she could sell online. She made several plans in the service of halting her life from careening to a disaster. Before she knew it, it was time to fetch Aila from school and take her to the gym.

She stopped by Appleberry's to get a treat. She shouldn't really, given Aila's strict healthy eating regimen for gymnastics but Malaika felt horribly guilty about the impending seperation. She wanted to bring a small beacon of joy to Aila's day. Aila was thrilled and devoured the treat in a ravenous frenzy on the way home.

She needed to find more work. This was her real challenge. Without more income she had no idea how she was going to make any of these getaway plans work. She had taken on extra private English tutoring lessons which, if she started operating on a shoestring budget, would go a long way. This is where she was starting from and she had to push her fear aside and step out. Putting herself out there was terrifying.

# 20

## Twenty

Malaika stared out the window. She didn't even register what the real estate agent was saying to her. It all sounded like Charlie Brown grownups, *mwueh mwueh mwuehing* in the background. Her mind kept replaying the last time she'd seen Paxon. They had had an argument and then he'd left, gone back to America.

He had bought an apartment for her and Aila. Just like that. She was happy, truly, and so painfully tempted to drop everything and move into it that very day. That was the problem. Paxon was like a magician, there to fix everything for her with his good looks, wads of cash, and an inexplicable capacity to withstand all of the mess that encompassed Malaika's life. She had let a man take the lead and "take care of her" before and she'd become one of the things he owned.

In the beginning, Malaika had tried to reason with Axel. During one particularly rage-fueled rant he had said,

"You will never be equal to me. If you want to live with me, you follow my rules. That's it!"

And it was. The incident had left her trembling. His features had leapt at her, making him look predatory and feral. From then on, Malaika had done what she was told without a single quip, ever. Even still, he reminded her every day that she wasn't enough. She didn't know when it happened, when his words, his voice had become her own. She would never make the mistake of being dependent on a man again. The problem was that there was no way to explain this without the supposition that Paxon would take on those same vile qualities that Axel had after having provided everything for her. Pax looked hurt at first and the more Malaika tried to explain, the look slowly turned to frustration and then anger.

"He broke you," Pax resigned. "Now I'm being punished for the shit he put you through. I am not that piece of garbage. I won't hurt you. What you are saying is the farthest thing from my thinking. I could never—" Malaika cut him off.

"Right now, I have nothing, and you would have to take care of me and at some point, you'll resent me. You won't see me as a woman. You'll see me as a child, and you'll lose respect for me and it will become—it's not about you being a bad person or like Axel. It's human nature."

"Bullshit. It's the nature of a small man with complexes or one who's replicating toxic masculinity cycles he saw growing up. It is not human nature." He shook his head disbelievingly. "You're so smart; how can you think that?" He exhaled in exasperation "There's no way for me to show you. Only time and getting to know me can do that, Lo," Paxon pleaded. "You'll never know if you don't try. Get to know me, Lo."

His face softened. "I want to know you, Malaika. I want your mind, your heart, your body, and your soul. I want them to be mine not so I can control you and feel all powerful— I want you because I know we could be amazing together. We could be amazing partners lifting each other up and loving each other the way we need." Paxon closed the space between them.

Malaika was silent, staring up at him.

"I love you Malaika. I loved you almost as soon as we met. I didn't choose this.  I am happy I got this," He leaned his forehead onto Malaika's tenderly and pressed his palm to her chest "you."

Malaika wanted to kiss him so desperately but she needed to keep a clear head.  They were an illusion.  While she had the strength and will, she took a step back. The effort felt like tearing away flesh. "Pax," she said in an insubstantial voice "It's all the same. I love you Pax, but I can't accept this. You're leaving, and I—you'll never belong to me."

"What does that mean? Why are you creating problems that aren't there?"

"Life doesn't work the way we'd like," Malaika parroted.

"Stop speaking in fucking riddles, Malaika. You're scared. You're pushing me away because you're too scared to make an actual decision."

Malaika remained silent.

Paxon shook his head. He lifted his hands up as if to show her that he had nothing else to give her. He ran a hand through his hair and then spoke "You always push me away and I just have to breathe you in while I can.  I'm always at your mercy and...and I don't mind."  He said that last part in an uncharacteristically small voice, like he was accepting defeat.

Malaika thought he'd say more but he didn't. It was like he was just telling her the facts.

"You're right, it is always the same. I'll always be wherever you are waiting for you to trust me with your scarred heart. I'd do it all over again, Malaika." He kissed her gently on the forehead.

Malaika closed her eyes and breathed him in. His quiet pleading broke her; tears streamed down her face.

He walked towards the door, calling back to her over his shoulder "You can keep the keys if you're gonna keep the place or turn them in to the guardian downstairs if not, Malaika." And as if this was the last and most important piece of house-keeping after she'd poured cold water on his hopes he said, "Just know that it pains me to leave." Then he was gone.

His words dragged at her heart like invisible arms. She stared after him for almost two hours before she could bring herself to move. She wanted to believe him, but she couldn't. She would not be the fool again. If only she could sink into his thoughts to see the motivations behind his love for her so she could see if it would be eroded by the difficulties of life and transfigured into cruelty and control. She had no way to know. Better not to know, she thought. Better to go it alone and have a single-minded focus on Aila and her own fledgling career. The ghost of his lips on her forehead suffocating her to the point of tears were all she was left with. Why did doing the right thing feel so wrong?

Now, three months later, she was still looking at apartments for rent. Being approved by rental agencies when you weren't on a permanent contract was like getting into the FBI. Fern had sent her a message about the wedding. They had met at Malaika's house on a weekday when Axel was at work.

Fern discovered Malaika with nothing but an oversized t-shirt on. The Dixie Chicks were blaring on a speaker.

"Country," Fern commented. "Things must be rough."

Malaika made no attempt at an explanation. She didn't tell

her that this was a vast improvement from Roxette's, "It Must Have Been Love," which had been on repeat for the past three months.

Fern excavated her expression and seemed to find what she was looking for. "It'll be okay," she said. "It'll be really fucking rough at first, but it'll be okay. I believe in you."

"Maybe I could wait it out. He's a lot older than me and men become pliable with age, no?"

"Absolutely not.  Average life expectancy is 75 years old. You're willing to live caged for what, 28 more years? That's crazy!" Fern, who was never economical with her words, said. "Besides, you're not a monster like him.  You don't want to control him."

Malaika just shrugged in defeat. "I'm confused."

Fern regarded her with concerned eyes over steepled fingers "You need to go to therapy and join a support group. I'll come with you to a few of the meetings if you want."

Malaika felt the weight of her words and then her brain slowed to an anxiety-induced halt. Getting free of Axel's grip required so much organization and rearranging and constantly being on top of things. Just thinking about everything she had to do was overwhelming.

Fern, ever intuitive, said, "Take it a day at a time. I think it would be beneficial to go to cognitive behavior therapy. I'm sensing you're having a hard time regulating your emotions which is understandable given all you're dealing with, but Geneva says it's helped him a lot, so..."

"I think you're right," Malaika laughed derisively.  She wondered what any of her family or the African Power Rangers would say? They'd think her weak. They'd say she'd forgotten who she was. We don't do therapy; leave that to the Europeans, they'd say admonishingly. She took a sip of her coffee and tried to mentally pinpoint the poor life decision that had brought her here. Maybe there were a series of bad decisions.

"What's new on the wedding front then? Malaika asked awkwardly segueing the conversation away from herself and into wedding planning territory.

Fern gave her all the wedding information and employed her as the unofficial wedding planner.

Malaika agreed to it because she needed the distraction and because she had the time. The irony of focusing on someone else's happily ever after while hers crumbled was not lost on her. Malaika was dreading the wedding day. On top of this, she was slated to be a bridesmaid. Malaika was happy to do it of course but upon reflecting that Paxon was in the wedding too as a groomsman, she groaned internally.

# 21

## Twenty-One

After Paxon left, while Malaika was still plotting her escape and roiling with ambivalence over her decision, her phone beeped.  It was a notification from the football league app. She'd forgotten to deactivate it . She made a mental note to do so and continued working on the copywriting she was doing for a client.

Her phone beeped again. This time it was a message from Fern. Malaika thought she'd get more unwarranted panicking from a nerve-wrecked bride but when she read the message, she stopped breathing. Paxon had been injured in a preseason game. Fern didn't know how serious it was but thought Malaika should know. Malaika didn't answer immediately. She checked the football app. It opened to a banner of Pax going down in what looked like a particularly brutal tackle. She didn't even read what it said. She called him immediately. The phone rang a few times before the call connected.

"Pax, I—are you ok? I mean, that's a stupid question because you're hurt. How hurt are you?"

"Why? So you can hurt him some more?"

"Vesuvio?" she said.

"Yeah, it's Vesuvio." He sounded disgusted and scoffed, "To think he thought you could be the one. What is it with you? Is this a game, pretending to care now to suck him back in? Leave him the fuck alone and focus on sorting out your own shitty life. Give him a chance to heal from you!"

The line went dead.

Malaika slid the phone from her ear. Was Vesuvio's acrid chastising right? If she really cared about him she'd stop hurting him. She decided then that she'd never contact him again. She sent Fern a quick message saying she hoped he wasn't seriously injured and that she'd keep him in her prayers. Fern replied with several question marks. Malaika didn't reply. She followed news on his injury and recovery on the app and fought back the overpowering urge to send him flowers, thinking they'd probably just end up in the bin.

With time, she thought she'd think less of him. She didn't; she just got better at suppressing how she felt when she thought about him. It came at the cost of shutting down her ability to feel in general.

The weeks that followed passed in a miserable blur. She was forced to organize all her documents to make sure she and Aila had medical insurance independent of Axel, just in case. She found out what support she was due from the government and registered for it. She fell back on 90's pop to get her through the sludge of emotions she compartmentalized in order to function. Me and Aila, she thought. Focus. One step at a time. One day at a time. One minute. One second. She thought about the sound track from Finding Dory, which she had suffered through at the cinema for Aila and now the annoying fish with the awful voice was playing in her head: Just keep swimming, swimming swimming. She did and internal eyeroll and sighed.

When she finally did have the lawyer draft the divorce papers and send them to Axel, it was a painstakingly anxious time for Malaika. He'd come home that day and found her and Aila's things evacuated from the house. He called her several times in quick succession. For the first time in over a decade Malaika was relieved to not have to answer. Her insides didn't knot in anticipation of orders barked at her in her ear. She thought that this time would be one of unadulterated celebration and happiness, but she found that she was skirting the edge of immobilizing depression. Realizing that almost every aspect of her life had been in bondage. Realizing fear had been her general state of existence living with Axel.

One day while at Camille's she burnt the quinoa she was making. She apologized profusely to Camille. It wasn't until Camille stopped doing what she was doing put a hand on her and looked her square in the eyes that she realized how abnormal her fear was. Camille's look of confusion was followed by her saying,

"It was a mistake, c'est pas la fin du monde." You don't have to apologize for everysing all ze time Malaika."

"What?"

"Not everysing is your fault and even, iz normal you can make some mistake."

Malaika didn't speak. She just nodded and gave Camille weak smile. Satisfied, Camille went back to what she was doing mercifully leaving Malaika to her baffled introspection. This is what she'd become: a pitiful husk of a person perpetually afraid and in self-doubt. Her feelings of shame, self-loathing, and fear coalesced in the following weeks. What kind of person had she been in the first place that Axel was able to affect her so much, to break her spirit? Was she so broken because she was so weak or he was so horrible?

Her therapist had her compiling a daily list of 25 things she liked about herself. The difficulty was in finding different things each day. The first attempt was a trial; she managed ten, then took a break and reconvened with the pen and notebook to add seven more. Just before bed, she thought of the remaining seven. As the days went on, she found herself being more mindful and it became easier to find things. The therapist also had her reading a book on toxic relationships with people with narcissistic personality disorders. In excavating her childhood, she found long repressed memories of being or feeling perpetually unappreciated. She also saw how she descended into the validation-seeking spiral. She saw it so clearly, the pattern. How had she not walked away earlier? What continued to exist in obscurity was how to break it. How was she going to walk away now?

# 22

## Twenty-Two

Malaika got out of the cab and stared up at the airport looming in front of her. She only had a large tote. It was silly, really, for her to think she'd just show up here and he'd be waiting with open arms. Vesuvio was absolutely right; Paxon's life would be better if she didn't keep showing up in it throwing him off kilter with all her drama. She loved him, at least she thought this was love seeing as after all the soul searching yielded the disturbing result that she'd actually never been in a healthy, fulfilling relationship. She got through check-in in record time and wandered about the duty-free shop looking for something to buy for Aila, Karim, and Camille.

Despite saying she'd never contact him again, Malaika flew to the U.S. when news of Paxon's injury broke. Now she was stood at the airport. She had gone to New York for a week to see her mother who spent four months a year there in her late husband's Manhattan condo. Malaika connected with Fern while she was there and, on her encouragement, found the balls to fly to Minnesota in the hopes of seeing if Paxon was okay. While waiting for the elevator at his apartment building, a javelin-thin woman stepped out. She recognized Bonnie from pictures and TV spots. She was much taller in person, Malaika noted. There was enough gold jewelry hanging from her neck, ears, wrists, and fingers to goldleaf the dome at Sacre Coeur.

"I told him the place we get needs to have lots of windows. You know how important light and an airy feeling is for me and my plants." Bonnie mused into her phone. "With the injury he has some time for once to—"

Malaika stopped listening. To say her heart sank was generous. She felt disbelief after everything he'd told her about not being able to go through with things with Bonnie. Yet here Bonnie sauntered. She'd taken all she could take. She needed to stop punishing herself by going backwards. When she got back to Paris a part of her was angry at her stupidity. She wanted to bury her love for Paxon for good. She told herself that if she met someone again, she'd do it right. She plopped on a bean bag and closed her eyes.

Her phone rang.

"Hey chick," Fern said happily.

"Hi," Malaika replied.

"I'm sorry it didn't go the way you wanted when you were here."

Malaika shrugged and realized that Fern couldn't see it through the phone "At least I know now." She said resigned "Anyway, I've gotta tell you I was worried about the bridesmaid dresses when I saw the pictures." She changed the subject.

"I know. I could tell by your comments."

They both laughed.

"I'm happy to report I have since come around. The dresses are perfect."

"Of course they are. I wouldn't have you guys looking like

shit on my big day. Besides, you have to stay in your dresses all day whereas I will be changing into another dress."

Malaika laughed.

Though Fern came from humble beginnings she had certainly grown into her glamorous diva shoes. Malaika loved her and appreciated this new, but true, friendship.

In the months that followed Malaika started a small editing business online and was hosting virtual workshops with a small but consistent customer base. Aila became an official Olympian, one of France's youngest. Axel seemed to be behaving with a modicum of civility whenever Malaika had to speak to him about things concerning Aila. Generally, things were looking good for Malaika.

The wedding felt like it snuck up on Malaika. Even though she said it wasn't necessary, Fern was making Geneva pay Malaika a wedding planner's fee. Fern assuaged any worries Malaika had about interacting with Pax at the wedding. Aila was dubbed holder-of-vows (the actual paper the vows were written on) and Fern's best friend's son was the ring bearer. The dresses were navy blue A-line pieces with keyhole fronts and backs and rhinestone rounded collars. All the bridesmaids looked regal in them.

The ceremony was held in the private garden at the Abbaye de Chaalis, owing to its picturesque and intimate quality. It was an arresting landscape with deep green grass carpeting the floor contrasted by decrepit grey stone brick that was once the catholic nuns' abode against a blue sky. The morning was spent at the official wedding accommodation, the Jaquemart Andre Musee, which was actually a castle that had been turned into a viewing museum for those who wanted to know how nobility lived. Camille was shocked by the great expense and vowed to get herself a football-playing husband.

As their makeup was done, the ladies drank champagne and wine. Fern sat, champagne glass in hand, with mascara streaked eyes wearing a pair of pajama pants as a make-shift hair ribbon holding her locks in a top knot, the aftermath of the previous night's festivities. Malaika had arrived the morning of. Hair was done followed by more alcohol and cream-cheese snacks. Malaika made herself the unofficial photographer and took photos of the flower arrangement resting in the bathroom sink, the copious amounts of drink and snacks littering the table, the girls getting their makeup done, the rings being shined by a jewelry cleaner, bridesmaids and groomsmen rehearsing the opening dance, Fern getting into her dress, and, of course, Aila.

She found Geneva sitting in one of the spacious suites in the castle between his sister and Vesuvio and decided against taking a picture. Geneva looked like he was going to turn purple-faced and barf at any minute. Vesuvio ignored Malaika. Malaika expected no less and didn't acknowledge him either.

"You ok?" Malaika asked, seriously concerned.

He nodded profusely though he looked anything but.

Malaika made eyes at his sister who simply said, "He wasn't earlier, but he is now." Malaika did not want to know. She didn't want to be the bearer of bad news when the groom either couldn't make it to his wedding because he passed out or split. She turned and left, glad to not be feeling anything other than pleasantly buzzed from all the morning drinking. Malaika walked out onto the grounds to get some shots of the location and the clouds in the sunny French sky. She didn't want to be left to her conflicted thoughts—truly happy for Fern and Geneva while grieving her own horrendous marriage. She looked at her watch. Even though there were still two hours left she really felt on edge. She wondered if it was too early to get dressed. Her aim was to be as busy as possible so her emotions couldn't rise to the surface to sabotage her publicly. She had the skill to fake it for however long she needed. She got changed and ran around helping with setting up for the reception. By the time it was time to drive down to the private garden for the ceremony she was bushed, and her system had worked the alcohol out. Man, did she need to top up on that. The drive was short and Malaika felt like a sardine in the car because of all the paraphernalia she was carrying for Fern and her bride's maids. Once they got to the garden and all the guests were seated, Fern told the wedding party not to go just yet. A tray of tequila was brought by a waiter.

Fern produced a saltshaker from within the bust of her diamond-encrusted dress and began salting the space between everyone's index and thumb fingers. "Here we go," she said and tossed the mild poison back, licked her hand, and bit into a lime.

They all followed suit. It tasted acrid and liquefied her insides but she awaited the boost to her fragile mindset.

They were under a canopy of leaves and sunlight streaked through making Malaika lose herself. They made their way down the aisle in a tipsy procession. Being paired with Vesuvio wasn't too bad. She leaned far too heavily on him for support. She watched her every footstep in fear of falling and eating shit in her heels. For once Vesuvio wasn't being a total ass and steadied her. The sunlight hung in a halo around Fern. Geneva was visibly struck down by the sight of Fern who somehow managed to look even more ravishing than normal. Malaika felt mildly affronted. The nuptial pair looked so sure and ready reading their own vows to each other. Their love for each other was palpable. Tears strung Malaika's eyes as she listened and watched the couple. She wasn't the mushy type. Bloody Tequila. She avoided looking at Paxon like it was her job. When the ceremony was done, they all had to stay behind for photos to be taken. Malaika was getting tired of avoiding Paxon. When it was all over, there was some debate about the order of proceedings. Malaika was only half listening. Paxon was pleading a case and then everyone was moving too fast for her to follow. She hiked up her dress so she wouldn't trip over it. She had it shortened by several inches but it was still long, or rather, she was still too short. It was possible the alcohol was affecting her dexterity.

Before she knew which way was up, she was swept up on a very muscular arm and being led forward. They stopped at the bridge and were handed flower petals. She knew whose arm she was drunkenly hanging on. She didn't look up to acknowledge him, though. They formed a human arch for Fern and Geneva to walk through and pelted them with the petals. Then they walked after them keeping a respectful distance so as not to be in the photographer's photos of the newlyweds.

Malaika carefully slithered out and away from Paxon's muscled arm and headed straight for the bar. She got a beer and drank it straight from the bottle. Aila was running around on the grass with the other children. The bar proved too popular for her liking so she slinked off to a lone chair in the shadows where she could lurk and still keep an eye on Aila. She remembered her own wedding—a thing of everyone else's design except her own. From the two-hour service in a decrepit church which wasn't hers at her mother-in-law's insistence, to the DJ Axel had hired who played West Indies music, completely forgoing the list Malaika had spent months compiling to the 250 people Axel invited who Malaika didn't know.  Axel himself spent nary a second with Malaika; he preferred socializing with everyone else save for the 2-minute dance they shared followed by a painfully awkward kiss. When the wedding was all over he insisted on staying at the venue to help clean up instead of coming home with Malaika, though he had paid for cleaners. They never had a honeymoon. She shook her head to clear it and tried to focus on where she was. At her friend's wedding in a lovely dress, enjoying a beer, and peace. She smiled to herself. The moment was short-lived.

"You enjoying yourself?" Malaika jumped and spilled a bit of her beer. She turned to face the groom and plastered on her most convincing scowl.

"Wonderful," she said, raising her beer as if it was proof. Malaika cleared her throat. "You two are #couplegoals," she continued awkwardly.

Geneva laughed.  "So will you be hiding here the entire night?"

Malaika wanted to protest but when she made eye contact with Geneva, she realized there was no point. "I'm just here to support Fern and you so I'm not really looking to use this as a site to find closure." She said, her tone flat. "Besides, Fern threatened that if anybody showed her up at her wedding, she'd announce a big endorsement deal or that she was having a baby at that person's wedding. I don't want that." Malaika chuckled.

"I'm glad to hear that."

Malaika looked at him with a quizzical expression.

"I'm glad, yeah, because you said you don't want that at

your wedding. You haven't given up hope on all this, on love." He gave her a goofy encouraging smile and Malaika rolled her eyes. Geneva nudged her with his shoulder. "You haven't been broken by..." he let his hand gesture finish his sentence for him.

"Okay," Malaika said dryly, to let him know that she wasn't taking anything he said seriously. "Believe me, it is better I stay hidden. Decking and heels are my enemy and this dress, though gorgeous, is conspiring against me. I think falling and eating shit counts as making a scene."

"Yeah, you look fantastic in the dress."

Malaika gave him an uncomfortable wide-eyed look.

"Relax," he said, understanding her expression "It's Fern's fault I noticed. After we met at the gym, she couldn't stop talking about how you have such a great bod and began plotting all the sly ways she could wrangle your secret workout routine out of you."

"No!" Malaika said, clearly disbelieving.

Geneva nodded with a laugh.

"Vesuvio uses it as an argument against you all the time."

"What?!"

"Yeah. He's always like, Pax bro, look I know she got a banging body, I'm not blind," he imitated Vesuvio's voice and over-emphatic mannerism "But c'mon, there are lots of bitches with bangin' bodies out there, man. Stop limiting yourself with this crisis of a woman. You know she got baby daddy drama. You don't want all that?" He squinted still impersonating Vesuvio.

Malaika frowned; it wasn't exactly a compliment when Vesuvio said it, but what else did she expect. He never liked her and she could understand that. He was looking out for his friend. "Thanks Geneva," she said softly. And then, "He pleads the case against me often?" she hated venturing into awkward conversation territory but her curiosity got the best of her.

"Pax and you. There's something there. It could be something real but your timing, both of you, is always really messed up."

Malaika had to laugh at this. "Fern already beat you to telling me about our unpropitious timing."

"Did she?" He gave her a skeptical look. "In those words?"

"I mean she said our timing is always super shitty but same thing." They both laughed.

"That's my potty-mouthed, brainy beauty." He said wistfully.

"Okay, enough of that. I can barely manage all the love vibes without you going all Bryan Adams on me here."

He laughed and shook his head then wrapped his massive arms around her and began ushering her to a more peopled area of the reception. She would have stopped him but he wasn't talking anymore so she went along with it. Malaika realized that the reason he was dragging her back to the crowds was because it was almost time for the wedding party to open up the dance floor. On top of being rhythmically challenged she was drunk and in heels. All conditions were ripe for her to make a fool of herself- the stars aligning for her embarrassing interlude. She took comfort in the knowledge that the day wasn't about her and likely no one would give a shit if she did something epically embarrassing. Fern glided over to them, the epitome of grace and beauty, her hips swaying hypnotically as she moved in her bodycon floor length gown.

Malaika made a slight bow and stood aside for her.

Fern swatted her on the shoulder. "You are ridiculous," she

joked with a wide and bright smile.

Malaika smiled back. She inhaled deeply and began scanning the space for her dance partner. She saw him properly for the first time today. Saying he was gorgeous seemed inadequate. She chided herself. For a wordsmith, she really was useless at describing what Paxon was. He was making his way over to her but before he closed in Vesuvio appeared in front of her.

"Hey partner," he said loudly. "Ready to boogie?"

Malaika's mouth was a thin slash and she nodded once.

He pulled her to him firmly.

She placed a hand on his shoulder and the other around his waist. She recalled the steps aloud, "Side, step-step, angled side, step-step, back, step-step, starting position, step-step."

Vesuvio regarded her with a strange sort of interest.

"I learned the waltz this morning, so..."

His mouth formed a silent ah with the accompanying apprehension. "It's the diamond first and then the box. It's fine, I'm leading and I'm a great dancer."

Malaika gave him a toothless half-smile. This was probably the first time Vesuvio had been civil to her in the time she'd known him.

"Trust me," he said and winked.

Malaika frowned. The melodious bells chiming out of the speakers started up, followed by Bruno Mars' silk voice. Malaika looked Vesuvio in the eyes with steely determination and then back at his feet. He called out the times when they needed to turn so she could follow. She trampled his toes too many times for her to care. To her surprise, he was an excellent sport about it. He laughed a couple of times and so did she. Was she having fun with Vesuvio? They danced clumsily right to the end with Vesuvio abandoning his counting and crooning along with Bruno Mars. He twirled her and added some of his special fanciful dance moves to it.

"Great job," he said when the song was over and sort of hugged her.

For some inexplicable reason she gave him that weird point at you, could be a gun hand sign and winked at him. She was officially in the twilight zone. She didn't understand what winks meant but here she was dolling them out to the one person who really, really did not like her. Malaika was smart enough not to mistake that happy moment with Vesuvio. He was probably drunk so being nice to her meant nothing at all. As she turned to walk away, she tripped. She wobbled a bit and thought she could save herself from landing face first when she caught her balance but the next step she took hooked in her lengthy gown and she went down. She fell into another one of the bridesmaids who caught her and helped her up. Malaika laughed and made a joke. She knew something ungainly would happen to her at some point in the evening. It was like her superpower... doing embarrassing shit. What a power.

"You recovered quickly," a bridesmaid said and Malaika wondered if there was a standing recovery time for embarrassing debuts. If so, how long was it? She thought she had better track down Aila and head to their hotel room.

Back in their hotel room, she put Aila to sleep. Malaika then went to the mini-bar and took out one of the energy drinks she had placed there. She gulped it down and followed it up with a 500 ml bottle of water. This was her hangover miracle aversion cure. She brushed her teeth, slipped out of her dress into a nightgown and collapsed into her bed.

23

# Twenty-Three

Geneva and Fern had asked Malaika to arrange activities for the travelling guests in the week after the wedding. Just fun insider things for people who've never been here before and not the obvious things for people who have Fern had said.

So here they all were at Les Bois de Vincennes, the largest park in Paris built by Napoleon the third. The weather was warm and humid and the wedding party members were dressed in light summery clothes lazing at a medium-sized wooden picnic table. Malaika had forced Camille to come along to this event. Malaika felt relaxed and relieved to have the wedding behind her. A few more days of this and then everything would go back to normal, she kept telling herself.

For tonight she had a reservation for dinner at a Japanese gastronomique restaurant in the 17th Arrondisement which she had found through one of her copywriting gigs. She and Paxon practiced social distancing, being sure to smile politely at each other when they came in direct line of each other. Otherwise Malaika focused her attention on everything but him. His perfectly defined cheekbones and jawline were worn away slightly by a few days' old stubble. It annoyed her that she noticed that.

Today was the day Malaika was collecting all their hotel room keys and everyone would be disbanding to their own accommodation arrangements. Malaika had her tablet with her and marked names whenever she received a key. She waited for people to bring them to her as she didn't want to seem pushy. She hated having to chase or follow up even in her personal life. This little fact made living in France, AKA home of bureaucracy, a hell. As she suspected, Paxon had not given her his and Vesuvio's key. If Paxon didn't give her the key by the leaving time, she would have to ask him. Malaika walked around politely making conversation with Camille glued to her as a discomfort buffer. The dinner would be the final opportunity for her to get all the keys.

Camille needed to go to the bathroom and complained bitterly about having to go in the bushes.

"You sink in France, 1$^{st}$ world ze parks can 'ave some toilet."

Malaika snorted while examining a chip in her manicured nail. She had them done for the big day and was annoyed to see that a good 40 euros spent didn't mean shit when it came to quality. "I mean this is also the country with gold star restaurants that sport Turkish toilets which are hazardous to the inebriated," Malaika said without thinking, the way she always talked when it was just her and Camille. When she remembered where she was, she amended, "But, there's probably a good, and possibly ecological, reason why."

Camille grumbled something in French too low and fast for Malaika to hear. Aloud she asked, "You 'ave papiere" It wasn't a question. Camille was low-key making fun of Malaika who had, years ago, made a habit of carrying everything anyone could possibly need in her sizeable bag because of how far she lived from Paris central. Malaika side-eyed her and proceeded to rummage through the contents of her bag. She handed Camille an umbrella, floss, lip gloss, a Leatherman, her wallet, a nail file, a small packet of Q-Tips, oil absorbers, hand-cream, hand sanitizer, and a small packet of Petit-Beurre biscuits before pulling a packet of tissues out triumphantly. Unfortunately, a stray tampon had attached itself to the packet and leapt off the tissues, sailing away from her in a direction neither woman was able to bring themselves to look out of embarrassment.

Camille fought back a smile and stared down at the earth beneath her feet.

Malaika closed her eyes and whispered hoarsely, "We're just gonna pretend that we have no idea."

Camille nodded and laughed in snorts.

Malaika retrieved all her things from Camille's now over-flowing hands and dumped the lot back in her bag.

"Hey." Pax's voice interrupted Malaika's humiliation.

At this, Camille burst out laughing. "I go, I go," she said, still laughing.

"Oh, come on Cam—" Malaika was struggling to keep her voice low. "Camille," she called after her friend in a strained whisper.

Camille darted off across the dirt path and disappeared into thick shrubbery.

"Traitor," Malaika whisper-shouted and slowly turned to the voice of her temptation to give him a stiff smile.

He was holding out his room key.

"Ah, great," she exclaimed, marking him off on her tablet.

"And there's also..." he pulled something out of his jean's pocket. It looked like a white bullet encased in plastic, her renegade tampon.

"Of course," she said to herself, her eyes fixed on it. She tried to think of something smart or funny to say but came up short. She finally settled on a perfunctory thank you.

"You coming to dinner tonight?" he asked.

Malaika nodded noncommittally. She did not want to come to dinner; she wanted to curl up in her tiny 2-bedroom apartment on her secondhand dark blue 2-seater which converted into a bed with Aila, eating ice cream and watching TV series. She didn't have a coffee table, so they ate off their laps. There was no real dining area or separation between kitchen and lounge. She had filled the interminable void where Paxon's love used to be with Ragnarok, a Scandinavian teen-hero drama, ever since she moved into her own space. She had always loved ice cream but the series was like a goldmine she'd unearthed. She watched it in the original version with English subtitles, reasoning that it made the viewing experience more authentic. Aila hated it because she spoke English and French and preferred to digest her media in those languages. She often switched between watching and scrolling on her phone.

Camille's head peered out from a bush in the distance. She waved as if Malaika wouldn't be able to see the only fancily dressed woman emerging from the thickets. Malaika did an internal eye-roll, shaking her head. When Camille came back to her, Paxon greeted her and she greeted him back, eyeing him and Malaika pointedly. Malaika made a big show of ignoring this. Then the pair left under the pretense of needing to return the keys. when really, Malaika had just had enough of peopling for the day.

Malaika wore jeans with a shiny top and a purple glitter encrusted blazer to dinner. The glitter was mild, not an eyesore. She had thrown some eye shadow, mascara, and lipstick on. She thought she would line her top lids but couldn't find the dedication required for that kind of symmetry. She had medium-sized gold hoop earrings on and wore wedged black espadrilles. She was impressed with her look. It had been a while since she'd gone out at night with other adults. She and Camille spent a lot of time together but not a lot of time out together. Malaika's hair was in a chignon, her go-to hairstyle when she had put too much oil in her hair and was trying to conceal the drowned musk rat look before she wither-washed her hair or the oil dried out over the next few days.

The dinner passed in a sort of murmured din. Malaika had small talk with the people seated beside her. Vesuvio entertained everyone with anecdotes and antics. Malaika sipped her Kir in relative silence. Overall, she was pleased to have come and was more pleased when the dinner drew to a close. She said her goodbyes and made her way out to her car. She couldn't wait to see what happened in the half-finished episode of Ragnarok she'd left to be there.

# 24

# Twenty-Four

"Malaika!" She heard someone call after her. Now what? Could she just go and be left to her ice-cream and TV catharsis? She turned to see Fern and felt guilty for being irritated.

Fern crossed the street quickly, bathed in a yellowy glow from the streetlights. "I have something for you."

Malaika hardly knew what to say so she smiled and remained silent.

Fern handed her a small orange box with silver lettering visible even in the dim night light.

Malaika took the box and asked, "What is it?"

Fern shrugged. "Take a look" Her huge blue eyes were alight with anticipation.

Malaika lifted the lid of the two-part box. Inside was a gold necklace with a cowrie shell pendant hanging on the chain. "It's beautiful," Malaika said. "Thank you."

"Read the..." Fern pointed to the white piece of paper attached to the inside of the lid.

Malaika hadn't noticed it.

*Malaika, You're more than the girl of my dreams—*

Malaika stopped and looked up at Fern.

"Don't look at me, I didn't write it."

Malaika made a quizzical gesture with her hands and narrowed her eyes.

"You know I love other people's secrets and interpersonal drama. Gossip is so humanizing." Fern smiled sweetly.

Malaika shook her head and carried on reading,

*I want you to be the girl in my reality. The times we are apart are always too long. Being with you is all that I am. I can't give you my heart- not my actual heart because it turns out I am scared of dying- but my emotions, my tenderness, my will, my soul- you're holding them all. However long it takes, as long as you come to me, everything I'll ever do, I'll do for you. Pax*

She'd gotten so drawn in that she hadn't noticed Fern disappear. When she looked up a hulking figure was where Fern once stood. Malaika laughed. "Who helped you write this?"

"What?" Paxon screwed up his face "I literally bleed on a page for you and you don't think I wrote it?"

Malaika shook her head at him with a smile.

"Not exactly the response I was hoping for." He ran his hand through his hair. "I'm a jock but I'm not a dumb one. You know that, right?"

Malaika gave him a disapproving look. "You know that's not what I meant." She took a deep breath. "It's not that. It's just—I've been seeing you kind of constantly for two weeks and you've been super economical with your words and then this." Malaika held up the little paper. "Also, no one's ever written me a love letter before so I'm not really sure what the appropriate response is. I know it should be some form of mitigated rapture..." She trailed off, looking thoughtful, as though trying to do a mental measurement.

"These were the things that enraptured me; listening to you microanalyse inconsequential things with words which, if I'm being perfectly honest, I sometimes have to look up."

"You feel like an illusion Paxon," she told him "Even if you weren't a football star, to think you care about me as much as you say is not totally outside the scope of possibility but it's highly improbable. I'm—" She wanted to say nobody but couldn't bring her mouth to say the word. She didn't have to; he was close to her and bent down to lean his forehead onto hers.

"Lo." His voice was soft, his words tender. "You are my sun, my joy, my little woman. You've been that for me from the moment we first spoke."

"I was in your city, you know," she blurted out. "I came to your city. Fern gave me your address and when I got to your apartment building, I saw Bonnie" She left it open. When he didn't respond she continued, "I called too, just when you got injured. Vesuvio answered and told me to stay away from you."

"I know about that." He shook his head as if in disbelief. "I talked to him about it. I never told him to do that."

Malaika nodded. She knew he was telling the truth. "And Bonnie?"

Paxon inhaled. "Bonnie was always around because we have history and live in the same city. When I got hurt, she came around all the time and I was just too, I don't know, I backed down and just let her help. That's what she was doing, helping with things, but when she tried to get back together, I told her I couldn't do it. Because I told you I'd be here when you sorted yourself out." He gave her a nervous smile. "I'm sorry you came all that way and didn't get to tell me what you wanted to."

Malaika smiled and shrugged it off.

"What did you want to tell me?"

"I wanted to apologize for hurting you. For everything really. I wanted to tell you that I pushed you away before because I was afraid, but you already knew that. That wasn't the most important thing though." She took in a sharp breath "I needed to be sure that what I felt for you, my wanting you was because of you and not because you, "saved" me from Axel. You are the only person other than Delano who's ever stood up for me to Axel. I wanted to rebuild my life and be sure that if any other person had done the same thing for me, it would still be you headlining my dreams and hopes. Because of what you do, people probably attach themselves to you for insincere reasons. But, you are sincere and wonderful, and I wanted to be with you without the backdrop of desperation. I wanted to be for you what you've always been for me, true. You've always been true."

"I accept some of the blame for the hurt, Lo. I know I hurt you too even though I didn't mean to."

"Lo, give me one good reason and I'll drop everything to make you my all." He paused and amended his statement, "Doesn't even need to be a good reason." He took in a ragged deep breath. "Forget the reason. I don't need one." He pinched her chin ever so lightly and drew it down with his thumb opening her mouth just enough to allow him access and kissed her. "I love you Malaika." he murmured softly into her mouth.

"I don't want to give up anything for me. I just want you to know who I am," she replied when she finally found her voice. "And if after that you still want t—"Her words were cut off when he leaned in and kissed her.

"There's no if," he said, coming up for air
Malaika smiled.

# 25

# Epilogue

Malaika was so nervous it felt like acid was burning down her throat in slow motion. She held her hands clasped tightly, as if she was praying. Aila was doing her final floor routine at the state championships. A group of her teammates stood off the floor cheering loudly, some already dressed in their tracksuits, adopting poses similar to Malaika's and taking labored breaths. Malaika had chosen DJ Ganyani's "Heaven" as her accompanying music. Malaika loved the song but couldn't enjoy it. She'd seen Aila go over the routine hundreds of times and knew all the moves that had posed difficulty when Aila was coming up with the choreography. Aila flipped and spun, moving with explosive energy. Her final move...Malaika closed her eyes. She was too nervous. The hall erupted in shouts and cheers and Malaika opened her eyes just in time to see Aila and her coach come running towards her. Aila had done it. This was gold. Malaika hopped up and down and yelled "My baby is gold!" Her and Malaika's coach joined hands and hopped in a circle together. Malaika peppered Aila with kisses and sandwiched her between her and her coach.

That night at Appleberry's Aila sat calmly at the table with both her parents. Axel had come with his girlfriend. Malaika had expected to feel jealousy or sorrow for this woman but found that she felt relief. They all ate and chatted and Malaika thought that behind all of Axel's assholery, was a spark of decency. That thought was quickly rescinded when the door to Appleberry's swang open and Fern and Paxon walked in. Axel's smile shrank by several molars. His girlfriend, noticing the sudden chilly draft in his temperament, looked in the direction of his gaze. Malaika smiled brightly at the pair as they walked towards them. Her moment of devouring Pax's immaculate frame was interrupted by her daughter

"Paxon and Tanti Fern!" Aila exclaimed and leapt from her seat. She ran to them and Paxon scooped her up into his arms and swung her up and over his shoulder like she was a toy.

Malaika grimaced in visible worry.

"Relax," Fern said, seeing Malaika's face. "Your child literally defies gravity every time she steps out onto a gym floor, but this worries you?" "When does your sister get here?" She picked one of Malaika's fries.

"Tomorrow."

Fern gave Axel and his girlfriend a superficial Theo Jansen wind sculpture wave.

Malaika didn't look to see how this was received but she heard Axel's wooden 'ello.

Aila dodged her way back to her seat, yelping as Paxon tried to grab her. She was holding a gift bag.

Malaika gave Paxon an approving raised eyebrow. Paxon shrugged, satisfaction written across his face.

He leaned down to give her an open mouth kiss. "Hey," he whispered.

She smiled.

He sat down and greeted the table.

Axel scowled and focused on Aila as she opened her gift. She beamed at everyone when she revealed the sports bag. It was from Paxon's collaboration with a big sporting brand. It had his name on it since the collection was inspired by him but customized with Aila's initials in the French flag colors.

"Thank you."

"Of course, kid. You're the star."

Axel began telling Aila loudly how he was planning on getting her a very expensive, fancy, sports bag.

Malaika and Fern exchanged a knowing look. Malaika leaned into Pax and said softly, "I am so glad you didn't get her a device. The last thing she needs is another device."

"I did good, didn't I?"

Malaika kissed him on the cheek and he grinned like an overgrown toddler. He took her hand and mingled their fingers, placing them on his chest.

"We should get going, we have to prepare for Chen season," Malaika announced. Fern made a quizzical face and Malaika began explaining.

"Chen will be here visiting, which is literally like a whole season. Long ago, she named her visits St. Chentine's." Malaika rolled her eyes. "And she's bringing the whole team."

"It's perfect then that you're now with me because: space. It's gonna be great— she's such a people person." Paxon said

"Ugh, people and people people," Malaika grumbled and called for the bill.

"I, for one, am looking forward to her being here. She's so much more fun than you are Miss workaholic bookworm," Fern said.

"Not you too," Malaika grumbled. "Do you know they call me Booklong as a nickname? Anyway, she's a workaholic too; she's just a social workaholic."

"Whatever makes you feel better," Fern quipped.

Pax stood and set his wallet in Malaika's lap before walking toward the bathroom.

"Which one?" she asked.

"Black," he called to her and was gone.

When the waiter arrived with the bill and the machine Malaika retrieved the card from Pax's wallet. She could pay with her own but felt a petty motivation. Axel never ever had given her any of his card information under the pretext that Malaika was the reason he was unable to become more successful. He blamed her, not his uncontrollable spending. She allowed herself the momentary satisfaction of shocking Axel. She wielded the card like it was her coup de grâce, slipping it into the machine and typed in Pax's code. She returned the card to its sleeve in the wallet and folded the receipt neatly, placing it with the card. When Malaika looked up Axel was staring, and she couldn't stifle a self-satisfied smile.

"Thanks for coming," she said sweetly. "See you on Friday when you come to get Aila."

He gave a curt goodbye and his girlfriend followed after him.

"Vesuvio will be happy to see Chen," Pax said on the drive back to their apartment. He took his hand off the gear shift and tangled his fingers with hers. Then, he lifted her hand to his mouth and kissed her fingers and her knuckles. Malaika could never get used to this, it always surprised her and always she was overcome by a feeling of peace and comfort that had now become her whole life.

"That's unfortunate because Chen said he is on her shit list."

"What's a shit list?"
Malaika eyed him from the side then chuckled sinisterly.
"Nothing good…"

# About the Author

Tendayi is a third culture individual and mom who writes fantasy fiction with strong female characters and diverse people doing incredible things all over the world. Based in France, she studied Global Communications and Civil Society at the Masters level at the American University in Paris and has been working as a digital content and communications expert in the city of light since.

**You can connect with me on:**

- https://www.tendayichirawu.com
- https://www.facebook.com/tendayiolgawrites
- https://www.instagram.com/tendayi_olga/?hl=en
- https://www.tiktok.com/@tendayiolga

# Also by Tendayi O. Chirawu

**Narinhi- The Man of the Lie**

Kai, a freshman at an international university in Paris, troubled by portent dreams since childhood is happy to be oceans away from her stifling hometown. She befriends Jarvis Chapter, a mysterious student haunted by the disappearance of his brother, Umbriel, in Southern Africa. While her duty to God is clear, she struggles to reconcile her hopes of fitting in among her peers and juggling the pressure of maintaining good grades. Unable to ignore the call placed on her life despite her insecurities and fears, her life is thrown into turmoil of biblical proportions when she is attacked by a humanoid in her apartment. She is forced to come to terms with the existence of the world in-between and her role in the fight for the world.

Made in the USA
Monee, IL
07 July 2026